Shine your shoes, sl...
and prepare for the ride of your life
in **Lauri Robinson**'s rip-roaring new miniseries

Daughters of the Roaring Twenties
Their hair is short and their skirts are even shorter!

Prohibition has made Roger Nightingale a wealthy man.
With his bootlegging business in full swing, and
his swanky hotel the most popular joint in town,
his greatest challenge is keeping his four willful
daughters in check!

Join
Ginger, Norma Rose, Twyla and Josie as they
fox-trot their way into four gorgeous men's hearts!

First travel with Ginger to Chicago in
The Runaway Daughter
Already available as a
Harlequin® Historical *Undone!* ebook

Then see Norma Rose go head-to-head
with Ty Bradshaw in
The Bootlegger's Daughter
Already available

Can Forrest Reynolds tame mischievous Twyla?
Find out in
The Rebel Daughter
Already available

And, last but not least, discover Josie's secret in
The Forgotten Daughter
Available now

Author Note

Welcome to the Roaring Twenties! A time in America where almost every citizen broke the law and new freedoms were discovered.

Significant change during this time period was the catalyst to bring about a new breed of women. The right to vote, opportunities to attend colleges and to pursue careers paved the way for younger women to embrace who they were. They flaunted the liberation of their generation and emphasized the separation of past rigid lifestyles with newfound hairstyles, fashion and actions.

Josie Nightingale is *The Forgotten Daughter* in this, the fourth book in the Daughters of the Roaring Twenties miniseries. Unlike her sisters, Josie doesn't concern herself with fashion, makeup or fancy parties, and embraces the concealment that living at the resort provides. It's allowed her to pursue other interests, that of helping others. Under the ruse of attending ladies' aid meetings, she sneaks north once a week to pass out condoms to women working the docks in Duluth. All goes well until she's arrested and has to call Scooter Wilson to get her out of the hoosegow.

My heart went out to Scooter from the get-go. He had his hands full with Josie, but he was the right man for the task.

I think this was the hardest book for me to write in this series. I knew it was the end of my visits with the Nightingales—for now.

LAURI ROBINSON

—

The Forgotten Daughter

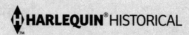

Recycling programs
for this product may
not exist in your area.

ISBN-13: 978-0-373-29854-9

The Forgotten Daughter

Copyright © 2015 by Lauri Robinson

Printed in U.S.A.

A lover of fairy tales and cowboy boots, **Lauri Robinson** can't imagine a better profession than penning happily-ever-after stories about men (and women) who pull on a pair of boots before riding off into the sunset—or kick them off for other reasons. Lauri and her husband raised three sons in their rural Minnesota home, and are now getting their just rewards by spoiling their grandchildren.

Visit: laurirobinson.blogspot.com, facebook.com/lauri. robinson1 and twitter.com/LauriR.

Books by Lauri Robinson

Harlequin Historical

Daughters of the Roaring Twenties

The Runaway Daughter (Undone!)
The Bootlegger's Daughter
The Rebel Daughter
The Forgotten Daughter

Stand-Alone Novels

Inheriting a Bride
The Cowboy Who Caught Her Eye
Christmas Cowboy Kisses
"Christmas with Her Cowboy"
The Major's Wife
The Wrong Cowboy
A Fortune for the Outlaw's Daughter

Harlequin Historical *Undone!* ebooks

The Sheriff's Last Gamble
What a Cowboy Wants
His Wild West Wife
Dance with the Rancher
Rescued by the Ranger
Snowbound with the Sheriff
Never Tempt a Lawman

Visit the Author Profile page at Harlequin.com for more titles.

To my brother Roger and his wife, Teresa.
Your involvement in these roaring twenties stories
meant the world to me!

Chapter One

White Bear Lake, Minnesota, 1925

If only this was something she enjoyed…

The outdoor dance floor covering the ground between the resort building and the water fountain overflowed with men and women set on having a good time. More people crowded the tables covered with alternating red, white and blue tablecloths that gave everything a patriotic feel, and the colorfully decorated Chinese lanterns hanging on the wires stretched from the tall corner posts added to the overall festive appearance.

Even the hill, as it gently sloped toward the lake on the other side of the fountain, was a flurry of activity, with people lined up outside the little red-and-white tents set up for them to change in and out of their swimming attire.

Her sisters had been right. As usual. People had come from miles around. Dressed in everything from fringed dresses and suit coats to beachwear. Age made no difference today. Betty Sandstrom, who'd turned ninety-one last month, sat in a chair with her cane hooked on one arm and on the other side of the table, Hannah Willis bounced her six-week-old baby boy, Henry. He was a cutie, with his tuft of blond hair and big blue eyes.

From her stance on the resort's balcony, Josie Nightingale held her customary role, that of being a bystander, wishing she could embrace all of this. She'd much rather be watching from her bedroom window, but that wasn't an option. She was expected to be in attendance today. Front and center, along with the rest of her family.

Resort employees served beverages by the trayload. Soda pop with striped straws and cocktails created to disguise the liquor filling the bottom half of the glasses. There was food, too. Lots of it. The scent of fire-roasted meat and corn boiled on the cob still hung in the air. Soon there would be dessert. Cake and ice cream.

The sigh that built in her lungs became too large to hold in. Too powerful. Josie let it out, feeling no relief when she did so. Everything was running smoothly. Extremely smoothly, but there was little pride inside her. Even less excitement.

There should be. A lot of work had gone into the party. The planning had started weeks ago. That wasn't unusual. Nightingale's Resort was known for its parties. What was different about this one was that it wasn't just a Fourth of July celebration—it was her sister's wedding.

Twyla and Forrest Reynolds had been married less than an hour ago. They were dancing right now, looking at each other with stars in their eyes. They'd been meant to be together. Josie had always known that. Had seen it with her own eyes years ago when they'd all been kids. She had a knack for that, seeing what others didn't always see, especially in themselves. Still, Josie's shoulders wanted to slump clear to her knees.

It wasn't that she wasn't happy for her sister. She was,

and not just for Twyla, but also for their oldest sister, Norma Rose, who would marry Ty Bradshaw in a couple of weeks, and Ginger, who'd married Brock Ness down in Chicago last month. Everyone had been surprised this morning when Ginger and Brock had shown up, having driven from Chicago for Twyla's wedding. Ginger and Brock, along with Norma Rose and Ty, were on the dance floor next to Twyla and Forrest, all of them looking happier than ever.

Josie tried to not feel it, but it was there. That deep, somewhat bitter sense of being the odd one out. The story of her life. For years, she'd told herself that was her choice. It still was. She truly didn't give a hoot about all the fuss and finery surrounding the resort, surrounding her family.

She did love them. Her family. And she was thankful for them. That's why she did all of this—planned parties she'd rather not attend, made beds and swept floors, even waited on tables and wrote out admittance tickets. The resort was the family business.

Today it was all just a bit unsettling.

Something must have changed inside her. In the past, she'd been better at putting on a smile—for show—when needed. Maybe it was just that currently, her life was in such disarray that keeping up the pretense that the world was as wonderful as her sisters claimed it was grew more impossible by the minute. She wanted to believe the world was a wonderful, happy place. She always had. But she knew otherwise. That notion weighed more heavily on her mind today than usual.

Another sigh built and burned inside her chest as an arm fell around her shoulders.

"Well, Josie-girl, it looks like it'll be just you and me."

The souring sensation in her stomach she'd had for days increased. Bucking up, for there was little else she could do, Josie planted a grin as big as her father's billfold on her face and leaned against his shoulder as he hugged her close to his side with one heavy arm. However, she made no comment in response to his statement.

Roger Nightingale was feared as strongly as he was revered by everyone, including his daughters.

He kissed the top of her head. "Dare I say I'm happy there's no man waiting in the wings to steal you away from me?"

The lump in her throat grew big enough to strangle a cow. Refusing to give in to the sadness or to peek toward the edge of the dance floor, Josie shook her head. "No chance of that, Daddy."

"Don't fret," he said with another kiss. "The right man's out there for you, too. Give him time."

"I'm not fretting." Lifting her gaze, because depending upon his answer, she knew things could get a whole lot worse, Josie asked, "Are you?"

"Nope." His grin was broad and his blue eyes shimmered. "Losing three daughters in a matter of weeks is more than enough. I'm going to hang on to you until the very end."

The strangling sensation happened again, and this time Josie couldn't speak around it. Scrounging up a painful smile that was as wobbly as her insides, she once again rested her head near the front of his shoulder. Her gaze wasn't controllable, either. Of their own accord, her eyes landed on Scooter Wilson. The sinking feeling within her could have sent her all the way to the other side of the earth.

Scooter was looking up to see if she was looking

down at him, and when their gazes met, he lifted a brow. Though the Chinese lanterns were hung and the music had started, night had yet to fall, and she could clearly see, and feel, the challenge Scooter sent her way.

Josie swallowed. Why had she called him, of all people, when she'd been arrested? Because he'd been the one person she could count on to get her out without too many questions. Way back when she'd worn pigtails and hand-me-down dresses, Scooter had been the one to come to her rescue when any of the other boys, or girls for that matter, had picked on her for one reason or another. He'd never told anyone about those incidents. True to form, just like he'd kept all her other secrets, he was keeping this one. Despite the ultimatum he'd laid down. Either she stopped her activities, or he'd tell her father.

Neither of which could happen.

"Did Scooter fix your car?" her father asked, his gaze following hers.

"Yes."

"Good," he said gruffly. "I still think I should have Ned look into that entire escapade. One of my daughters being arrested for speeding is ludicrous. They should have told you to slow down and nothing more."

Getting Sheriff Ned Withers involved would completely blow her last bit of cover. Her father thought she'd given Colene Arneson a ride up to Duluth to see a niece and that the speeding incident had happened on the way back home. "It was like Scooter said, Daddy," Josie replied, her nerves hitting a high gear. She'd never blatantly lied to her father, and it didn't settle well with her. It hadn't settled well with Scooter, either. "The gas pedal stuck. He promises it won't happen again."

"It better not." Her father spun her around by the

shoulders to directly face him. "Matter of fact, it won't."
He grinned broadly. "I told Scooter you need a new car.
Come Monday, he'll go with you over to Big Al's to pick
one out."

Her stomach sank. Avoiding Scooter hadn't been easy
over the past weeks, not when she'd had to arrange for
him to set off the fireworks later tonight, but she had no
intention of going anywhere with him, not even to pick
out a new car. When searching for an excuse didn't re-
sult in one, Josie asked, "Couldn't it just be delivered?"
The way her father frowned made her add, "I mean, with
Twyla married, she won't be here to help and Norma Rose
is busy planning her wedding, and—"

He kissed her forehead. "No, it can't be delivered. I
know you. You'll want Scooter to check it from bumper to
bumper. Being the only one of my girls here, you'll need
a car—one you can depend on—while Norma Rose and
Ty are on their honeymoon. They'll be moving into the
farmhouse when they return, and don't worry, she'll be
taking over the helm again before the end of the summer."

It wasn't the work at the resort Josie was worried
about. She didn't mind covering the front desk and helping with all the parties. Just like she'd never minded
cleaning rooms and doing laundry. The resort was her
responsibility as much as it was anyone else's. She just
didn't know how she'd manage everything with Twyla
gone. Unlike her, Twyla thrived on being the life of the
party. She'd been thrilled to step up and help Norma
Rose and had completely plunged herself into making
sure the events at the resort were top-notch. Twyla had
planned tonight's party, in fact she'd planned the whole
day of activities that included the entire town of White
Bear Lake, and it had been a success.

When her sister moved into town, to live at the Plantation with Forrest, it would create a hindrance to Josie's other duties, namely her Tuesday runs. Twyla had assured her she'd come and help while Norma Rose was on her honeymoon, and afterward, whenever they needed her assistance.

Norma Rose was planning ahead, too. The resort had been her first love—although many people had thought Forrest Reynolds had been Norma Rose's first love. Josie had known Norma Rose had never been in love with Forrest, just as she knew Norma Rose would never relinquish the resort to someone else. Not even one of her sisters. Norma Rose had made Nightingale's what it was today.

While her father had been busy amassing a fortune from bootlegged whiskey, Norma Rose had been busy making the rest of the world believe the family's resort was where they'd struck it rich. *Hospitality* was what she called it.

Josie had been very thankful for Norma Rose's, and her father's, drive and ambition. While her father had been focused on getting Minnesota 13 shipped worldwide and Norma Rose had been busy catering to the rich men their father did business with, Josie had had the freedom to pursue other adventures.

Twyla and Ginger had complained they were little more than prisoners, sent up to their bedrooms as soon as the sun went down. Freedom, Josie suspected, was like most everything else. Each person perceived it differently. Crawling into her bed while the parties below were still going strong had never bothered her. She'd been exhausted most nights, and more than ready for a good night's sleep.

Her sisters would never understand that, and she'd

never admitted it, not to anyone. Just like she wouldn't admit she couldn't fill in for her sisters *and* keep helping the Ladies Aid Society.

It wouldn't be forever.

Just for the next couple of months.

She'd manage.

That was if Scooter didn't follow through on his threat and put a stop to it all.

That's what truly couldn't happen.

There were simply too many lives at stake.

"I'm not worried," she told her father. Another lie, but he'd been waiting for her response. "Norma Rose hasn't booked another large party until Labor Day." Taking a deep breath, Josie added, "Everything will be fine. Just fine."

"You've always been the most sensible and level-headed one of the bunch," her father said. "I've always appreciated that. Even if I haven't told you." He kissed her forehead again. "You've never given me the worries your sisters have."

Once again her smile wobbled.

"Must be that Ladies Aid Society you're so involved in," he said.

Josie closed her eyes, fighting harder to keep the smile on her face.

Letting go of her shoulders, her father straightened the maroon suit coat over his black shirt and vest. "I'm going to mingle," he said. "It's not every day a man gets to rub elbows with Babe Ruth. You should have some fun, too—visit the dance floor. Looks like your sisters are having the time of their lives."

Her sisters all had reasons to be having the time of their lives. They'd not only found love, but in a sense they'd also found their freedom. Being one of Roger Nightingale's daughters wasn't an easy road. Up until a few years ago, they'd been just one more poor family among many others in the area. That had changed. Wealth changed a lot of things. Once again she told herself to be grateful for that. Luck had been on their side. If not for their father, and his determination, their lives would be very different.

"There's Babe," her father said, pointing toward a man as large as he was, and just as boisterous. "You coming?"

Inviting Babe Ruth had been Twyla's idea, and the stunt had worked. People from all across the state had driven to the resort in hopes of meeting the baseball legend. "In a bit," she said. "I have a few other things to see to up here." Gesturing toward the empty ballroom—most of the tables had been moved outside, leaving a mere smattering of them in the adjoining dining room—she added, "Now that the barbecue is over, I want to check on dessert and make sure the chefs are making hors d'oeuvres for later on. The fireworks won't go off for hours. We wouldn't want anyone getting hungry. Especially Babe Ruth."

Prohibition restricted the sale of alcohol, but the resort didn't sell drinks. It sold tickets that included all the food people could eat. The tickets weren't cheap, but people paid the price because along with the food came free drinks. Her father chuckled and patted her shoulder. "That's my girl. Your momma would be as proud of you as I am. Of all of you."

Josie nodded and watched him walk to the stairs leading to the ground. Reggie, the resort's long-standing bartender, had set up a portable bar beneath the balcony. Now that she was alone, the noise—that of the people beneath her, the music, the gaiety in general—vibrated against her eardrums. This was by far the largest party the resort had hosted and the entire day had gone without even the tiniest mishap.

She was thankful for that, but would be even more grateful when the day was over.

Josie spun around and walked through the open double doors leading into the resort's ballroom. Once nothing more than an old dance pavilion her grandfather had built to entertain weekend visitors to the lakes, the room now rivaled ballrooms in California and New York. Leastwise, that was what Norma Rose claimed. Her sister would know. She'd spent hours studying pictures of those places while designing the renovations on this room.

Stopping near one of the few tables left behind, Josie wrapped one hand around the back of a chair to steady herself while adjusting her shoe with the other hand. Blisters were forming on her heels from the hideous shoes she'd been requested to wear.

Her matching dress, identical to the one Twyla had bought to wear today, was just as bad as the shoes. The entire ensemble was an ugly pea-soup green—green was Twyla's favorite color. Josie much preferred her soft-soled slip-on shoes, dungarees and loose-fitting blouses. They were not only more comfortable, but they also didn't stand out. In them, a person could easily hide in a crowd.

After adjusting the second shoe, she wiggled her hips to shake the handkerchief hemline of the silk dress back into place. Cut above the knee in the front, but almost touching the floor in the back, the dress was as repugnant as the color. And the matching beaded headdress covering her hair had long ago started to itch. Fashion was not her thing. Thank heavens Twyla had been too busy to put much effort into insisting she pierce Josie's ears before the wedding.

That was all she'd have needed. Swollen earlobes.

Then again, they probably would have taken her mind off her aching feet. In all honesty, she should be glad it was *only* her feet aching. Modesty had never been Twyla's biggest trait. A lavish wedding would have been more her sister's style. It was rather amazing that other than the green dresses, the actual wedding had been a simple affair. Granted, it had happened in the middle of the largest Fourth of July party the state had ever known. That made up for the simplicity of the wedding in Twyla's eyes, no doubt.

Norma Rose's wedding wouldn't be simple. She'd been planning it for weeks. That, too, was a bit surprising— how easily Norma Rose had accepted Twyla getting married before her. If Josie had been more herself, she'd have questioned all of those things. Both of her sisters insisted she'd understand some day—how the most important thing truly is who you're marrying, not where or when it's taking place, or even what you're wearing.

Hearing either Twyla or Norma Rose say that was as out of the ordinary as roses blooming in winter. Never one to voice her opinion when it wasn't necessary, Josie had held her tongue. It wasn't as if she had plans of marrying anytime soon. If ever.

"I mean it this time, Josie."

The voice startled her so deeply that if not for the chair still nearby, she'd have toppled over. With both hands gripping the back of the chair, she took a stabilizing breath before lifting her gaze.

One foot braced on the lower brass rail, arms crossed and leaning against the bar a few feet away, Scooter

Wilson stared her down like a John would a whiskey runner. Scooter was about as formidable as a copper, too. Over six feet tall and as beefy as any of her father's men, Scooter's size alone made people think twice before questioning him. That was just one of the things she'd admired about him. Or used to admire when they'd been kids. His attitude of late had her questioning if they'd ever been friends.

The other thing she used to admire had been his looks. His slicked-back black hair, parted on the side and combed behind his ears, made women of all ages stop at his gas station just to get a close look. Some didn't even need gas in their tanks or air in their tires.

"I mean it," he repeated.

Looks were as deceiving as friendships. They both faded over time.

"I heard you the first time, Scooter," she replied. "And earlier today, and yesterday, and last week, and—"

"And I'm tired of saying it."

Josie refrained from saying she, too, was tired of hearing it. This was Scooter. He didn't care what she wanted. There wasn't much he cared about. Other than his gas station and flirting with the girls who visited it.

If those girls could see him right now, in his black suit, with a white shirt and shiny black boots, they'd be pulling in to his station two at a time. Then again, they probably had already seen him. Everyone for miles around was here today.

"Why aren't you dancing?" she asked.

He didn't so much as blink an eye. "Don't change the subject, Josie."

"That would be a little difficult," she snapped. "Considering the way you've hounded me."

Scooter didn't just step forward, he lunged, and took her arm in a tight hold. "Enough is enough, Josie." The sound of giggles on the balcony made him lower his voice. "You need to be glad you only got arrested for speeding in Duluth."

Enough was enough all right, and she'd had more of Scooter than she could handle. "I got arrested for speeding on purpose."

The instant the words left her mouth, Josie repented.

Scooter's sapphire-blue eyes narrowed and his lips tightened. "You got arrested on purpose?"

She wasn't intimidated easily, but Scooter had a way about him that unsettled all sorts of things inside her. Lying to him would be useless. "Yes," she hissed.

He cursed under his breath and released her arm when a man and woman, whispering and giggling, entered the ballroom. Josie kept her gaze averted as the couple made their way to the sweeping staircase leading to the second and third floors above.

She knew exactly when they were far enough away not to hear. Not only had their giggles faded, Scooter had grabbed her arm again.

"What about her?" he asked. "Are you going to save her, too?"

Josie pinched her lips together. Answering wasn't worth her breath.

"You know what they're going up there to do," he said.

Normally not embarrassed by talk of sex, it had become a common subject in her life—her underground life—Josie chided herself for the sting in her cheeks. "Of course I know."

"And you're fine with that?"

Once again Josie told herself not to answer. Not to respond to his nit-picking.

"You're a hypocrite, Josie Nightingale," he said. "Right under your own roof, you live with and condone the very thing you get on your soapbox to preach against."

The air in her lungs turned fiery as her spine stiffened. Josie wrenched her arm from his hold. "I do no such thing."

"Like hell you don't," Scooter retorted, planting his face so close to hers the tips of their noses almost touched. "Nightingale's is known for the women on the third floor."

"It is not," she argued. "Most people don't even know about it." Justifying the activities at the resort was not something she'd ever had to do before, but she'd justify the very air she breathed to get Scooter off her back. "Those women choose to rent rooms during large events, just like everybody else. Nightingale's has nothing to do with it, nor does it take a share of their profits. And," she added, emphasizing the point Gloria Kasper took pride in, "Dr. Kasper checks every girl who enters, making sure they're healthy and not here against their will."

"Securing your investments."

Scooter's words were lined with loathing. The twisting in Josie's stomach intensified, gnawing on her backbone. "Fine," she snapped. "Believe what you want. It makes no difference to me."

"Well, it makes a difference to me," he growled. "I'm sick and tired of waiting to hear if you've come up missing or not. I told my mother—"

"You what?" Josie bit her lips together and glanced around to make sure the ballroom was still empty.

"I told my mother to tell Gloria you're done."

Relief that no one had heard her shout disappeared. Josie grabbed the lapels of Scooter's suit jacket. "It's not for you or anyone else to say when I'm done. And," she added with all the fury spiraling toward the top of her head like a champagne cork let loose, "you need to remember where Maize might be if not for Gloria."

Her stomach sank before the words had completely left her mouth.

Eric Wilson, otherwise known as Scooter because of the motorcycles he'd coveted since seeing his first one around the same time he'd learned to walk, hadn't been this angry since he didn't know when. Josie Nightingale knew how to get him fired up, and she'd had him running on all cylinders for the past two weeks. Before then, too, but not to this degree. Passing out condoms to prostitutes was one thing, but her recent activity—attempting to steal girls away from their pimps—was far more dangerous than her pretty little brain could fathom.

"I know exactly where Maize would be," he replied. "That's exactly what I'm trying to prevent." Grabbing her shoulders, he gave them a quick shake. "To stop you from ending up where my sister did."

"I'm not going to end up anywhere," she retorted.

Scooter wanted to shake her harder, maybe rattle some sense into her, but he knew that wasn't going to happen. Josie thought herself untouchable. Not just because she was one of The Night's daughters, but because her ruse had worked too well for too long. He knew exactly when it had all started—three years ago, when his sister Maize had been found missing after taking a job at the Plantation nightclub. Galen Reynolds had owned it back then—and he was a crook like no other. The man had been selling women, and like most everything else of the criminal nature Galen embarked in, he'd gotten away with it.

Scooter knew all about Gloria Kasper, too. She was now the resident physician at Nightingale's but back then, when Maize had gone missing, Gloria still lived in town, in the house she and her husband had lived in for years. Long ago, when Gloria had been a young bride, she'd discovered her husband was doing more than tending to certain patients while on house visits and had put a stop to it. However, she'd been a bit too late. Her husband had already been infected. Gloria took it upon herself to find a cure, or at least a way to stop the disease he'd caught from spreading. She'd jumped on the condom bandwagon faster than the army. A few years later, after her husband died, she had become a doctor.

She'd also become a vigilante. Gloria understood prostitution was the oldest profession known to man, and knew no amount of protesting or rallying would put a stop to it, so she set out to make it as safe as possible for those involved. Men and women.

Astute, but also very secretive, Gloria had known about Galen Reynolds's trafficking. She'd also been the first person Scooter's mother had contacted when Maize hadn't come home one night. Which was also why— though it had never been proven—her home had been burned to the ground after Maize had been rescued. Another reason Scooter was dead set on stopping Josie. Galen Reynolds may be in prison for counterfeiting, but Josie was getting herself involved with other people, men and women, some far worse than Galen.

He wanted to tell Roger everything he knew and put an end to Josie's shenanigans, but that could backfire.

Just like his plan had backfired years ago when his sister had gone missing. He'd gone to the Plantation that night, to find out what Galen had done to Maize. If Brock Ness hadn't been delivering milk the next morning, Scooter had no doubt he'd have died in the ditch he'd been pitched into.

Brock had hauled him home and, to Scooter's shock, when he'd awakened, his sister was home. No amount of questioning had gotten him a straight answer from either his mother or sister, but he cobbled enough bits and pieces together to know Gloria had been behind Maize's rescue. Since Josie's arrest, he'd discovered she was Gloria's right-hand gal, and that her father knew nothing about it.

The Night had a reputation that far preceded him, and would be furious to learn what his daughter was up to, but that wasn't what scared Scooter. It was what Roger would do that frightened him. Roger would go after the top dog, barrel in to put a stop to it, much like Scooter had done when he'd gone to see Galen Reynolds. That had taught him a valuable lesson. Top dogs were always protected. Roger Nightingale was no fool. Scooter understood that, and the man had a fair amount of protection circling him and his family, but Roger's night watchmen wouldn't be enough in this case. People—namely Josie—would get hurt.

Scooter had thought long and hard about this. He had no choice; it kept him up at night. The girls on the third floor of the resort proved Roger didn't believe prostitution rings were dangerous. Scooter, however, knew the opposite. He hadn't been able to rescue Maize, hadn't been able to protect her from what had happened, but he wasn't about to let history repeat itself.

Some of Josie's anger had receded, as had his. Scooter let go of her shoulders. In truth, his fury should have increased. She had no idea of the danger she was playing with, how close she may be to having her life snuffed out.

"Dang it, Josie," he growled. "This has to stop."

"I don't have a choice, Scooter," she said, rather despondently.

"Yes, you do," he insisted.

The shimmering green beads covering her blond hair flapped near her shoulders as she shook her head. "No, I don't. I'm the only one who can get in and out unseen."

Frustration filled his stomach. "You aren't getting in and out unseen, Josie. Pants don't make you invisible." He stopped shy of stating she looked even more fetching in her britches and shirts than she did in the green dress she wore right now—although the color wasn't very flattering. Normally he didn't notice such things, but Josie usually, when she did wear a dress, chose one of simple colors. White, blue, yellow. The one she had right now was a pond-scum green. Twyla had probably picked it out for her wedding, as she and Norma Rose had on identical dresses.

"I have to go," Josie said. "There are things I need to see to in the kitchen."

He didn't doubt that. The party had just gotten started and would continue for hours. Both Twyla and Norma Rose were otherwise occupied, which would leave most of the work to Josie. When she'd started taking on a bigger role at the resort a month or so ago he'd hoped that would curtail her other activities. It hadn't. Her phone call from the Duluth jail had dropped his heart clear to his knees two weeks ago.

Scooter took hold of her elbow as she started to walk away. "Why'd you say you got arrested for speeding on purpose?"

The shock in the depths of her sky-blue eyes said she'd hoped he'd forgotten that tidbit of information.

She sighed heavily, but just as she was about to say something, they were interrupted.

Chapter Two

"Isn't this party swell?" Twyla asked excitedly as she and Forrest crossed the room.

"Just swell," Josie muttered under her breath. Remembering—as if she'd been able to forget—Scooter stood beside her, she pulled up a brilliant smile. "Yes, it is," she told her sister. "One people will long remember. Who could ever forget Babe Ruth?"

"He's so funny," Twyla said, using Forrest's shoulder the same way Josie had used the chair to hold her balance as she fiddled with one and then the other shoe. "He told me every woman should love baseball for the pure fact it's played on diamonds."

Josie merely grinned. Babe had been saying that to women all day. She almost found an ounce of comfort knowing the shoes were hurting her sister's feet as badly as they were hers, but didn't. It was Twyla's wedding day, and nothing, not even tight shoes, should dampen her enjoyment.

"I was on my way to the kitchen," Josie told Twyla, glad for the opportunity to escape Scooter. "Want to come with me? We can get something for our heels."

Twyla laughed as she graced her new husband with a somewhat sheepish grin. "That's exactly what I came inside for."

"I told her she should have bought a larger size," Forrest said teasingly.

"It's not the size," Twyla insisted. "It's the style. These were the only ones that were the same color as our dresses."

"Lucky shoes," Scooter drawled.

Josie twisted her neck to hide the laugh that caught in the back of her throat, but Scooter caught it. His grin, as well as the glint in his eyes, said he thought the dresses were as ugly as she did. That made her want to smile, but she wasn't about to let him think they shared the same thoughts on anything—not one tiny iota. Josie reached over and grabbed Twyla's free hand. "Come on. Moe has bandages in the kitchen."

Dramatic as Twyla always was, her sister held on to Forrest's hand as she started walking, stretching her arm out as if Josie was pulling her away from her new husband. When she finally let go of Forrest's hand, Twyla said, "Don't let him out of your sight, Scooter. I don't want to have to go looking for him."

Josie's ability to keep her thoughts to herself momentarily disappeared. "Good heavens," she whispered. "You'll only be gone a minute."

"I know," Twyla whimpered. "But a minute away from Forrest feels like hours."

Josie bit her lips together to keep her from pointing out that little over a month ago Twyla had been selling kisses for a dime apiece to any man who walked past the cotton candy stand at the amusement park.

She'd barely taken another step when a solid grip wrapped around her elbow.

"Actually," Scooter said, "Josie wasn't on her way to the kitchen. She and I were discussing something and weren't finished."

Dumbfounded, it took Josie a moment for her mind to kick in. "Yes, we were finished," she said. The undercurrent of tension surrounding them could sink a ship.

Twyla and Forrest obviously sensed it, too. "Did something happen to the fireworks?" Twyla asked.

"No," Josie and Scooter answered simultaneously.

They hadn't broached the subject of fireworks. There had been no need. Scooter was as reliable as Father Time. He said he'd handle the fireworks, and he would, without fail or complications.

Twyla always had to dig deeper. "Are you sure?"

"Yes," Scooter said.

"The fireworks will go off as planned," Josie assured her. At least once a day, usually more often, for the past week Twyla had talked about how Forrest was taking her up in his plane to watch the fireworks, cooing about how romantic it would be. Josie had to admit it did sound romantic, but right now, it made her want to be sick. Probably because of the way Scooter's hold tightened on her arm. It plainly reminded her romance would never be a part of her life. Ignoring Scooter, she said to Twyla, "It's almost time to cut your wedding cake. I was on my way to see if the ice cream was ready."

"Twyla and I can do that," Forrest said, glancing between her and Scooter. "Sorry to have interrupted you."

Josie clenched her back teeth together so hard her jaw stung. She took several deep breaths through her nose as Twyla was led off by her new husband. Once they were out of sight, she wrenched her arm free from Scooter's hold. "That was terribly rude," she spat out.

"So?"

"So?" she repeated, even more furious at his callous attitude. This was not the Scooter of yesteryear. The one she could have laughed with over the color of her shoes.

He shrugged, as if being rude made no difference to him in the least. "Our conversation wasn't finished. Why'd you get yourself arrested?"

Huffing out a breath, she used the time to gather her wits. Flying off the handle would only make matters worse. If that was possible. She'd already told him more than she should have. He had the uncanny ability to get things out of her like no one else. "That is none of your business," she said, sounding much calmer than she was. Catching a glimpse of Norma Rose on the balcony, Josie took a step in that direction. "And our conversation is finished."

"I've made it my business, Josie," he said.

The conviction in his tone made her spine shiver, but she didn't turn around.

"There you are," Norma Rose said, pausing in the open doorway. "We need to move a table into the center of the dance floor for the cake." Waving a hand, she continued, "Scooter, we could use your help."

Josie held back her opinion on that as she crossed the threshold and followed Norma Rose across the balcony. When a hand settled on the small of her back, sending fire and ice up and down her spine, she willed herself not to flinch. Half the country was watching them.

"Smile," Scooter whispered.

"Shut up," she replied, seething.

He laughed.

She planted a smile on her face for the onlookers while elbowing him in the ribs.

At the bottom of the steps she gladly separated herself from him, and took a spot on the sideline to keep people back while Norma Rose cleared the dance floor and gave directions as to which tables needed to be carried over. When Moe, the assistant cook, appeared, he was followed by several serving girls carrying trays of little glass bowls holding scoops of ice cream drizzled with chocolate syrup and topped with a mint leaf. Josie stepped forward to ensure he had a clear pathway to the tables. The last in line was Silas, the head cook, carrying a cake so tall he could barely see over it.

"I still can't believe Twyla agreed to ice cream," Moe whispered as they walked. "But Silas says it's not the Fourth of July without ice cream."

"Twyla's so in love she'd eat mud pies today," Josie replied. Silas was a bit temperamental, but Moe was always smiling and was the real one in charge of the kitchen.

Moe winked at her. "That's how a girl should feel on her wedding day."

Of their own accord Josie's eyes settled on one of the two men carrying the last table to the center of the floor. She wanted to pull her eyes away from Scooter as badly as she wanted to pinch the bridge of her nose, where a headache was starting to form. "I suspect you're right."

"We'll start serving the hors d'oeuvres around nine," Moe said. "Before the fireworks start. By then people will be hungry again."

"Sounds perfect," Josie answered. "Thank you."

He set down his tray and directed the girls to start unloading the bowls of ice cream onto the table. "Hurry now, the cake is coming and we don't want things to melt."

Turning to her, he said, "You go enjoy the day, everything in the kitchen is under control."

She hadn't taken a step when a hand took a hold of her elbow. Stepping out of the way of the serving girls, she hissed, "You're worse than a bad penny today."

"Thank you," Scooter said, leading her toward the edge of the platform.

"That wasn't a compliment," she said.

"I know."

Josie bit her tongue as others gathered near. Being the center of attention had never been her way. That much hadn't changed.

"There sure are a lot of people here," he said.

"Yes, there are," Josie answered, noting how others were nodding, having heard his comment. "It's because of Babe Ruth," she said, hoping no one noticed how Scooter held her arm. Her subtle attempts to shake off his hold hadn't worked and anything more strenuous would be noticed. Even with the distraction as Babe Ruth approached.

The ballplayer stopped next to her father, who was in the center of the dance floor along with Forrest and Twyla. A hush came over the crowd when her father held up a hand. He made a brief speech about how he'd known Forrest his entire life and was proud to call him family, and then Babe Ruth said a few words about having flown with Forrest on the east coast and that he was honored to have attended his wedding. He also remarked on how beautiful Twyla was and that if he wasn't already married, he'd have stolen her away from Forrest.

The crowd roared, especially when Twyla proclaimed that although Babe Ruth was famous, and handsome, she'd still have chosen Forrest, mainly for his airplane.

Josie scanned the area behind her, looking for an escape route, but didn't have any luck. As she turned back around, Scooter's chuckle irked her. Pretending it didn't she asked, "You didn't have any problems with the fireworks, did you?"

"No," he answered. "They're all set to go. Dac and I built a raft and anchored it out in the middle of the lake. That's where we'll light the fireworks."

Scooter was a member of the volunteer fire department and took all fires or potential fires seriously. She figured it was because his father had been with the fire department until he'd lost his life battling a blaze at one of the resorts closer to town several years ago. Nodding, she said, "Twyla's excited about them."

"Forrest, too," Scooter replied. "He's going to fly over them."

"I know," Josie answered.

"Have you ever gone up in his airplane?" Scooter asked.

"No."

"Afraid?"

"No."

He chuckled again and the shine in his eyes, the one that said he'd been teasing her, made her drop some of her guard. They had been friends for years, and he was likable, when he wanted to be.

"It's fun," he said. "You should try it."

"I'm sure I will, someday," she answered. Forrest had been giving airplane rides all afternoon. Even her father had taken one and upon landing had proclaimed he was going to buy his own plane. He most likely would.

"Want to know a secret?"

She frowned and her mouth went dry as she once

again brought her gaze up to meet his. "What secret? Whose secret?"

"Twyla's," he answered. "She asked Dac and me to set up a tent out on the island."

"What for?"

"For her and Forrest to spend the night."

"Tonight?"

He nodded. "She said the island is her and Forrest's favorite place."

Josie didn't doubt that. All of her sisters, not just Twyla, had favorite colors, favorite places and favorite things. She didn't. Not really. That had never bothered her before today. Once again she chalked it up to the feeling of dread inside her. Maybe it wasn't necessarily that something was going to happen, but the fact that something had happened. In a matter of a few weeks, everything around her had changed. She was still one of four sisters, but those sisters had all moved on, moved out. Pretty soon it was just going to be her. When Norma Rose and Ty moved into the old farmhouse where they'd all lived before the resort had been built, it would be just her and her father occupying the family area of the second floor.

First Ginger had left, then after tonight, Twyla would no longer be there and soon Norma Rose would be gone—although, while Norma Rose thought no one knew, she hadn't been sleeping in her room for weeks. She spent most nights at Ty's cabin. One of the twenty the resort owned that lined the lakeshore.

All that could cause her to be out of sorts. After all, her father would surely notice her comings and goings a lot more in the future. Meaning she'd have to be a lot more careful. Along with making sure Scooter didn't snitch on her.

He was frowning and looking at her curiously.

"A tent, huh?" Josie said, pretending she hadn't been thinking about other things. She let her gaze wander around the fountain, toward the big island in the center of the lake. "We all used to play out there," she said. "Back in the day."

"I remember your foot being bandaged when school started one year. You'd stepped on a nail out there."

She'd like to have said she'd forgotten about that. Some of the other kids had teased her and Scooter had put a stop to them. Trying to forget that part, she said, "My grandmother said I was going to get blood poisoning from that nail and insisted I keep my foot above my heart at all times." Shaking her head, she admitted, "I thought she meant forever. I was afraid I'd die right at my desk when school started."

"I'm glad that didn't happen." With a wink, he added, "Old Mrs. McGillicuddy would have died right alongside you. Besides being as blind as a bat, she was afraid of her own shadow."

"Probably because you boys were so mean to her," Josie suggested.

"Mean? We weren't mean to her," he said. "She was so easily frightened we couldn't help but put a stick or two in her desk drawer. She's the one that *thought* they were snakes."

Josie almost laughed at the memories, until she recalled she was still mad at Scooter. Standing here laughing over foolish childish pranks wouldn't—or at least shouldn't—lessen that. "Well," she said seriously, "Mrs. McGillicuddy was a much better teacher than Miss Jenkins."

Scooter lifted an eyebrow before he leaned closer.

"Miss Jenkins," he whispered, "was too busy chasing after the older boys to teach anyone anything."

For some unfathomable reason, heat stung her cheeks. It didn't have anything to do with Miss Jenkins. She barely remembered the woman. The influenza epidemic had hit shortly after she'd taken over as teacher and school had been closed for months.

"She married Dac's cousin," Scooter said. "They live over by St. Cloud and have five or six kids, last I heard."

The cheering crowd brought her attention back to the dance floor, where Twyla and Forrest were embraced in a rather heated kiss. Along with everyone else, Josie watched, and wondered. Many things had changed in her life. Teachers. The epidemic that had taken her mother, brother and grandparents away in a swoop. She'd missed them terribly at first, still mourned the losses, but not even their deaths had left her with the uncanny sense of dread she felt today.

Perhaps because she'd been too young. She was twenty-one now, an age where she understood cause and effect, and consequences.

After a roaring round of applause, girls started passing out ice cream and cake. Josie once again looked for an escape route, but people were crowding closer, vying for the next bowl. Scooter handed her one that held both cake and ice cream, and a spoon.

"Let's move over a bit."

She started to protest, but was cut short when someone bumped into her.

Scooter caught her bowl before it toppled. "This way," he said.

Josie followed him a few feet, to where he stopped

next to Ty and Norma Rose. She'd barely taken a bite when Norma Rose shoved another bowl in her direction.

"Hold this." Her sister then grabbed Ty's bowl and Scooter's. "We have to get those tables off the dance floor."

"Why?" Josie asked as she took the bowls Norma Rose handed her. Having waited tables plenty of times, balancing all four was easy.

"That's why," Norma Rose said.

Josie turned in the direction her sister pointed. Their other newly acquired brother-in-law, Brock Ness, had positioned himself behind the piano that had also been transported outside as another round of applause echoed through the air. Brock was an excellent musician and the locals had missed his performances since he'd left for Chicago.

"Once he starts playing, people will crowd the floor, tables or not," Norma Rose said.

Ty and Scooter followed Norma Rose. Frustration filled Josie as she glanced down at the four bowls full of untouched cake and ice cream. Spying a waitress nearby now gathering empty plates, Josie wasted no time in getting rid of all four. A touch of guilt ensued, but she ignored it. Scooter, as well as Norma Rose and Ty, could get more cake and ice cream. There was plenty.

She'd made it almost to the far side of the dance floor when a familiar hold once again caught her arm.

"Where do you think you're going?" Scooter asked.

"I have things to see to," she said, twisting her arm.

"No, you don't," he said. "I heard Moe tell you everything was under control."

"In the kitchen," she said. "But there's—"

"Nothing you need to see to right now." Turning her toward him, he said, "Let's cut a rug."

"I don't want to dance," she said, spinning around. The flash of a camera bulb momentarily blinded her. Newspapermen were everywhere today, hoping to get a picture of Babe Ruth.

"Too bad," Scooter said. "Whether you want to or not, we're dancing."

She truly didn't have much of a choice. Others were pushing their way onto the dance floor, hurling her and Scooter forward with their momentum.

Brock hit the piano keys and the first notes ripped through the crowd like a buzz saw. People shouted, their hoots and hollers loud enough to frighten the seagulls from the air.

Josie stifled her protest as Scooter glided her into his arms and she allowed him to whisk her across the floor. He was an excellent dancer, especially of the Charleston. The two of them had been paired up in an impromptu dance-off a few weeks ago, which had been more fun than she'd had in ages.

The tempo of the song increased and she and Scooter held hands as they spun forward to rush through the steps of the popular dance. People bumped into her and Scooter pulled her closer before swiftly guiding her around to his other side.

"I don't want someone to step on your toes," he shouted above the ruckus. "Your feet have already been damaged enough from wearing those ugly green shoes."

Josie had to laugh. "Thank you," she shouted in return. "Your gallantry is outstanding."

In the middle of his fast dance steps, he gave her a brief bow, which had them both laughing. Having grown up with him, she'd never felt uncomfortable around Scooter, as she'd felt around others, and she'd gone to him, on more than one occasion, when she'd needed things. Mechanical things usually. Having a car she could count on was an important aspect of her life.

They danced through the next two songs Brock played, and when, after striking the final chords as only Brock could, he stood up from behind the piano, Josie was more than a little winded.

Scooter was, as well, or at least he acted that way, and said, "Water, I need water."

Laughing, Josie led him away from the dance floor, to where a table of nonalcoholic punch and soda was set up. She picked up a soda and drank half of it as Slim Johnson made his way to the piano. Wayne Sears, another musician they'd hired for the night, was somewhere at the resort, too. When the dance-off started, they'd need more than one. A large number of people had signed up for the contest.

Her father was beside Slim and as the musician sat down, her father once again held up a hand, drawing everyone's attention to him. "Ladies and gentlemen," he began, as a hush came over the crowd. "I want to thank all of you for attending this first ever Fourth of July barbecue here at Nightingale's." Once the applause died, he added, "It's been so successful, we'll have to make it a yearly event." Finding the baseball player amid the crowd, he asked, "What do you say, Babe?"

Babe Ruth held his glass up in salute, and once again the crowd went wild.

"You've all met my daughter Twyla," her father then said, "the girl who got married today, and I want to introduce you to my other daughters."

Josie's heart sank. He'd never publically introduced

them before. Although she was proud of her father, never being in the limelight suited her. She liked being the mediocre sister. The one no one recognized. It meant she could wear britches and go barefoot when she wanted to.

Scanning the crowd, her father said, "Norma Rose, you and Ty come up here. Twyla, you and Forrest. Ginger? Where's my baby girl? Aw, there she is. Brock, bring her up here. And Josie...?"

She wanted to slink under the table. Particularly when her father said, "Scooter, bring Josie up here, will you?"

"Come on," Scooter said.

Scooter's hand landed in the middle of her back. It might appear he was simply guiding her forward, but in actuality, he was shoving hard.

"Everyone's watching," he said, without making his lips move.

"I know," she answered in the same manner.

"It'll only take a minute," he said.

The dread that had been inside her doubled. She'd always known it would happen someday, that she'd be pointed out as one of The Night's daughters, and that it would change her life. She'd no longer be able to hide in the shadows.

She and Scooter arrived near her sisters, but the pounding of blood in her ears was too loud for her to hear what her father was saying. Something about Nightingale's being a family business, and that this was the family. The family. Her sisters claimed they'd felt like prisoners, trapped in their bedrooms, but this was where she felt the iron bars surrounding her. Being a Nightingale had come to mean being something she wasn't. It had given her a station in life she'd never wanted. And it was full of expectations. There were things being a

Nightingale provided, but the list of things they couldn't do was longer. Unfortunately, those were the things that made her who she was.

Eventually her father stopped talking, and the clapping and cheering slowed. Josie wasted no time in making her exit. She made it all the way to the resort building, but didn't go up the balcony steps—there were too many people—instead she headed for the corner of the building and the side doors there.

"Good grief, do you have wings instead of feet?"

Josie hadn't realized Scooter was still at her side. The fact he'd been pulled center stage along with her overrode any lingering anger. "I'm sorry about that."

"About what?"

"That," she said. "Being pointed out."

"Your father's proud of you, Josie, of all of his daughters. He just wanted to acknowledge that."

"Maybe some of us don't want to be acknowledged," she answered, finally arriving at the side door that led to the storeroom. Josie clasped the doorknob, worried Scooter was going to start another argument. That would take more energy than she had right now. This day truly couldn't end soon enough.

But it wasn't Scooter's voice that had her spinning around.

Chapter Three

Scooter stepped aside so Josie could see past him. Having recognized Gloria Kasper's voice, he hadn't turned around. Anger once again stirred his insides. The fury had left him for a few minutes, while he and Josie had been dancing. Now, seeing the shadows back in her eyes, he wanted to tell Gloria the same thing he'd told his mother. Leave Josie alone. Find someone else to do their dirty work.

"Hello, Eric," Gloria greeted him.

He bit the tip of his tongue before turning about. "Hello." The bitterness in Gloria's eyes told him exactly what he'd already known. His mother had told the other woman what he thought. What he knew. Not that it would matter to Gloria. She had her own agenda. As always. Short, round and gray-haired, she looked as fierce as an angry badger as she strolled toward them.

"I know you won't mind, Eric," she said formidably, using his given name as if that gave her authority. "I need to speak with Josie."

"Actually, Gloria, I do mind," Scooter said. Normally, out of respect, he addressed her as Mrs. Kasper.

He wasn't feeling overly respectful right now. "Josie and I are busy."

Gloria's wrinkled lips pursed while a gasp sounded from Josie.

"Well, I never," Gloria snapped, her nostrils flaring like a bull's. "I insist on speaking with Josie this very moment." She reached out and grabbed Josie's arm, tugging her forward. "What I have to say is extremely important."

Scooter grabbed Josie's other arm. "I can't believe it's that important."

"Eric," Gloria snarled, "don't do this." She pulled Josie toward her again.

He tugged her back his way. "I could say the same to you, Gloria. Now is not the time or place."

Gloria gave Josie another hard pull. "Young man, I—"

"You'll what?" Scooter challenged, pulling Josie back. "I—"

"Stop!" Josie twisted until neither of them held her arms. "Stop it, both of you."

Regret washed over Scooter. He was acting like an idiot, to both Gloria and Josie. The older woman wasn't bad; she'd helped a lot of people, including his family when they'd needed it, and continued to assist others. He just didn't want her sending Josie out on another run. Not today. Not ever. It had grown too dangerous, yet he seemed to be the only one to realize that.

Josie glanced between him and Gloria. The sorrow in her eyes stabbed at him, and left him feeling about as low as a flat tire. He had no right to step in, but his intuition said he had to.

"I have to talk with Gloria, Scooter," Josie said, almost apologetically. "I won't be long."

He'd fully expected her to tell him to get lost. It wasn't as if she'd invited him to wait for her, but what she'd said could give that impression. "I'll wait here," he said.

A tiny smile tugged at her lips and she shook her head. "Go back to the party. I'll see you there."

He shook his head. "I'll wait here."

Gloria rushed Josie through the door before any more could be said. It was just as well. Scooter didn't have much more to say. He wouldn't until he figured out a way to stop Josie. Telling her to stop wasn't working. Josie had a mind of her own. He'd always admired that about her, long before any of this nonsense had started.

Even as a kid, Josie had caught and held his attention. Although she'd always been quiet and thoughtful, when riled, Josie had stood up for the underdog like no other. That had all been years ago, before he'd left school to become the family breadwinner.

Whenever he heard someone complain about how slowly time seems to go by, he wanted to tell them to start paying a few bills. They'd soon see how fast the first of the month rolled around, how quickly another month's rent was due and how gallons of milk could disappear as if they'd never been there in the first place.

He'd never known his family was poor. At least his parents had never complained about it. After his father died, Scooter quickly discovered the few dollars he made delivering groceries on his motorized bike wasn't enough to keep a family of mice in cheese. His hobby of tinkering with motors came in handy then. The location of their house along the highway played in his favor, too. Little by little he'd added services, but it wasn't until Nightingale's took off that he'd started making enough money to truly live on. That had been a godsend, and he knew it could disappear just as fast. Without Roger Nightingale and the business the man brought in, this entire area would dry up faster than yesterday's bread left uncovered on the counter.

A lot had happened in the past ten years. He'd been fourteen when his father had died, and three years later, his brother-in-law had been killed while serving in the army overseas. Maize had just given birth to Jonas when they'd received word about John. Shortly thereafter, Maize could no longer afford to stay in the house she and John had rented since getting married, and she had moved back home. When Jonas had started school three years ago, Maize had gone to work over at the Plantation, and had come up missing less than a month later.

Another bout of disgust, or guilt, assaulted Scooter's guts. He wasn't exactly sure what had happened back then, but he knew Gloria had been behind Maize's return. Scooter understood he was indebted to Gloria for bringing his sister home, but he couldn't let what had happened to Maize happen to Josie. Gloria had to realize not even Roger Nightingale was in the same league as the gangsters that were responsible for the girls working the docks in Duluth.

It really was a tangled mess.

If Josie was captured, there was no guarantee she'd be rescued like his sister had been. The Ladies Aid Society his mother and Gloria were associated with was the way Josie had become involved. Dressed in britches, she visited the shipyards of Duluth regularly to pass out rubbers to the women working the docks, selling their wares to the sailors.

None of this was something a Ladies Aid Society should be a part of.

It wasn't all of them. Just a select few knew the activities taking place under the concealment of their meetings. Most of the women thought all of the members were busy throwing birthday parties and putting on bird-watching symposiums. A good number would faint dead if they learned about Josie hauling condoms up to Duluth every Tuesday.

He'd only learned about it because his mother had told him a car had been delivered to the station that needed to go faster. Seeing the vehicle was Nightingale's hadn't surprised him. He'd rebuilt carburetors, put in larger radiators and fitted extra fuel tanks in all of the automobiles Roger Nightingale's hired men drove. A month later he'd discovered the latest coupe he'd worked on was being driving by Josie. Bronco, Roger's number one man, had brought the car over to get fuel, as he did for all of the cars the daughters drove, and had mentioned Josie sure used a lot of gas going to her Ladies Aid meetings.

Scooter's stomach fell almost as hard and fast now as it had in the past. He should have put a stop to it then. That had been his first mistake. His second had been keeping his mouth shut all this time.

"Hey, Scooter."

"Hey, Dave," Scooter replied, as Josie's uncle walked through the manicured trees. Dave Sutton lived in one of the bungalows on the other side of the pine trees. Not wanting to have to come up with an excuse as to what he was doing hanging around the resort's back door, Scooter asked, "How's your Chevy running?"

"Good. Those new tires you put on sure made a difference."

"Glad to hear it. Firestone makes a good tire, but only Fords come off the assembly line with them. Henry Ford knew what he was doing when he formed that partnership," Scooter said, trying not to look at the door behind him. He should never have let Josie go with Gloria. They had to be up to something.

"It's all about who you know, not what you know," Dave said before he asked, "How are Maize and Jonas?"

"Good," Scooter answered. The baseball bat, mitt and ball that had been left on the family's porch a couple of weeks ago had been from Dave. Just like several other birthday and Christmas gifts that had magically appeared on their porch over the years for Scooter's nephew. For whatever reason, Dave didn't want anyone to know he was the one that dropped them off. "Jonas had a birthday a couple of weeks ago, turned eight."

"Time flies," Dave said. "I remember when John got the letter from Maize saying the baby had arrived and that it was a boy."

A moment of silence spread between them. Dave and John had been shipped overseas together, and though the other man never spoke of it, Scooter had heard Dave was at John's side when he died. Even though Dave had been Josie's mother's brother, he'd moved back in with the Nightingales when he returned home, and now was Roger's top salesman. He carried around a suitcase full of resort brochures, but sample bottles of whiskey—Minnesota 13—were tucked inside hidden compartments. The home brew was better than the stuff the Canadians made and had become world-renowned. Thanks to Roger.

Everyone knew that, but no one mentioned it. A man might as well cut his own arm off if he did. The entire area thrived because of Roger's business, and no one wanted things to go back to the way they'd been.

"Jonas is here somewhere," Scooter said, still trying

to keep the conversation off what he was doing. He nodded toward the crowd that littered the slope leading toward the lake. "He's excited to stay late enough to see the fireworks."

"It is the Fourth of July," Dave said. "And those nieces of mine outdid themselves with this party."

"They sure enough did," Scooter agreed, glancing toward the door.

"I'll mosey around, see if I can find Jonas and say hi," Dave said.

"Try the beach," Scooter said. "He was convinced he'd learn how to swim today. Otherwise just listen for the popping noise. I bought him several rolls of firecrackers."

"I bet that made him happy."

"It sure did," Scooter said. The firecrackers were only a nickel for a hundred, and he'd gladly paid the minimal price. There had been times in his life where a nickel had seemed like a dollar. Now, thanks to Roger Nightingale's success, his fueling station allowed him to spend money a bit frivolously once in a while. He'd picked up several boxes of sparklers, too, for Jonas to share with his friends later on in the evening.

"I'll see you around," Scooter said, stepping closer to the door. Josie should have returned by now.

Dave nodded and waved as he took his leave. Scooter grabbed the doorknob but didn't have time to pull it open.

"Hey, Scooter, hold up."

His fingers clenched the door handle before he let it loose and Scooter pulled up a smile for the couple walking hand in hand toward him. Getting hit by a Studebaker couldn't have shocked him more than the sight of Brock and Ginger pulling up to his gas pumps that morning. He and Brock had been friends since childhood and Scooter had questioned if he'd ever see Brock again when his old pal had headed down to Chicago to perform on the radio several weeks ago.

Brock had defied Roger Nightingale by refusing to perform solely at the resort and leaving town, which had been an act few men would have the guts to follow through on. Marrying Ginger, Roger's youngest daughter, could have gotten Brock killed, too. Scooter figured Brock didn't have a chip on his shoulder; he had an angel.

"Where's Josie?" Ginger asked.

Scooter gestured toward the door. "Inside, talking with Gloria Kasper."

Ginger shot a concerned glance at Brock and then asked, "Why? Is she not feeling well?"

It was still hard to believe Brock and Ginger were married. Then again, Scooter had been shocked to see Norma Rose at his gas station with Ty Bradshaw earlier this summer, and again when he'd heard Twyla had gone flying with Forrest in his airplane. A lot had changed this summer. Maybe all that contributed to his urgency to make Josie stop her Duluth runs. The fact her sisters weren't around to keep her in line meant it was up to him.

He doubted any of the sisters knew of Josie's activities. They'd have told their father and Roger would have put a stop to it all long ago. "She's fine," he answered. "It was probably something to do with the party."

"I can't believe all that's happened in the short time we've been gone," Ginger said. "It's like I left one world and returned to another." Her sparkling eyes were once again gazing up at Brock.

The two of them looked as love-struck as two doves on a telephone wire. Feeling a bit like an intruder, Scooter looked the other way when Brock leaned down to kiss her, and didn't turn back until Ginger spoke.

"I'm going to find Josie," she said. "The dance-off is about to start."

The prize for the winner of the dance contest was a hundred bucks. Not for the couple to share, but a hundred bucks each. Scooter had read that in the advertisements. Add Babe Ruth, Twyla's wedding and fireworks, and it was no wonder half the state was in attendance. Those who lived out of town and couldn't find rooms to rent had set up tents in empty lots and backyards. This would be an event the town would remember for a long time.

When Ginger disappeared through the side door, Scooter once again attempted to shift his attention off how long Josie had been gone. "I thought I was seeing things when you pulled into my place this morning."

Brock laughed. "Your face said as much."

"That new car you're driving says things turned out real swell for you in Chicago." Scooter stated the obvious.

"If I hadn't lived it, I wouldn't have believed it." Brock's gaze shot back to the door where Ginger had disappeared. "Some days I still don't believe it."

Scooter playfully punched his friend in the arm. "We all knew you'd make it big."

"I don't think I would have if not for Ginger," Brock said. "She's the reason we're home. When she heard about Twyla's wedding, she told Oscar—Oscar Goldman, he's the owner of the radio station, that we were coming home. She promised to bring back a case of baseballs signed by Babe Ruth to give away on the radio." Brock laughed. "She already has two cases, signed, in the trunk."

Scooter chuckled. "I'm sure Babe Ruth couldn't say

no to Ginger." Curious, he asked, "How'd she end up in Chicago?"

"Now, that, my friend, is a long story," Brock said. "And calling Roger to tell him I'd found her under the tarp of my truck when I'd stopped for fuel on the other side of Wisconsin was one of the scariest things I'd ever done."

"Under the tarp of your truck?" Scooter shook his head. "I put the tarp on your truck while you were locking horns with Roger about leaving."

"I know," Brock said. "And she climbed in right afterward." Growing serious, Brock added, "Don't let any one of those Nightingale girls fool you. They're sneaky when they want to be."

"Ain't that the truth," Scooter mumbled under his breath.

"You dating Josie?" Brock asked.

"Nope."

When Scooter didn't elaborate, Brock said, "I guess I assumed you were when Roger called you and her over with the rest of us."

"I was just standing next to her," Scooter explained. "A case of being in the wrong place at the wrong time."

Brock grinned. "If you say so."

"I say so, all right," Scooter said, withholding the truth. Trying to keep Josie from being shipped to some foreign land came nowhere near dating her. Changing the subject, he asked, "When are you heading back to Chicago?"

"Monday," Brock said. "Want to spend some time with my mom and dad tomorrow."

That reminded Scooter of another case of being in the wrong place at the wrong time. Last year Brock's dad had been shot while delivering milk down in St. Paul.

A raid had been happening nearby and the bullet that struck Rodney Ness had left the man paralyzed from the waist down.

"Ma said he's been getting out a lot more lately," Brock said. "Says that wheelchair has made all the difference."

Scooter guessed it wasn't so much the chair that made the real difference for Rodney as the fact Brock had bought it with earnings he'd made by singing on the radio. He figured Brock knew that, as well. Rodney Ness couldn't stop talking about his radio-star son.

They conversed a bit longer, about nothing in particular. All the while, both of them kept sending curious glances toward the door. When Ginger appeared by herself, Brock grinned while Scooter frowned.

"I can't find her anywhere," Ginger said. "Norma Rose will be furious. She said none of us could win the prize, that wouldn't look right, but we all have to participate in the contest."

"That didn't stop her from winning the last dance-off," Scooter said, when really he wanted to ask Ginger where she'd looked. The place was massive, with three stories covered in inch-thick red carpet, varnished oak wainscoting and stair rails, and velvet curtains covering more windows than a man could count. It was a palace in comparison to his humble home, and Josie had to be in there somewhere.

"You know Norma Rose," Ginger said.

Not as well as he knew Josie. Unable to stop himself, he asked, "You checked everywhere for Josie?"

"Yes," Ginger answered. "The offices, the bedrooms, the kitchen."

"Maybe they went out another door," Brock suggested.

Scooter spun around to stare at the garage full of cars,

all owned by Roger. Surely he'd have heard if one had started. "You look 'round the back," he said. "I'll go out front."

Brock grabbed his arm before Scooter had taken more than a step. "What do you know that we don't?"

Scooter was sick of lying, but didn't have much choice. "Nothing. Other than the wrath of Norma Rose."

Brock's gaze said he didn't believe that, but his friend must have chosen not to say more in front of Ginger.

"Bring her straight to the dance floor if you find her," Ginger said. "We'll do the same."

Scooter didn't bother answering and kicked his feet into a sprint. The garage was full, every car in its place, including Josie's red-and-black coupe. Walter, another one of Roger's men, was there.

"Have you seen Josie?" Scooter asked.

The portly man dropped the book he'd been reading and leaped up from his chair just inside the door. "No, why? What's happened?"

Scooter attempted to disguise a bit of his distress. "Nothing," he said, heading for Josie's car. Unlatching the hood, he lifted it and reached in to disconnect the ignition wire. Closing the hood, he told Walter, "I'm making sure it stays that way. Don't tell her I was here."

Walter lifted a brow.

"Trust me." Walking out of the open doorway, Scooter spun around. "Don't let her in another car, either."

"I'll pull the keys," Walter said, "but does Roger know?"

"There's no place she needs to go today," Scooter said. "Roger will agree with that." Turning around, he headed for the front door of the resort. Cars of all makes and models filled the parking lot. Some he recognized as belonging to regular customers, others he'd never seen before. Josie could jump in and drive away in any number of them; more than half had the keys sticking in the ignition.

Scooter shook his head as he entered the resort's double front doors. Someday people would learn to take their keys with them. Car theft didn't happen in these parts, but someday it would.

He checked the offices, the ballroom, the kitchen and storerooms, along with every other door he came upon before taking the back staircase to the second floor. Halfway down the hall he came to a heavy door that obviously separated family rooms from the rest of the guest rooms.

Opening and closing doors, he concluded whose room was whose by the colors of the walls. Pink for Ginger, red for Norma Rose, green for Twyla and white for Josie. The rooms were empty and he didn't bother checking the third floor. Josie wouldn't be up there.

Scooter jogged back down the hall and the staircase that led into the ballroom. Then, with his footsteps echoing, he crossed the floor and passed the empty bar to exit the building onto the balcony. Searching for a pond-green dress, he found Twyla and Norma Rose, and then Ginger, although the youngest sister was wearing a red polka-dot dress. But there was no sign of Josie. His mother, however, was standing next to the cake table on the far side of the dance floor.

"Hello, Eric," she greeted him as he arrived at her side. "I'm getting Jonas another piece of cake. He's certainly enjoying the day."

His nephew was usually at the top of Scooter's list, but

even Jonas had to take second place right now. "Where's Josie?" Scooter asked. "And don't tell me you don't know. Gloria ushered her into the house." Adding gravity to his tone, he added, "To talk."

His mother opened her mouth, but closed it as she glanced around. When she turned back to him, she leaned closer to whisper, "This is none of your affair, Eric."

This was the woman who'd given birth to him and kept him alive through those days when food was short and heat almost nonexistent, yet, at this moment, she was nothing more than a barrier. "Where is she, Mother? Today is not a day to send her off on one of your missions. I won't put up with it and neither will Roger."

Startled to the point her slice of cake toppled off the plate in her hand, she asked, "You haven't told him, have you?"

Scooter didn't answer, just stared her down.

One of the many girls hired to keep guests happy by serving glasses of their choice and keeping the place neat and tidy appeared with a new slice of cake on a clean plate. She took the plate from his mother's hand and, after scooping the cake off the ground, the girl disappeared just as quickly as she'd come.

Thankfully, for he didn't want a family showdown in the middle of the party, his mother realized how serious he was.

"She's with Gloria. In the Willow."

All of the resort's twenty cabins along the shoreline were named, and he knew the Willow was settled between two large willow trees among the north set of cabins. Spinning around and forcing his feet to move at a normal pace in order to not draw attention to himself,

Scooter headed toward the pathway that led to the cabins. All the while, his heart rate increased.

Once the trees hid him from most of the partygoers, he increased his speed. His mind raced, too, telling him over and over that he shouldn't have let Josie out of his sight. That had been his plan and he should have stuck to it. Shortly after collecting her from Duluth, a truck driver with a flat tire had pulled into his station. The truck was from the huge US Steel plant in Duluth. While working on the tire, Scooter had mentioned he'd recently been in Duluth. The man asked if he'd visited the docks and the girls there. With a few innocent-sounding questions, Scooter had learned all sorts of information from that truck driver and none of it was anything Josie should be involved in.

Upon arrival at the little green-and-white cabin, he leaped up the two steps and threw open the door.

Gloria was still jumping up from a chair at the table when Scooter slammed the door shut behind him. "Where's Josie?"

A single glance toward the bedroom door told him all he needed to know.

"You can't go in there," Gloria declared, as he started in direction of the door.

"You can't stop me." He was already pushing open the door, and what he saw not only stopped him in his tracks, but it also sent his temper soaring. "Get your dress back on."

Josie finished buttoning the top of her white blouse before spinning around. A combination of anger and relief surged across her stomach. Going with anger, she planted her hands on the waistband of her dungarees. "I will not."

"Yes, you will."

"No, I won't." This sounded a lot like the conversation she'd had with Gloria a short time ago. That argument she'd lost. This one, she wouldn't. Scooter had no say in what she did or when she did it, and it was beyond time he realized that.

He strode forward. "You either change back into your dress, or I will."

"Go ahead," she said. "It's an ugly dress, but I doubt it'll fit you."

The anger in his eyes was enough to make her flinch, but he didn't notice her reaction, not with Gloria storming into the room.

"Eric, this is none of your business," the woman insisted. "Now leave."

"I'm not going anywhere," he said, "and neither is Josie."

Josie had half a mind to tell him he was wasting his breath, but some people just had to learn that on their own. She had learned it years ago. Offering an opinion when no one was willing to listen was as useless as raking leaves during a storm.

"Do you honestly think she can sneak away on one of your missions today?" he was asking Gloria. "The entire family is looking for her. The dance-off is about to start, and Roger wants her on the floor along with her sisters—

Gloria frowned. "What dance-off?"

Since the doctor was now looking her way, Josie answered, "It's for the guests."

"Not just for the guests," Scooter said none too quietly. "Your sisters say it can't start until you're there."

"Why didn't you tell me about this?" Gloria asked.

Josie wanted to scream. She had told Gloria sneaking away today would be too difficult, but when it came to her cause, Gloria dismissed any obstacles in her way. Normally, Josie did, too, but today things just hadn't *felt* right. Hence the relief at Scooter's arrival that softened her spine. She wouldn't tell anyone, or let it show, but the thought of traveling to Duluth today frightened her. In all honesty, the past couple of missions had scared her— ever since she'd been arrested for speeding.

"You must have known about it," Scooter said to Gloria. "It's been in all the advertisements about the party."

"Blast it," Gloria said as she took to pacing the floor. "With Francine Wilks and her number one henchman here, we have a chance of discovering where those girls are."

Josie flinched, and noted how Scooter noticed this time. He was sharp, and Gloria should have realized how much information her babbling was giving away. Then again, Gloria was no fool, and most likely knew exactly what she was doing. To be fair, Scooter probably knew that, too.

He took Gloria's arm with one hand and pointed at the pea-green dress with the other. "Put that back on," he said, while pulling the other woman to the door. "And be quick about it."

Josie feared quick wouldn't be quick enough. It would still give Scooter time to question Gloria about their activities. Francine Wilks had a warehouse in Duluth where she kept girls "that weren't ready," as the madam had put it. Francine didn't mind her working girls receiving the free condoms Josie passed out along the waterfront, but the woman didn't let anyone near her captives.

Scooter didn't need to know any of that. Josie headed for the door as he pulled it closed, and she grabbed the knob before the door shut.

"You can leave, Scooter." Josie knew he wouldn't leave just because she told him to. "Please go tell my sisters I'll be right there. I don't want them looking for me."

"I'll wait," he said. "Deliver you to the dance floor myself."

"That won't be necessary," she said.

"It won't be necessary for me to put that dress back on you, either," he said staunchly, "but if you don't hurry up, I will."

"Hurry up, Josie," Gloria said. "I'll keep Scooter company while you change."

That was exactly what she didn't want to happen. She didn't need Scooter learning more than he already knew about her Tuesday adventures. He'd never understand.

"Are you waiting for help?" he asked.

"No," she snapped.

"Then get dressed."

Josie slammed the door. Maybe he and Gloria should pair up and leave her completely out of things. It had gotten to be more than she'd bargained for lately.

Her anger melted away like the swan-shaped ice sculpture near the fountain. The ice had yielded to the sun before Twyla and Forrest's wedding, and now Josie had to yield, too, to the truth that things had only become more than she'd bargained for because of her.

The rules were that she passed out condoms and brought back any bits of information she gathered. However, when one of Francine's girls had told Josie about the warehouse, she'd had to investigate. One of the guards had seen her sneaking around and had given chase. Afraid her little car couldn't outrun his larger one, she'd taken the road that led directly past the police station, hoping an officer would see her speeding by.

One had.

She'd been arrested.

And she'd called Scooter to come and get her.

Chapter Four

Scooter hadn't been lying. Her sisters had been looking for her, and the expression on her father's face said he wasn't impressed.

"I'm sorry, Daddy," she said, rushing up to where he stood next to the piano. Other instruments had been set up, too. Swallowing, she added, "There were things I had to see to."

"Like what?" Norma Rose asked. "We looked everywhere for you."

"There were some issues with one of the cabins." Josie felt her insides sinking again with the number of lies she'd told lately.

"We have maintenance people for that," her father said.

"It's all settled now," Scooter said. Giving her father a nod, he started to step away.

"Not so fast, there, son," her father said. "Josie needs a dance partner." With that, her father stepped forward and called for the crowd's attention.

"I have fireworks to set off," Scooter said to her. "You're going to have to find yourself another partner."

That would have suited Josie just fine, however, she

didn't need her father's fury. "And irritate my father further?" she snapped. "Not on your life. We'll bow out of the contest in plenty of time for you to set off the fireworks."

His eyes narrowed. "And plenty of time for you to still sneak away?"

"No," she snapped. Then, because there hadn't been time earlier, not with the way he'd dragged her from the cabin to the dance floor, she asked, "What did you and Gloria talk about?"

His glower grew darker. "Let's just say we have an understanding."

"That neither of you will tell my father what the other knows," she concluded. Her father would be furious. "Maybe I'll tell him about both of you."

"Go ahead," Scooter said. "It's what I've wanted all along." Snapping his fingers, he added, "He'll put a stop to your shenanigans that fast."

"They aren't shenanigans," she insisted.

He grabbed her hand. "Whatever they are, you aren't doing them tonight. You're going to be glued to my side like chrome on a bumper."

Josie didn't have time to respond. The moment music filled the air, people ran to snag an inch on the dance floor. Scooter shouldered their way into the very center, and there he held her so close she could barely breathe, let alone dance. Being this close to him increased her anger.

"Good grief, Scooter." She pushed at his shoulders with both hands. "You're smothering me."

"It's not me. We're packed in here tighter than whiskey bottles in a crate."

It was only then that Josie realized his hands barely rested on her sides; the pressure forcing her against him was from someone pressed against her back. She'd danced with Scooter many times over the past few weeks, and had never experienced the sensations she was feeling right now. Every inch of her body was sizzling. She'd like to believe it was her anger, but knew it wasn't. This was different.

In fact, she wasn't mad at Scooter for interrupting her journey to Duluth. That had been a bad idea from the minute Gloria had suggested it—the two of them would surely have been missed. She was mad because he wanted her to stop. That wasn't an option. Not even if she wanted it to be.

She'd never gotten a good look at Francine Wilks or her henchman. For her to pick them out in the crowd tonight was impossible. There were too many people. She was comforted knowing the same was true for them. There was no way for them to make a link between the woman handing out condoms and her or the resort, not unless they recognized her car. To be on the safe side, for the past couple of trips she'd made to Duluth, she'd swapped cars with Twyla, who'd been so busy planning this party she hadn't questioned why. Neither of their cars was so unique they stood out in a crowd, so even if Francine or her man saw the family vehicles in the garage out front, they still wouldn't know.

"What are you thinking so hard about?" Scooter asked.

Snapping her head up, Josie replied, "Nothing, other than I wish there was more room."

Scooter started to lead them sideways, which was a slow task.

"Are we bowing out?" she asked, not sure whether she was pleased or not about that idea.

"No, but I see Dac. I'll ask him to move some tables

and give us some room on the grass. If either of us leave to do it, we'll be eliminated."

She joined his efforts, elbowing people aside, all the while dancing, until they were at the side of the dance floor. Scooter yelled for Dac Lester, who quickly found a couple of other men to assist him. Drawing her hand over her head, Scooter twirled Josie around, off the dance floor and onto the grass. Other couples followed. Soon the grassy area was as full as the dance floor, but at least there was room to actually dance.

When a few people started shouting for disqualifications Slim Johnson yelled above the noise of the piano that the grass area was officially part of the dance floor.

"Goodness, people sure are serious about this contest," she said when the next dance had them in each other's arms once again.

"A hundred bucks means a lot to people," Scooter said. "Some of the folks here don't make that much in a month or more."

They were so close his chin was just over her shoulder, making his breath tickle her ear. Josie leaned back to look him in the eye. She hadn't been any more enthusiastic for this dance-off than she'd been the last time, but she'd gone along with her sisters. As usual, she'd do anything to keep the focus away from her. "I understand that. I'm the one who suggested the prize be cash. Norma Rose wanted to give away a bottle of whiskey again."

Scooter did have a rather fantastic grin. It was one of those smiles that fed others. "And a snow globe?"

Josie, although grinning, shook her head. "That is one of Norma Rose's prized possessions. It was back then, too, she just couldn't admit it that night."

"And now she can?"

"Yes, Ty won it for her at the amusement park."

He nodded and pulled her close to lean over her shoulder. Josie once again scanned the crowd, her thoughts returning to Francine Wilks. Guilt was eating at her, too. There were young girls in that warehouse Francine kept under guard. Girls that needed to be returned to their families. Gloria was sincerely disappointed, and Josie had to admit, she was, too. Uneasy or not, she could have put more effort into sneaking away. Those girls had little hope. Now that she'd participated in the dance-off, no one would be looking for her. Not even Scooter. He'd soon be too busy setting off fireworks to give her a second thought.

"What are you thinking so hard about now?"

She leaned back again. "Why do you keep asking that?"

"Because you keep becoming as stiff as a board," Scooter said. "And that tells me you're conjuring something up."

Just as her mind was coming up blank, Josie's gaze landed on Scooter's sister, Maize. She was standing on the sidelines, watching the dancers with a hint of longing in her face. Certainly not a wallflower, Maize could be dancing with any number of men. She chose not to. Once very lively and outgoing, Maize had been changed by the incident with Galen Reynolds.

"I'm just wondering," Josie said, turning her attention back to Scooter, knowing he was awaiting her answer, "why your sister never came to the resort for a job, rather than the Plantation."

Scooter shifted slightly as he glanced over his shoulder toward his sister. "I'd say that would be because of your uncle."

"Dave?" Josie asked, rather confused.

"Yes, Dave," Scooter answered. "He and John were friends."

Everyone knew Uncle Dave and John Blackburn had been friends. However, Scooter made it sound as if there was more behind it than she knew. Josie didn't have the energy to contemplate that notion any more deeply. Not right now. The music had changed to a faster beat, and with her mind elsewhere, her feet became tangled up when Scooter twirled her around.

Scooter's hold on her hand tightened, but it was too late—she was going down.

She landed on the grass, and he came down on top of her. The grassy area turned into a game of dominoes with people toppling over one another. Josie closed her eyes and tucked her head against Scooter's shoulder, hoping no one would land on them. For a few seconds she heard nothing but grunts and thuds. And music, which never stopped. Slim didn't so much as miss a beat.

"I think it's safe to get up now," Scooter said a few moments later.

She lifted her head. Others around them were scrambling to their feet.

Scooter pushed off her. The absence of his body pressing against hers left behind a tingling sensation from head to toe that she couldn't call relief. Unwilling to contemplate such things, Josie readily grasped the hands he held out and leaped to her feet.

Shaking her skirt back into place as soon as her toes touched the ground, she asked, "Dare I admit I'm glad that's over?"

"Only if I can, too," he replied.

"Deal."

He laughed. "Let's get out of here before we're knocked

down again," he said, taking her hand to lead her toward the tables.

Ginger and Brock stood there, among several others.

"Are you two all right?" Ginger asked.

Josie nodded.

"Well, applesauce," Ginger said, brushing grass off her skirt. "That was one huge mess. I thought I was going to get trampled."

Brock wrapped both arms around Ginger and pulled her back against his chest. "I wouldn't let that happen, doll. You know that."

Ginger grinned and looked up at him with sparkling eyes. "Yes, I do."

"Looks like your other sisters are still going strong," Scooter said.

Josie scanned the crowd and found Twyla and Norma Rose, dancing with their partners, completely oblivious to what had happened on the other side of the dance floor.

"Need a drink after that, Scooter?" Brock asked.

Scooter shook his head. "No, thanks, I have to go get the fireworks set up."

"Need any help?" Brock asked.

"Dac's helping," Scooter said while wrapping a hand around Josie's arm. "So is Josie. You and Ginger are welcome to row out in another boat if you want. Could be fun."

"Yes, let's," Ginger said, looking up at Brock, who nodded.

"I'm not helping you," Josie whispered, as Scooter forced her to start walking beside him.

"Yes, you are." His lips had barely moved. "I said

you'd be glued to my side for the rest of the night, and I meant it."

"I have things to do," Josie hissed.

"Not anymore," he insisted.

Ginger grabbed her other arm. "This is going to be so much fun," Ginger said. "I've never lit fireworks before. Have you?"

"No," Josie admitted. "And I'd prefer not to."

"Why?" Ginger asked.

"They scare me."

"Liar," Scooter whispered in her ear. Then, loud enough for everyone to hear, he said, "Don't worry, you'll be safe with me. As safe as a baby in her mommy's arms."

"My mother is dead," Josie said sarcastically.

Ginger flashed her a frown, but Scooter laughed.

"Sticks and stones may break my bones, but words will never hurt me," he said.

"Ducky, Scooter, how old are you, ten?" she asked.

"If the shoe fits," he said, lifting an eyebrow.

"I'm not the one acting childishly," she snarled.

"Aren't you?"

"Fine," she said stubbornly. "I'll help light your fireworks."

"But?"

"But what?" she asked.

"You normally add a *but* to everything you agree to do."

"I do not, but I will remember you think I do."

He lifted a brow again.

"I said that on purpose," she retorted.

Ginger laughed. "Stop teasing her, Scooter. The two of you are sounding like Twyla and Norma Rose."

They'd stopped on the far side of the crowd.

"Norma Rose and Twyla argued?" Brock asked teasingly.

"Like a Siamese cat and a bulldog," Ginger said. "You can guess which is which."

They all laughed. Even Josie. Ginger had never minded letting people know what she thought.

"Where are the fireworks?" Brock asked.

"Dac and I anchored a raft out in the middle of the lake," Scooter answered. "We have two boats full of fireworks down by the south cabins." Gesturing toward the boathouses at the bottom of the slope, he added, "You two may want to take a boat out of one of those houses. I have to get my motorcycle. There are things I need in the saddlebags."

Josie recognized the chance for an escape. "I'll go with—"

"Me," Scooter interrupted. "I need your help."

"Perfect," Ginger said, tugging on Brock's arm. "See you on the water."

As the other couple started walking away, Josie said, "You don't need my help."

"No, I don't," Scooter said, spinning her to face him with a firm hold on her elbow. "But I'm not letting you out of my sight. Remember?"

"How could I forget?"

Dac Lester, a tall, thin man with a permanent grin on his face, caught up with them a few steps later. "We heading out to the raft?"

"Yes," Scooter answered. "It'll be easier to get everything set up while there's still some daylight."

"Sounds good to me," Dac said. "You joining us, Josie?"

"Yes, she is," Scooter answered.

"Good enough," Dac said, nodding toward the resort.

"My cycle's on the other side of the parking lot. I'll meet you at the boathouses."

As Dac jogged away, Josie told Scooter, "I have a mouth and could have answered him myself."

"I know," Scooter said. "Trust me, I know."

Josie pulled her arm out of his hold and ignored the way he laughed.

He stayed right at her side, no doubt ready to grab her if she attempted to make a run for it. She might have tried it, too, if there was anywhere for her to run. But that was unlikely tonight. It wouldn't be worth the effort, either. He'd catch her with these stupid shoes on her feet.

Eventually, they arrived at his motorcycle parked near the garage. Walter, the man in charge of looking after the family cars, stepped out of the garage as they arrived. He merely tipped his hat toward Scooter and reentered the side door. She wondered what Walter did in there all the time. He was nearly always there, unless he was in her father's office or walking the grounds.

Scooter lifted his flat leather hat off the seat and set it on his head. "I'll get it started before you climb on."

She'd always been intrigued by his motorcycle, which was bright red with *Indian* painted in flourished gold lettering on the fuel tank, but still she insisted, "I'm not riding that. It's dangerous."

"And speeding through downtown Duluth isn't?"

She glared, but turned as Dac whizzed past them on his motorbike, waving.

The start of an engine had her turning back to Scooter.

He had straddled the seat of his bike. "Climb on behind me," he shouted above the noise. "But don't let your leg touch that." He pointed to a long cylinder. "That's the muffler. It'll burn you."

"There's no room," she pointed out. The leather seat was clearly made for only one person.

"You can sit on this." He patted a flat metal platform that rode above the back tire and was attached to the back of his seat. A set of old-fashioned leather saddle-bags was strapped onto the platform and hung over both sides. "Jonas does all the time."

"You allow a child to ride on this thing?"

"Jonas loves it," he said. "Climb on. Even my mother has ridden on it."

"Well, I'm not," she insisted.

"Yes, you are," Scooter said, grabbing her arm.

She could argue. There wasn't much he could do. However, the idea of climbing on behind him was making her heart skip. She'd often wondered about riding on his motorcycle. Josie played with her options a moment longer, mainly to irritate him, before eventually stepping closer.

His smile said he'd known she'd give in. "Pull your skirt up and tuck it between your legs so it doesn't get caught in the tires or burned by the muffler."

"I told you this was dangerous," she said, unable to think of anything else.

"But you want to ride it," he said, grinning. "I know you do."

Josie wouldn't admit that if her life depended on it. Which it almost did. He could still tell her father about her activities at the docks anytime. Life certainly would be much easier if she was more like her sisters—in love with fashion or money or men.

Gritting her teeth, Josie hitched up her skirt and swung one leg over the seat behind Scooter.

"Put your feet on top of mine," he said, "to keep them out of the way."

Closing her eyes against the shocking sensations zipping up her thighs, Josie did as she was told, tucked her skirt under her legs and held her breath. This was outrageous.

"Hold on," Scooter said over his shoulder, still shouting above the noise.

"To what?" she shouted in return.

He grabbed one of her arms and pulled it around his waist. "To me."

The cycle shot forward. With a squeal, Josie grabbed his waist with her other hand, as well. She slid closer to his back, too, despite the way her inner thighs stung from the contact.

After the initial shock of the tires moving, and of riding on two wheels, she settled in, let out the air she'd been holding in her lungs and realized she was smiling. It was fun. The wind in her hair. The way Scooter leaned slightly left or right while maneuvering the curves along the road leading past the cabins toward the lake. It was all exciting in a daring sort of way. She wasn't surprised, either. For as long as she could remember, she got a thrill out of things her sisters always found a bit frightening. Of course, back then, it had been frogs and snakes or salamanders and mice. It was what had made her become involved with Gloria's crusade.

She'd also always secretly coveted Scooter's motorcycle. Slipping in and out of the dock area in Duluth would be so much easier than in a car. There wouldn't be any place to store her goods, though, and that would be a problem. She also needed a backseat for someone to hide in. She'd considered that issue when Twyla had been trying to persuade their father to buy a convertible.

Thankfully, convincing him how dangerous a car with no top could be had been a simple feat.

The motorcycle slowed and Scooter placed his feet on the ground as it came to a stop. "Careful of the muffler," he reminded her as the engine went silent.

Josie had been in the process of dropping her feet to the ground, and she stopped. Holding her legs out to the sides, she asked, "How am I supposed to get off, then?"

He chuckled. "You don't have to be that careful, just mindful," he said. "The muffler is tucked under the frame, but it still gets hot." He leaned to the left, angling the motorcycle slightly. "There, step off."

Josie slid off with almost no problems, other than her ugly pea-green skirt getting caught on the saddlebag. She managed to get it loose without doing damage to the material, which would not have broken her heart. Stepping back, she waited while Scooter kicked down a metal stance bar and pushed the cycle backward to balance upright on the stand.

"Is it heavy?" Josie asked.

"Is what heavy?" Scooter asked, climbing off.

"Your motorcycle," she said as he spun around to search in the saddlebag. "Is it heavy? Hard to lift onto its stand?"

"No," Scooter answered, seconds before an eerie sensation tickled his spine. Turning slowly, he spied the thoughtful expression covering Josie's face. Sometimes her thoughts were as easy to read as a billboard. "For me," he clarified. "For you, it would be way too heavy."

"I'm stronger than I look."

He pulled out the rest of the fuses and punks he'd assembled to light the crates of Roman candles, sky rockets, mortars and flying torpedoes Josie had requested that he order for the evening's enjoyment and shoved them in his back pocket. At first he'd questioned the amount of money she'd given him to place the order, but upon learning about the rest of the day's events, he'd spent every dime. Nightingale would want the night to end with a bang, and it was his job to make sure it would.

Right now, though, it was his job to get whatever idea Josie had brewing out of her pretty little head. He took her by the arm and steered her toward the boathouse down the hill. "You could never handle a motorcycle, so quit thinking you could."

Her attempt to wrench her arm out of his hold failed.

"You have no idea what I can and can't handle," she said.

"Oh, yes, I do." He marched her down the hill and onto the dock. There he handed over the things from his pocket so they'd be kept dry. "Hold these and wait here."

"What are these?" she asked, taking the items.

"Fuses and punks to light the fireworks," he said, stepping off the dock toward the boathouse built into the sloping hill. "Don't let them get wet."

Each cabin had its own dock and boathouse, which were small sheds built of rocks and thick logs to store the boats and other items guests might find enjoyable to use. Lawn chairs and such. The cabins were old, having been constructed years before, when the resort had originally been built, but they'd been refurbished, or at least some had. Others were still being worked on. The two where he'd chosen to store the fireworks had just recently been fixed up. He'd chosen them for the new locks on the sturdy doors. He'd known kids would be all over the resort today and he hadn't wanted a couple of sneaky young ones to play with things they shouldn't.

Dac was already in the second house when Scooter unlocked the door and entered the other dimly lit shed. He quickly checked the boat, making sure the barrels and crates hadn't been disturbed before he stepped around the boat to unlatch the heavy double doors facing the lake.

The boat slid down the sandy slope into the water next to the dock. After closing the double doors, he jogged along the sand and jumped onto the wooden planks of the dock, catching the boat as it floated close. "Go ahead and climb in," he told Josie, holding the boat steady with a rope.

She did so without mishap, and sat down on the farthest of the three plank seats that stretched from side to side. "Don't you want one of the boats with motors?" she asked.

Nightingale's had several boats with motors that they rented out to guests, and he'd purposely chosen ones with only paddles. "No," he said, stepping down into the boat.

"Why?"

Settled on the center seat, he held out a hand for her to pass him the equipment. "Because of these. Fire and gas don't mix."

She nodded and looked away.

After stuffing the fuses and punks in his pocket again, he grasped both oar handles.

Dac waved from his boat nearby. "All set?"

"All set," Scooter answered. Dusk hung on for hours during the summer. It would be some time before it was dark enough to set off the fireworks, but getting them all set up would take time.

Josie was facing him, and as if that bothered her, she kicked up her feet and, without standing up, she spun around to face the other way. The beads on her green headdress clicked together. He laughed. "You can take that silly thing off your head."

One hand rose and she patted her head, then the other one rose and she pulled the headdress off. Setting it on the bench beside her, she fluffed up her hair with both hands. "This is all fireworks?" she asked, referring to the cargo filling the bow in front of her.

Her hair was the color of sunshine and bobbed near her shoulders. Why she'd wanted to cover it up with those pond-green beads was beyond Scooter. Then again, why she did most things was beyond him. "Yes," he answered. "It's all fireworks."

"What's in Dac's boat?"

"More of the same."

She turned to look at him over her shoulder. "Isn't that a lot?"

"It's what you ordered."

Nodding, she turned back around. "Twyla wanted it to be a day no one will forget."

"Twyla wants every day to be one no one will forget," he said.

She twirled back around, her knees folded so her feet didn't skim the bench as she spun. The action caused a bit of her thigh to show and Scooter averted his gaze. Momentarily. A strong force had his eyes going right back.

Josie was facing him now, so he focused on keeping his eyes on her face. Which was almost as disturbing. She was so pretty. Always had been. Every part of her was eye-catching and more than a bit appealing.

"Why do you say that?"

"Say what?" He honestly didn't know. Another glimpse of her shapely thigh had burned a hole in his brain.

"That Twyla wants every day to be one no one will forget," she said. "What's wrong with that? It is her wedding day."

"Yeah, I know," he said. "And it will end with a bang."

Crossing her arms, Josie lifted her chin. "You could have said no."

Momentarily confused, he asked, "To what?"

"Setting off the fireworks," she said. "I could have found someone else."

That galled Scooter. She could have asked someone else, and they'd readily have agreed. Saying no to her ranked up there with saying no to her father. Very few men did that, and those who did faced the penalty. Just ask Jeb Smith, who was rotting in the hoosegow and would be for years. Although Jeb had had it coming. He'd attempted to double-cross Roger. Smitty, as Jeb was known, had run shine for years for Roger, until he'd decided to start skimming bottles off the top and reselling them himself. He'd boasted about refusing to tell Roger who he was selling the "extras" to when Scooter had filled his tank one night, mere hours before he got arrested in St. Paul.

"I could have, you know," Josie said. "You're not the only one who knows how to light fireworks."

"I know," Scooter answered. He also knew the consequences of not being on the up-and-up when it came to her father. Roger took pride knowing what was going on in all aspects of his business, and Scooter imagined that when it came to someone claiming his actions had put one of his daughters in danger, Roger would be furious. "But you didn't," he said, almost with remorse. He should have told Roger what he'd discovered right after talking to that trucker, whether the man would have wanted to hear it or not. Now, after this length of time, Roger could claim that Scooter withholding the information was just as bad as attempting to double-cross him.

Josie fidgeted, but kept her arms crossed. "Only because Twyla suggested I ask you."

"Back to Twyla again, are we?" That was fine with Scooter. It was a safer subject than the one rolling around in his head. "The life of the party. The center of attention. That's Twyla." Leaning closer, while still rowing with both arms, he continued, "While you, Miss Josie Nightingale, love being the mouse in the corner. You don't want anyone to see you, but you certainly don't want to miss anything, either."

"I do not." Shaking her head, she insisted, "I don't care what I miss, and I do not hide in the corner."

"Yes, you do," he said. "You hide and you listen. Your only saving grace is that you rarely repeat what you've heard."

Her lips pinched together as she glared at him.

He chuckled. "Cat got your tongue?"

Her eyes narrowed.

"Did you know the British proclaimed the Germans had cats and dogs spying on them during the war?" he asked.

She unfolded her arms and fluffed out her skirt around her knees. "You're making that up."

Scooter had no idea why that bit of trivia had entered his mind, but figured it was because he was desperately trying to sidetrack his other thoughts. "I'm not making it up. Ask your uncle Dave."

"I will," she said snootily. "And next time we need fireworks, I'll ask someone else to organize them."

"That'll be fine by me," he said.

"Me, too."

Scooter's fists tightened around the oar handles as he rowed with more vigor. "Call me nuts for saying yes this time," he muttered.

"That's not a very nice thing to say."

"Just the truth," he said. "A man has to be nuts to get tangled up with any of you girls."

"Ducky, Scooter," she sneered.

"It's the truth," he snapped. "Ginger hiding under Brock's tarp, Twyla and her kissing booth—" He snapped his lips closed. Those were nothing compared to Josie's escapade. But the way her lips were puckered made him think of kissing her. If Josie had a kissing booth, he'd pay more than a dime. He would have even years ago, when he couldn't have afforded it. That inner confession didn't settle well, and he turned his focus back to rowing the boat.

They were nearing the raft he and Dac had anchored in the center of the lake earlier. Two other boats were already there. Dac's on one side, and Brock and Ginger's on the opposite side.

Josie flashed him a playful smile, before she spun around. "Hey, Brock," she shouted, "do you know Scooter thinks you're nuts?"

"Yep," Brock shouted in return. "He's told me that more than once."

Scooter leaned forward again. "Satisfied?" he asked, although he was a bit surprised she'd said that to Brock. Josie normally kept her mouth shut. Normally they would have a hard time getting something out of her.

His brain, which for whatever reason wasn't functioning as smartly as usual, kicked back into gear. She was mad at him. Had been all day. His attempts to put a stop to her shenanigans must have her seeing red. She'd been trying to start a fight with him, probably so she could finagle a way to make her getaway.

Glad to once again be thinking straight, Scooter said, "I'm not letting you out of my sight. So get over it."

She didn't comment, but did stand up and grasp the edge of the raft, to keep the boat stable as it glided to a stop. Brock and Dac had tied the fronts and backs of their boats to the corner posts, keeping the rowboats flush with the floating platform. Scooter did the same to his and Josie's boat.

"Applesauce," Ginger squealed as she climbed onto the raft with Brock's help. "You have enough fireworks for the entire state, Scooter."

"I was just following Josie's orders," he said, stepping onto the boards before turning around to offer Josie a hand.

She took hold of his hand, but once on the floating platform, let go. The raft had been plenty large enough when he and Dac had built it, but now, with all five of them standing on the boards, it seemed to have shrunk.

"So, what can we do to help?" Ginger asked.

"You," Brock said, flicking the end of her nose, "and Josie can sit down on the edge by our boat and stay out of the way while Scooter, Dac and I unload the boats."

"All right," she said, stretching onto her toes to kiss Brock's chin.

Scooter couldn't say he was jealous. *Envious* would be a better word. Josie would never take kindly to being told to stay out of the way. She'd never, ever, readily agree to it, either.

Ginger took a hold of Josie's arm, pulling her toward the side where Brock's boat was tied. "Let's sit over here. We can't lift those heavy crates."

Josie's glare told Scooter how unimpressed she was with her little sister's immediate compliance. He grinned and lifted a brow.

She squinted and spun around.

Before she'd taken more than a step, it dawned on him that she could easily jump in the other boat and start paddling away. He wouldn't put it past her. Wouldn't put anything past her. Stepping forward, he grasped her shoulder.

Stiff as a board, she spun around.

"Hold these again, would you?" he asked, pulling the fuses and punks from his back pocket. "I don't want them to get wet."

Scooter pulled off his suit coat, glad to finally be rid of the thing. The heat of Josie riding behind him on his cycle had somehow become trapped inside his coat, making all sorts of crazy ideas dance in his head. He tossed the coat into his boat before he started directing Dac and Scooter as to which crates to unload first and where to stack them. He kept one eye on the sisters sitting on the edge of the raft, with their feet resting on the bench seats of Brock's boat. They were doing a lot of whispering, and he wanted to know what they were saying. He'd bet his last gallon of gas Ginger didn't know anything about Josie's Duluth trips, but he could be wrong. He had been before when it came to Josie.

"Those two barrels need to be on this edge," he told Brock and Dac. "They have the big mortars in them. The ones we'll use for the grand finale." Setting down the crate he'd hoisted out of his boat, he further explained, "We'll start with these crates. They're full of Roman candles. I built a metal stand so we can launch four at once. That'll give the crowd a good show. Then we'll shoot off some sky rockets and torpedoes. I have stands for them, too."

"You put a lot of thought into this," Brock said.

"As always," Dac agreed. "Which is why Josie asked him."

Josie turned around at the sound of her name, and her eyes went directly to Scooter. He figured the sun must have been warmer than he'd noticed today because all of a sudden his cheeks felt sunburned.

"You actually had to build stands for the fireworks?" she asked. "Besides this raft?"

"Yes," Dac said. "He's been working on them every spare minute. Up until midnight last night."

Scooter wanted to tell Dac to shut up. His cheeks were growing warmer due to the way Josie's expression had softened. "They're called *fire*works because they involve fire. You can never be too careful when it comes to that." Looking around, trying to focus on something besides the blue eyes gazing up at him, he muttered, "This thing seemed bigger when we built it."

"The raft?" Dac asked.

"Yes, the raft," Scooter answered. "Once I set up the stands, there won't be room for us."

"Where are the stands?" Brock asked.

"In these two crates," Scooter said. "Along with the tools and hardware I need to assemble them." Scratching his chin, for the space was awfully small, even with Josie and Ginger sitting off to the side, he added, "Let's get them put together and we'll figure out what to do from there."

It didn't take long to bolt the metal pipes he'd cut in varying lengths onto the frames he'd welded. The stands were then bolted to wide square metal bases to keep them from tipping over. The plan was to drop the mortars into the pipe. The bottom of the pipe had several holes for him to light the fuses through. The other pipes, for the sky rockets and candles, held the fireworks upright so they'd shoot skyward when the fuses were lit.

When it came to fire of any kind, he always took extra precautions. It had been a lesson his father had taught him while he was growing up.

Once assembled, the stands took up a good amount of space. Scooter was considering all the options, when Josie said, "I have an idea."

Chapter Five

Scooter checked her hands to make sure she wasn't holding both paddles, preparing to leave, before he asked, "What's that?"

"You could set up one stand on each side of the raft," she said. "Then, you, Dac and Brock could all stand in your boats. You could each light a different kind of firework."

While Scooter contemplated the logistics of that idea, Dac, Brock and Ginger started talking, sharing their thoughts on Josie's suggestion. They all agreed that it wasn't a bad idea, and would keep the fireworks far enough away from each other. It would also put Josie back in his boat, where he could keep a closer eye on her. He still didn't trust her not to try to sneak away while he was lighting fuses.

"All right," Scooter agreed, having worked through his thoughts. "Dac, you set up the sky rockets to be set off on your side. Brock, you do the Roman candles. I'll do the torpedoes, along with a couple of the mortars. We'll keep rotating until the end, then light the rest of the mortars."

"Sounds like a great plan," Brock said. "Josie, you best

climb back in Scooter's boat before we get everything set up. There won't be room afterward."

Scooter was glad Brock had made the suggestion. Josie wouldn't question Brock to the extent she would him. Without a word of protest, she climbed onto the raft and walked to his boat. She even took his hand to assist her steps down into the boat.

"I'll pass out the fuses and punks once everything is set up," he told her. "Just hold on to them for now."

She agreed with a nod, which was all he expected. Josie had always been the quietest sister. Up until the two of them had started arguing every time they saw each other.

Night was now falling fast, and all three of the men scurried to get the stands positioned and secured, and move the crates of fireworks near the correct stands. There was no wind to speak of, and Scooter was glad of that. It made their job that much safer.

A faint buzz soon became a rumble overhead that had them all looking up.

"It's Forrest and Twyla!" Ginger squealed.

The plane swooped lower, flying over the lake and then the resort. A roar of laughter and clapping from the crowd filling the beach echoed over the calm water.

"That has to be cherries," Ginger said. "Just cherries."

Scooter's eyes weren't on the plane or Ginger. They'd settled on the way Josie watched the sky with an intensity he didn't know how to take. It wasn't excitement. Josie was too secretive to ever let that show, but there was something there, a wistfulness that went deep.

When her gaze dropped to his, she said, "They're coming back this way. I think that's our signal to get started."

"I think you're right," he said. "Again."

She smiled slightly. "You need these now?"

"Yep." He took the punks and fuses. After giving careful instructions to Dac and Brock, Scooter stepped down into his boat.

Josie was sitting near the back of the boat, giving him room to straddle the center bench. The boat rocked gently, bumping the platform, but the movement wasn't enough to cause concern. "You ready?" he asked her.

"Yes. Is there anything you need me to do?" she asked.

"No, just enjoy the show."

"Will it be loud?"

"No more so than on the beach," he answered. "Other than some hissing from the fuses. The loud explosions will all happen in the air."

"Isn't this just swell?" Ginger asked.

She was at the front of Brock's boat, which almost bumped the back of the one Scooter and Josie were in. The sisters were sitting almost side by side.

Josie pulled her gaze off Scooter to glance at her sister. "Yes, it is," she answered. Glancing up to the sky that was turning darker as they spoke, she searched for Forrest's plane. Twyla was up there, newly married and probably having the time of her life. Josie couldn't say she was resentful, but she wouldn't mind having what her sister had. What each one of them had. They'd found their freedom, something she might never find. It was funny, because for years, she'd had more freedom than any of them.

After spending the day in Scooter's company, she was questioning if what she'd considered freedom had, in truth, been just the opposite. She hadn't been caged up at the resort like Twyla claimed. Although her sister had crept out more times than the rest of them put together. Attending the Ladies Aid meetings and making the trips to Duluth had been her escape, but that hadn't been freedom. Even then, she'd always been following orders. Specific directions. She'd never been alone, either. Other than the day she'd got caught speeding. That had only happened because Hester Williams had unexpected company and couldn't go with her.

The first hiss startled her, but only because she'd been thinking about other things. Dac had lit the sky rockets. The pop and a flash of light high above them were quickly followed by a second, third and fourth.

Brock then lit four Roman candles, each one shooting ten small balls of fire into the air that all burst apart high in the sky. Scooter then set off four torpedoes. They whistled as they shot upward and the boom that followed was louder, as was the roar of the cheers coming from the crowd on the beach. As soon as the last torpedo shot out of the metal stand Scooter had built, he lit two mortars.

The crowd really cheered then. The mortars were the ones they'd come to see. High above the lake, they exploded with a great bang and illuminated the sky with red and green sparkles that reflected off the water, making a spectacular show.

Dac lit off his sky rockets again, which were followed by Brock's Roman candles and then Scooter's torpedoes and mortars. The men set a steady rhythm that was timed perfectly so there was always a firework exploding, even before the previous one faded. Besides the crowd cheering on shore, several other boats were on the water, with people watching the show.

"Wow," Ginger said. "This is fabulous."

"Yes, it is," Josie agreed, scooting herself forward so

she could lean her head against the back of the boat. "It really is."

Ginger was lying in her boat, in much the same way. "This is the best way to watch fireworks, don't you agree?"

"I guess I do," Josie agreed.

"The only thing that would make it better would be if Brock was lying next to me," Ginger said wistfully.

"Then there wouldn't be any Roman candles," Josie pointed out. "Be happy he's standing next to your feet."

Ginger giggled. "You're always the sensible one. Happy with whatever you have. Making the most of everything. Sometimes I wish I was more like you."

"No, you don't," Josie answered honestly.

Ginger was quiet, perhaps because Scooter had let off two more mortars and the booms were loud. When the quieter sky rockets shot into the sky, Ginger asked, "Why do you say it like that? Is something wrong?"

"No," Josie answered. Knowing her sister wouldn't give up without a reasonable explanation, she added, "No one should ever wish to be like anyone else. You are your own person. Appreciate that."

"Now that sounds like you," Ginger said. "The sensible one."

Silently they watched the sky light up again. Josie couldn't help but wonder if that was what was wrong with her. That she was tired of being the sensible one. When two mortars exploded simultaneously their blue and white lights intermingled, along with their booms. Oohs and aahs floated from the watchers on the beach. Josie closed her eyes as the lights faded, holding the sparkles in her mind for a second longer. She took her own words to heart. No, that wasn't it. Sensible or not, at this moment she was very glad to be who she was. Where she was. Glad that she hadn't crept away. Doing so would not have been sensible. Then again, she hadn't been overly sensible lately.

She didn't want to admit that. Didn't like admitting it. But it was the truth. Whether she wanted to believe it or not. Getting involved from the beginning hadn't been sensible, but she liked helping others. She liked knowing she was making a difference to even one other person in some small way. Going to Duluth was exciting, and the secrecy had been challenging and thrilling, until lately... Scooter was right. It had become dangerous. She wasn't a fool, and only fools continued when they knew they were in over their heads.

But she couldn't stop. It was impossible. It was also a part of her. A part she liked.

She'd liked tonight, too. Especially being with Scooter. Fighting or not, with him at her side she didn't feel like the odd man out. It had always been that way with Scooter. His mother and hers had been close friends, and Josie clearly remembered being little, very little, and telling her mother she was going to grow up and marry Scooter. A crazy notion, dreamed up in a child's mind. He'd probably stopped one of her sisters from picking on her or something—

The boat rocked hard, and her eyes snapped open as she shot upright.

Scooter was yelling. So were Brock and Dac.

Josie stood. A boat, with a motor, sped toward them. "Who is that?" she asked.

"I don't know," Scooter yelled, before shouting for the boat to slow down.

From that moment on, everything turned crazy.

The boat didn't hit them, but the wake it left as it

swerved sent the raft and all three of the boats tied to it rocking uncontrollably.

Someone yelled, "Fire!"

Scooter shouted to untie the boats. Josie found the rope on her end while he did the same on his. As the knot slipped loose, Scooter grabbed her arm.

"Get down!"

She landed on the floor of the boat, between two of the bench seats, as the explosions started. A scream escaped her throat and when something covered her head, she clutched on to it. The scent and feel of the material told her it was Scooter's coat, and that, despite all the noise and commotion, provided a sense of security.

The boat was moving, gliding fast over the water. Josie lifted her head slightly to peer out from beneath the coat. Scooter was behind her paddling with both oars. She was on the floor of the boat, sitting between his knees. She twisted to glance toward the raft, which was now several yards away.

Fireworks were shooting off in several directions, a dozen at a time. A loud boom, accompanied by sparks that engulfed the raft and spit into the air, made her pull the coat back over her eyes.

When the boat slowed, Josie once again lifted the jacket. They were almost to the shore. Gradually, the boat spun around to face the raft, where fireworks of all kinds were exploding.

"Are you all right?" Scooter asked.

"Yes." Twisting to look up at him, she asked, "Are you?"

He nodded as his gaze went to the floating platform. Sky rockets, torpedoes, Roman candles and large mortars were all going off at once. Most were still shooting skyward, but a few shot off the edges of the raft, landing in the water and disappearing.

"What happened?" she asked.

"Whoever was in that motorboat threw something into one of the crates. Something that was on fire."

A shiver rippled through her so fast she shuddered. Scooter settled his coat tighter around her and then rested both hands on her shoulders. "We're safe here," he said. "Far enough away. Dac and Brock and Ginger are far enough away, too."

Josie nodded even while she scanned the lake, looking for the others. The constant flash of lights in the air made it easy to see them. "Who would do such a thing?" she asked.

"Don't know. Maybe someone thinking it would be a fun practical joke." Scooter tugged her backward. "Lean back. We might as well enjoy the show. The fireworks were packed in sawdust inside those crates and barrels. It'll take a while before they're done."

The mass of explosions overhead was something to see. Red, blue, green, yellow and white lights lit up the sky. All at the same time. There was no waiting in between, just constant booms, pops and bursts of color. Josie maneuvered her legs out from beneath the bench seat to stretch them in front of her. "Want to sit down here?" she asked. "You won't have to bend your head so far back."

"I'm fine," he said. "But you make yourself comfortable."

"All right," she said. Resting both elbows on his knees, she leaned all the way back, until her head touched his chest. "You make a pretty good chair, and it is a rather spectacular firework show."

"Yeah, it is." His hands were still on her shoulders,

and when they started to gently rub, she closed her eyes. There was no rhyme or reason to the pops and booms of the fireworks, and she could almost see the lights through her closed lids. Once again, she admitted she was glad to be where she was at this very moment. Normally, she'd never admit that, never do this, but tonight, she wanted to be more like her sisters. Like those fireworks. Wild. Unconventional. Free.

All day, all week actually, she'd watched Twyla and Norma Rose snuggling and kissing the men they loved. Both had continued to work, to ensure this party would be a success, but even then, while working at her side, her sisters had giggled and talked about Forrest and Ty. Moments ago she'd caught Brock and Ginger in their boat in an embrace that said they were certainly not watching fireworks.

She'd never had anything remotely close to what her sisters had, and wondered if she ever would. Nestled between Scooter's knees, with fireworks exploding overhead and the gentleness of his hands easing the tension from her shoulders, here she was as close as she'd ever come.

Scooter's arms folded around her shoulders from behind and he rested his chin on the top of her head. "It's quite the display, isn't it?"

She opened her eyes and gazed heavenward, toward the bursts of light. "Yes. I'm sure the crowd is loving it."

"Are you?"

She twisted slightly to look up at him. The fireworks were reflecting in his eyes and his smile was one of those that had her wanting to smile in return. A wave of warmth rushed up inside her, making her want to sigh, and all the while her heart picked up the pace of its beats. He truly was a handsome man, and right now, for whatever reason, that fact seemed to be sweeping her out of her world and dropping her in one she didn't know, but was excited to enter.

"Are you enjoying the fireworks, Josie?" he asked again, while brushing her hair off her forehead.

"Yes," she answered, although her whisper was so soft he may not have heard. Her voice didn't want to work. Nothing wanted to work.

Scooter leaned closer. The idea of what he was about to do struck her so swiftly Josie gasped and pulled her head back to look him in the eyes. He grinned and lifted one eyebrow. Excitement shot clear to her toes, leaving her tingling all over. She bit her bottom lip, even as she leaned forward.

The moment his lips touched hers, Josie wondered if the fireworks were going off inside her instead of over their heads.

The warmth of his mouth was divine and a greedy need burst forth inside her. *You shouldn't be doing this*, she told herself as she moved her lips against his. *It can only make things worse.*

But I want to do this, she argued with herself. *I want to do this more than I've ever wanted to do anything. If just to understand what all the fuss is about.*

Scooter's arms tugged her upward. She twisted about and tucked her knees beneath her. Then she wrapped her arms around his neck, and kissed him with all the passion that had been building inside her lately.

Scooter's hands, rubbing her hips, her back, her shoulders, gave her encouragement.

The fireworks continued to rumble in her ears, flashing before her closed lids, but Scooter held her attention. She'd never been kissed and was utterly enthralled by each movement of his lips. How they pressed against hers, how they parted briefly and met hers again. He caught her bottom lip between his and tugged slightly, making her want to smile. She couldn't help it.

His hands were on the sides of her face as they separated. He was smiling, too. She'd truly never experienced a blush like the one burning her cheeks.

Scooter leaned forward again, and this time, when his lips parted, she instinctively copied the action. His tongue swept inside her mouth so swiftly she grasped his shoulders at the wave of pleasure flooding her system.

The kiss continued until she was breathless and felt rather boneless. Her entire body would have sunk to the bottom of the boat if he hadn't been holding her. Or if she hadn't been holding on to him. She no longer told herself she shouldn't be doing this. Now her thoughts were more along the lines of never wanting to stop. This was certainly something to fuss about. And something to indulge in.

Scooter was the one who stopped, backing out of their kissing with such slow tenderness Josie slumped against him.

"The fireworks have stopped," he whispered next to her ear.

"No, they haven't," she replied just as softly. They were still going off in the recesses of her mind as brilliantly as ever.

His chest rumbled as he chuckled. "Listen."

Eyes closed, Josie focused on hearing. Although it was hard. Scooter smelled so wonderful and his enveloping warmth offered comfort she'd never known. Eventually, she had to acknowledge there were no echoing booms, but there was the faint sound of a plethora of cheers and clapping. Letting out a sigh, she opened her eyes and lifted her chin to peer up at him. "Maybe they are over."

"Maybe?"

She sighed again. "Yes, maybe."

He laughed again and kissed her forehead while wrapping his coat around her shoulders once more. Josie didn't want to move, not even when he gently lowered her. Her body seemed to have lost all coordination as she sank back down to the bottom of the boat between his knees.

She'd never been here before. It was as if she was teetering somewhere between dreamland and reality. The splashing of water from the oars and the movement of the boat slowly brought her senses around. Letting out another sigh, Josie asked, "Is it safe? What if they all haven't gone off?"

"They've all gone off," Scooter said.

"How can you be sure?"

He gestured toward the water with a nod of his chin. "The raft is on fire, so I think it's safe to say they all went off."

Dropped into reality like a rock pitched off a dock, Josie spun around at the same time she asked, "What?" Sure enough, a ball of flame sat on the water directly in front of them. "What do we do now?"

"Throw some buckets of water on it," Scooter said rather lazily.

Disbelief rippled her spine. "Aren't you upset?"

"No sense being upset," he said.

Little by little, she drew her eyes away from the fire and turned to look up at Scooter. He was still grinning, and the way he winked sent the blood rushing into her cheeks again. This was the Scooter she'd always known. He took life in stride, with a smile. Until— Oh, what had she done? *Please don't let him say something about kissing.* She wouldn't know how to reply.

Spinning around, she gathered up his coat and then went ahead and stuck her arms in the sleeves. While they rowed closer, and her mind conjured up all sorts of embarrassing bits of conversation, she climbed onto the seat in front of her, edging close to the side so Scooter could see around her.

Brock and Ginger were approaching the fire from one direction and Dac from the other. What if they'd seen her and Scooter kissing? They'd been some distance away, but the fireworks had been bright.

"That was one hell of a show!" Dac shouted.

Josie's stomach dropped to the board beneath her feet. Lower even.

"It sure was," Brock replied.

"Everyone all right?" Scooter asked.

"We are," Ginger answered. "How about you?"

"We're fine," Scooter replied.

The boat was rocking. Josie turned to watch Scooter dip a bucket over the edge.

"Looks like it's just the crates and barrels burning," he said. "Let's get it put out and see if the platform can be salvaged."

The other men started using the buckets in their boats and the fire was soon extinguished. Scooter then rowed the boat up to the edge of the raft, and Dac and Brock did the same.

"Soaking the platform before we anchored it was a good idea," Dac said. "It's barely charred."

A fourth boat rowed up beside Dac's. It was Ty and Norma Rose. Josie wanted to groan. An accident like this was sure to upset her sister.

"What happened?" Norma Rose asked.

Ty grabbed the edge of the platform to keep their boat from colliding with Dac's. "We saw a motorboat speeding past, and the flames."

"Do you know who it was?" Scooter asked.

"No," Ty said. "They were too far away for us to get a good look. Do you know?"

Scooter had climbed onto the platform and was pushing debris around with his feet. "No, but it was one of the resort's boats."

Josie hadn't noticed that. Then again, there hadn't been time to notice much.

"Need any help here?" Ty asked.

"No," Scooter said. "I'll take the stands with me and come back in the daylight to clean up the rest of it."

"We'll head back and see who took out boats with motors."

"I don't think those on the shore know what happened," Brock said.

"Me neither," Dac agreed. "Not with the way they were cheering."

"Let's leave it that way," Scooter said. "Not give whoever did this the satisfaction of knowing how close they came to ending the show just as it got started."

The glances shared between the men said they were attempting to make light of the situation. As Josie questioned why, a consensus to agree with Scooter's suggestion was made. Shortly afterward, with the stands loaded into their boat, Scooter started rowing toward shore.

Stars glistened overhead, reflecting off the water, and music filtered through the air from the resort, disrupted only by the steady splash of the oars hitting the water. Dac was rowing toward shore a short distance away, and

Josie tried to hold her attention on why the men wouldn't want to discover who was behind the fire. She didn't have much luck with that, not with the way her mind continued to bounce back to something else. No one seemed to have seen her and Scooter kissing. As much as she didn't want people to have seen them, she wanted to kiss him again. That was disconcerting.

Her entire being filled with warmth just thinking about it. There were a few impious sensations swirling around her head and body, too. Things that had never entered her before, not in anyone's company. Certainly not in Scooter's presence. He had been around her entire life. He'd been there whenever she'd needed things. Tangible things, like new tires or someone to light fireworks. Or a ride from Duluth.

Josie couldn't hold in her sigh. What was happening to her?

Scooter's long exhale sounded from behind her. "About what happened tonight," he said.

She closed her eyes. Here it comes, his regret at what they'd done. Her teeth clamped together in preparation, but it didn't help. She lifted her chin. "Don't think anything of it. I'm not."

Chapter Six

Scooter, watching the way Josie's back had stiffened, pinched his lips together. Kissing her may have been the biggest mistake of his life, but he wasn't regretting it. Not in the least. The perfect curves of her five-foot frame had haunted his dreams for years. So had that delectable mouth. She didn't slather bright red lipstick over her lips like her sisters did. He appreciated that, and recognized that that was Josie. She didn't mask who she was. Not in that sense. In other ways, she was as secretive as a turtle tucked into its shell.

She'd released herself during their kiss, and that had thrilled him in ways not even motorcycles did.

"You're not thinking of the fire?" he asked, withholding his grin. Inside, though, he was chuckling. She must be thinking of the kiss they'd shared, and was most likely mentally beating herself up over letting it happen. Josie liked to pretend she held no interest in men, but he knew she'd wanted him to kiss her as badly as he'd wanted it. "Not thinking about who may have thrown that fireball?"

She spun around. A frown tugged on her brow while her eyes displayed a hint of surprise.

"That's what I'm thinking of," he said. "How some-one wanted to spoil your party."

"You said it was probably a practical joke."

He knew she didn't believe that any more than he did. Whoever had started the fire had had more in mind than a joke. Scooter had nothing to go on but instinct, but that was enough. A man of Roger Nightingale's stature was bound to have enemies.

Big shots and no-name gangsters, and those in be-tween, had all been in attendance at today's party, but Scooter's gut told him none of them were responsible for the fire. He had a horrible suspicion that, whether it had happened before tonight or when Roger had introduced his family to the crowd, someone knew Josie was the girl infiltrating the prostitution rings at the docks.

His stomach clenched. That firebomb suggested they wouldn't stop until she did. Or worse.

She spun all the way around to face him. "You told—"

He interrupted, "Because I didn't think you'd want them discovering your secret."

Her lips snapped shut as her eyes widened.

"You need help with the stands?" Dac yelled, as he climbed out of the boat near the dock a few yards up the shoreline.

"No, thanks," Scooter replied. "I'll come get them in the morning."

"See you at the party," Dac answered.

"See you," Scooter replied, while gliding the boat up next to the dock they'd launched from earlier. While sta-bilizing the boat by grabbing hold of the dock, he ges-tured for Josie to step out. Several sizes too big for her, his coat hung down to her thighs and the sleeves com-pletely hid her hands. The sight also stirred his insides more than any other outfit she'd ever worn. Climbing out, he grabbed the rope at the front of the boat and tugged it along the side of the dock as they walked to shore. There, he walked through the damp sand, pulling the boat toward the boathouse.

Josie didn't follow, and he didn't expect her to. Those ugly green shoes would get stuck in the sand. A grin crossed his lips. His coat was an improvement on the dress that matched those shoes.

A spit and sputter echoed over the lake, signaling Dac had climbed on his cycle and was heading back to the resort building. Scooter released several feet of rope, letting the boat float out into the water a bit in order to line it up with the double doors he pulled open.

The boathouse was pitch-black when, after hauling the boat all the way in, he closed the double doors facing the water, yet he knew Josie stood just inside the other door. Not just because he'd heard the door squeak, but because his internal awareness honed in on her presence—as it always did.

With the stealth of a cat stalking a mouse, he maneuvered his way between the boat and the side of the building, listening for any sound she might make. She was silent. Perhaps she was hoping to scare him. She'd been known for doing that, years ago, when they'd played hide-and-seek as kids.

He paused at the sound of a twig snapping. An almost silent hiss said Josie had heard it, too. It also told him exactly how close she was.

Scooter reached out and grabbed her arms. "Gotcha!"

She squealed, and then pushed at his chest. "That was not funny."

There was laughter in her tone. His, too. "Oh, and standing in the dark, prepared to scare me, was?"

"I wasn't—"

"Thinking about scaring me?"

"Fine," she said with a sigh. "I thought about it, but only because I want to know what secret you were talking about."

The boathouse was darker than a barrel of oil and he could barely see her eyes, but he really didn't need to. She was right before him, and his lips could find hers without him seeing them. "Not the one about us kissing," he whispered.

Her protest was little more than a murmur. His lips had found hers. They were warm, lush and sweet, and met his with an intensity that said they'd wanted another bout of kissing as much as his lips had. For a man who was cautious around fire, he sure was playing with it right now.

When her arms reached up to circle his neck, he took a step closer. His hands found their way inside his coat to run up and down the trim curves of her sides before grasping her hips to hold her against him. The heat of the contact, of her body aligned with his, sent warning signals to his brain.

He was making the second-biggest mistake of his life, but he might never get this chance again and was not going to let it slip away. One faint click wasn't enough to make him stop kissing her, but a second one was.

She let out a little mumble and he pulled her closer. "Shhh. Listen."

A snap sounded, like the one he'd heard earlier, as if someone had stepped on a twig. A tingle spiraled up Scooter's spine. There were no twigs inside the boathouse. It was all sand. Clean sand, from when it had been refurbished.

The double doors on the far side of the structure rattled slightly before something clanged and clicked.

"Damn," he muttered.

"What?" Josie asked.

"I think someone just locked us in here." Scooter side-stepped, keeping one arm around her as he felt for the handle of the door that he knew had to be just behind her. Finding the handle, he grasped it and gave the door a hard shove. It barely moved. Someone had fastened the padlock outside.

"Who?" she asked. "Dac?"

"Dac wouldn't lock us in here," he whispered. There was another sound and the eerie sensation it created made him add, "Listen."

After a brief silence she answered, "That's just the waves splashing."

Every sense Scooter had kicked into full awareness. "That's not water. It's gas." Grabbing Josie's hand, he spun around and rushed toward the back of the boathouse. The lock on the double door would give way easier than the smaller door.

"Gas?"

"Yes, someone is throwing gas on the building." He let go of her hand. "Stay back."

A well-aimed, solid kick sent the double doors flying open. "Stay here!" Scooter shot out of the building and ran around one swinging door. A can rolled down the bank as he dashed up it. He raced all the way around the building, but didn't catch so much as a glimpse of any-one. The smell of gas filled the air, though, and he ran down the bank on the other side of the building.

Josie stood near the door. "Who was it? Did you see anyone?"

"No," he said. "But we interrupted them before they could strike a match."

"Who would do such a thing?"

Dismay and fear shimmered in her eyes as she looked up at him. A great storm of emotions collided inside him. He stepped closer, wrapped both arms around her and kissed the top of her head as her body, trembling, snuggled closer. Earlier he'd wanted to tell her someone had learned who she was, what she was doing. Now he wanted to protect her from that possibility as much as everything else.

"Probably just another prankster," he said.

Her arms were around his waist, holding on tightly. "Don't lie to me, Scooter," she whispered. "You don't believe that. I know you don't."

Not saying anything about what he did or didn't believe, Scooter held her close for several minutes before gathering the will to step back. "Come on, let's get back up to the party."

A lost kitten couldn't have looked sadder than when she lifted her eyes to his. "You think this is my fault, don't you? The fire and—" she waved a hand "—this."

Scooter grasped her cheeks. "I didn't say—"

She grabbed his wrists and pulled his hands away. "I didn't ask if you'd said it, I asked if you were thinking it, but never mind, I know the answer."

He let his hands fall to his sides as she started walking away, but then he lurched forward and grabbed her arm. "Hold up. We have to shut these doors. Help me grab a couple of rocks to keep them shut for now." He didn't remind her someone might still be close at hand, waiting for her to take off alone.

While he closed both doors, she positioned decent-sized rocks in front of them to keep them shut. She didn't pull away when he took her elbow to help her maneuver through the sand, either. Once on the grass, she stepped away and stopped near the gas can.

"That looks like an old milk can to me."

He reached down and picked up the can by one of the two handles welded near the top. The cap was a few feet ahead of them and he walked forward to scoop it off the ground. Demonstrating how it fit, he explained, "See, the lid screws on."

When she made no comment, he added, "You can't tell me you don't smell gasoline."

Huffing out a sigh, she said, "Yes, I smell gasoline."

Scooter set the can down by the front of the boathouse and when they arrived at his motorcycle he gave it a thorough examination, making sure no one had tinkered with it in their absence. Once satisfied, he climbed on and gave it a good wrench backward to release the stand. After locking the stand in place, he stomped on the kick-starter. While the engine sputtered to life, he held out an arm. "Climb on."

Cautious of the muffler, she climbed on. He waited until she had her skirt situated, had set her feet upon his and had placed her arms around his waist before he shifted into gear. Her hold tightened and every place where her body touched his awakened a renewed awareness within him.

So focused on ignoring what was happening inside him, Scooter almost missed the image of a man flashing before the beam of the single headlight on the cycle.

He braked and brought the motorcycle to a stop near the edge of the road. Recognizing Bronco, Scooter thanked the stars above that his luck had finally kicked in.

Cutting the engine so they wouldn't have to shout, he said, "Where're you headed?"

Bronco glanced at Josie before he said, "Just making a round."

"Ty talk to you?" Scooter asked.

Bronco's nod was slight, and meant only for him to see. An impossibility. Josie had eyes like an eagle.

"Head down to the last boathouse," Scooter said. "I'll be back there in a few minutes."

With a nod, and a final glance at Josie, Bronco started down the road at a faster pace.

Scooter leaned the bike slightly to the left. "Hold your leg out of the way while I kick the starter," he told Josie.

She did as he said, and then wrapped her arms around his waist again as they started up the road. The fact she hadn't commented on what he'd told Bronco weighed heavily on his mind. She couldn't be trusted to stay at the resort. Not left alone, anyway. Roger's men were out searching the grounds, so leaving her with one of them would be impossible. He didn't trust her sisters much more than he trusted her. If she told them what had just happened, they'd all be out looking for the culprits.

Just then Scooter recognized Tuck Andrews stepping out of the row of pine trees. Tuck was another one of Roger's men. Scooter swerved the bike to the side of the road. This time he didn't bother shutting off the engine. "Meet us at the last boathouse," he said. "Bronco's there."

Josie bit back the grin tugging on her lips. Scooter had changed his mind. He'd been going to deliver her to the resort and then go back to tell her father's men about the incident, but now, as he turned the motorcycle completely around, she realized he was taking her with him. By not saying a word, she'd gotten what she wanted.

Although she wasn't exactly sure what that was— what she wanted. Other than to know who was behind such dastardly deeds. Someone playing practical, albeit dangerous, pranks made more sense than what Scooter thought. No one knew her from her trips to Duluth. She'd been careful. Extremely careful.

She momentarily lost her train of thought when Scooter leaned as the bike followed a curve in the road. Holding on to his waist, she leaned with him. This was by far the most fun part of riding. Swerving with the bike reminded her of dancing. The steady whine of the engine could very well be music and the road a dance floor.

Just like the first, this ride ended too soon. And it was just as well. She had to keep her wits about her, and that couldn't happen while she was musing over how wonderful it was riding on Scooter's cycle. Josie shook her head, trying to shake loose the thoughts that did no good. All of them included Scooter, and how he'd kissed her. Twice. She truly hadn't expected that second kiss. Perhaps that was part of what made it so thrilling.

"What happened here?"

Bronco's voice was like a plunge into cold water. She even shivered, and then realized Scooter had already turned off his motorcycle and was waiting for her to climb off. She did so rather hastily, and was thankful when he grabbed her arm to steady her. She had to get her thoughts in order. There were far more important things to worry about than kissing Scooter. Bronco was sure to tell her father what had happened, and that could ultimately lead to him discovering her Tuesday trips to Duluth. That would put a stop to her future, too. The one she'd covertly planned.

When Scooter let go of her arm, he answered Bronco. "Someone locked Josie and me in the boathouse while we were putting away the boat."

"Why do I smell gasoline?" Bronco asked.

With the bike on its stand again, Scooter climbed off and took her arm as they walked down the grassy slope. "Someone splashed it against the outside of the boathouse," Scooter said. "I kicked open the double doors and they ran off before they could strike a match."

Tuck, having cut across the grass, had arrived in time to hear what had happened. "Did you get a look at anyone?" he asked.

"No," Scooter replied. "Not even a glimpse. But they left their gas can behind."

Bronco picked up the can. "It's the resort's. The one we use for boat-motor gas." Setting the can back down, he asked, "Do you think it was the same person who threw that fireball?"

Josie held her silence. They expected Scooter to answer, so she let him. However, she did make a mental note that it hadn't taken long for someone to report what had happened to Bronco. That was Norma Rose, no doubt. Unlike Scooter, her sister wasn't thinking that Josie had anything to do with the fire, so at least she had that in her favor. If Norma Rose had any suspicions, her father would already have learned of them.

"Yes, I do," Scooter answered.

An eerie sensation fluttered its way up her spine. What if Scooter was right? That somehow all of this had something to do with her? She could be putting her entire family in danger.

"Any idea who?" Bronco asked.

Josie didn't know she was biting her lip until the sting almost made her yelp. Scooter hadn't answered, and she hoped beyond hope he wouldn't implicate her.

"No," he said heavily. "I don't." He shrugged. "Could be some whiskey runners mad at Roger, or one of Galen Reynolds's old cronies who wanted to get back at Forrest for seeing Galen never gets out of jail."

"Yeah," Bronco said. "Could be, or there are a few others I can think of. This place was crawling with gangsters today, a few I'd rather never see the likes of anywhere near here."

None of what either man said should have caused her to feel relieved, but Josie did.

"We'll take care of this," Bronco said. "Rinse away the gas so there's no worry of fire. The two of you can go back up to the party. It'll be going strong for another few hours, I imagine."

"All right," Scooter said, steering Josie around by the elbow. With a nod, he told Tuck, "Catch up with you later."

Tuck nodded and Josie had the distinct feeling the men had said a whole lot more than she'd heard. It was that way with her father and his men, and she'd learned to read between the lines.

She held her tongue, biting it at times to keep it in place, until after she and Scooter had ridden his cycle back along the winding road that ended in the resort's parking lot. He left his leather hat on after he'd secured the motorcycle on its stand. It looked nice on him and went well with the way he had his white shirtsleeves rolled up to his elbows. Even with the narrow suspenders, the hat and rolled-up sleeves made him look more like Scooter, rather than just another man in a suit.

She grasped the lapels of the coat she still had on. "Here, you'll want your coat back."

Scooter caught the coat before it fell off her shoulders and pulled it back up. "Naw, you keep it on." Grinning, he winked. "It looks a lot better than that green dress."

"It is somewhat homely," she admitted.

"Somewhat?" he asked. "There's no somewhat about it. It's ugly, plain and simple."

"Twyla picked them out," Josie explained. "They were the only green dresses that would fit all three of us. There wasn't time to order any others."

He patted her shoulders before dropping his hands to his sides. "I figured as much."

With a wave, he gestured to start walking toward the resort.

Music and the sounds of people laughing and having fun filtered through the parking lot. Josie had no desire whatsoever to rejoin the party. "Just like you figured I was behind what happened tonight?"

He rubbed a hand across his mouth, as if stopping himself from speaking.

"That's what you implied earlier," she persisted.

Shaking his head, he let out a sigh. "And I shouldn't have. I'm sorry. I probably shouldn't have done a lot of things tonight."

She instantly knew he was referring to kissing her, and a ball of fire that made the blaze on the platform look small ignited in her belly. He was accusing her of making him kiss her. He hadn't said that, but that was how it felt. As if it was all her fault.

"It was most likely just what I told Bronco," he said.

"Someone upset with your father, or someone associated with Galen Reynolds. He had dealings with some tough characters."

Josie didn't know if she was mad or hurt, or a mixture of the two. All she knew was that it felt as if steam might soon shoot out of her ears. She now understood how foolish she'd been. Wanting him to kiss her. Letting him kiss her. She wasn't like her sisters, never would be, and pretending she could have what they'd found was ridiculous. She didn't need all that, either. It certainly wouldn't fit in with her future. "Galen Reynolds had dealings with a lot of people. Are you going to tell me that was my fault, too?"

"Your fault?" He shook his head. "No, Josie, I'm not saying anything is your fault."

"Oh, you're not?"

"No, I'm not."

She'd never wanted to cry so much before. Well, other than the day she'd been arrested. As a matter of fact, Scooter was the reason she'd wanted to cry that day, too. He'd been so mad. About as mad as she was right now. "Yes, you are. You think everything is my fault." Skipping over the kissing part—which was the most painful—she stated, "No one in Duluth knows who I am, Scooter. No one."

He grabbed her by the upper arms. "Josie, calm down. I never said—"

Pushing at his chest with both hands, she informed him, "You don't have to say it. I know what you're thinking."

"Do you?"

"Yes, I do."

"Then you know I'm thinking about doing this."

His lips landed on hers so fast she didn't have time

to respond. Verbally or mentally. His kisses completely shut off her thinking capabilities. Her lips, however, knew how to respond. They went into action, flying against his with all the frustration and fight she held inside. That soon changed. Her frustration. It turned into a need like no other.

When his tongue swept into her mouth, she grabbed on to his shoulders in order to plaster her entire length against him. There was no denying that was exactly what her body craved.

As her mind grew hazy, it momentarily snagged on an iota of reality. This couldn't be what she craved. What she wanted. Scooter would be the last person to understand why she was helping Gloria.

Josie snapped her head back so fast her neck popped. The action caused a bit more common sense to prevail. All this kissing was making things worse. She pushed at Scooter's shoulders, harder this time, and took a step backward. Then she did something she rarely did.

She ran.

Footsteps followed behind her, and she took a moment to shout over her shoulder, "Leave me alone, Scooter Wilson. Just leave me alone."

Entering the resort through the front door, she was thankful the entire party was outside. There were no obstacles in her way whatsoever. She ran all the way to the second floor, through the door that separated the family living quarters from the rest of the resort, and into her bedroom, where she slammed and locked the door.

Chapter Seven

Josie slept in later than usual. She hadn't fallen asleep until dawn was breaking. The clock beside her bed said it was well after ten. Pushing eleven, if her second glance was right. As flustered as she'd been the night before, she threw back the covers. At some point, she didn't exactly remember when, she'd gotten undressed. The pea-green dress lay on the floor like a glob of moss.

She headed for the closet, trying not to glance at the black coat draped over her dressing table chair, but her eyes wouldn't cooperate. She stubbed her toe on something, sending a shooting pain up one leg and making her hop on the other. She crossed the room like that, off-kilter and uncoordinated, until she caught herself from falling on the floor by slapping both hands against her closet door. Her nose smacked against the wood in the process, making it sting and her eyes water.

Pressing her forehead against the door, she waited for her toe and her nose to stop throbbing before she lifted her head.

A deep breath helped, so she took a second one, and a third. Then she pulled open the closet and chose a white blouse and dungarees. Gathering up a pair of soft-soled shoes with almost no heels, she snatched clean under-clothes out of her dresser on her way to the door.

The bath, though she'd made it a fast one, helped her mood, and before leaving the bathroom, she pressed a couple of finger waves into her damp hair. A quick and final glance in the mirror gave her the satisfaction to nod at herself. At least she looked normal. Like the Josie she'd known her entire life. The one who had never—ever—spent half the night kissing Scooter Wilson.

That had been so foolish. So unlike her. She'd made up her mind some time ago as to what she wanted, and it didn't involve Scooter. It didn't involve any man. The events of late had confused her. Her sisters all getting married, for example. All that had interrupted her plan and she had to get back on track. She should look at all this as a blessing. Leaving wouldn't be nearly as hard now, at least not once Norma Rose returned home. She'd have to accept that her father would need her for the next few weeks, but afterward she'd be free to proceed. On her own.

Well, not entirely alone. She'd still need Gloria.

A second wave of remorse overtook her. The reper-cussions of what had happened yesterday, when Scooter had stopped her and Gloria, were another issue. Some-thing she'd need to resolve.

Determined to get back on an even keel, Josie marched out of the bathroom and down the hall.

The other bedroom doors lining the corridor were closed and silence echoed in her ears. For a place that had been overflowing with people a few hours ago, things were awfully quiet.

Then again, her father was an early riser. As was

Norma Rose; her sister had been even before she'd started sleeping most nights in Ty's cabin. The only one who might have slept in the family quarters last night was Ginger, but Josie doubted Brock would have wanted to sleep in Ginger's bedroom. Everything in there was pink. Entering that room was like walking into a ball of cotton candy. Whether they'd slept in there or not, Ginger and Brock had probably already left. They'd planned on visiting Brock's family today.

Josie pulled open the door that separated this portion of the second floor from the guest quarters and stopped dead in her tracks.

Scooter was there. He was stretched out, with his feet on one chair, his body on another and his hat pulled low over his face. A smile tried to creep onto her lips as a softness spread through the inner cavity of her chest.

She tugged her gaze away to glance up and down the empty hallway. He still had on the same clothes as last night. Right down to his high-topped boots. And suspenders. His white shirt was partially unbuttoned, exposing a long V of skin and dark curls.

Fighting to inhale enough air to keep from passing out, Josie weighed her options. She could back up and pull the door closed, or sneak past him. The sight of him was confusing her, making her forget why she'd been so mad at him last night. She was already unsure about exactly what had made her so angry. She'd wanted him to kiss her. She just hadn't wanted to like it. She still didn't.

There was only herself to blame for the pickle she was in, and she was the only one who could get herself out of it.

Josie eased the weight off her heels and tiptoed into the hallway.

An idea crossed her mind—that of kicking the chair out from beneath his feet. Twyla would do something like that and then wait to be chased. By Forrest, of course, not Scooter. Josie could almost see it happening, Twyla squealing and Forrest kissing her once he'd caught her. The image in her mind quickly changed to that of her and Scooter.

"I can hear you."

His voice startled her in one way. In another, she'd expected it. She'd thought he'd twitched.

"I can see you, too," he added.

Planting her heels on the carpet, she crossed her arms. "Then why were you pretending to be asleep?"

He pushed back his hat and flashed her a grin. "I wasn't pretending. At least not until you opened the door."

Refusing to be affected by him in any way—ever again—she asked, "What are you doing here? It's eleven o'clock in the morning."

"Actually, it's almost noon," he said. "Do you always take that long in the bathroom?"

The way his eyes roamed from her toes to her hair sent fire-like heat zipping beneath her skin. Especially her breasts. His gaze had stalled on them briefly, making her tighten the arms she'd crossed over them. "You'd better hightail it out of here," she warned. "Men are not allowed in the family quarters."

He kicked his feet off the chair and swooped to a stand so quickly she took a step backward.

"I'm not in the family quarters," he said, advancing toward her. "I wasn't all night."

"Father won't like—"

"Your father saw that I was brought a pillow and a blanket." He stopped far enough away to give her breath-

ing room, and twisted his neck left and then right, stretching the muscles. "I should have taken him up on the bed
he offered. Those chairs weren't too comfortable."

"You slept there all night?"

He stretched his arms wide. "Yep."

Josie had to pull her eyes away from his shoulders,
and the way the muscles rippled. "Why?"

"Someone had to make sure you didn't creep off."

She opened her mouth, but closed it before doing much
more than swallowing a gulp of air. Then she recovered.

"Well, I didn't sneak away, and I'm not going anywhere today, so you can leave now."

"Can't."

"Yes, you can."

"No, I can't."

Arguing was useless, and flustered her, yet with him
she couldn't stop. "Why not?"

He snagged her arm and spun her around. "Because
I don't trust you."

They were headed for the stairs, so she didn't protest. Once downstairs she'd find an excuse, a chore that
needed to be done. One wouldn't form in her mind right
now, but there would be lots of them. There always were.

Halfway down the staircase that ran along the wall
leading into the ballroom, she ducked slightly to see
through the arched doorway and into the dining room.
The tables had all been replaced and set with tablecloths,
napkins and silverware, ready for whomever chose to
sit down, but no one was sitting. The room was empty.

"Where is everyone?"

"Family or guests?"

"Both," she replied.

"Probably because Norma Rose was whipping out

orders to disassemble the dance floor before the birds started tweeting, most of the guests left shortly after breakfast. I suspect a lot of them had long journeys home and tomorrow is a workday."

Josie glanced up at Scooter and let her aversion to his smart attitude ooze from her gaze.

He grinned. "Your father decided last night that he'd drive Babe Ruth back down to New Ulm. Well, actually Walter drove them, in your father's car. He and Babe decided making Forrest fly back down there the first day of being married was asking a bit too much. I agree with them. It was a nice sentiment. They left right after breakfast, too."

Her sigh hadn't fully escaped before he continued.

"As far as I know, Forrest and Twyla are still out on the island. Ginger and Brock left at the same time as your father and Babe."

Stepping off the last stair, she pulled up her mouth into a false grin. "Well, in that case, I'll go and see what Norma Rose needs help with."

He hadn't let go of her arm, and he tugged her backward when she attempted to walk away. "I just told you she's been cracking the whip since the sun came up."

"So?" Josie asked.

"So, she's not here."

"Not here?" Josie shook her head. "Norma Rose would never leave the resort unattended."

"She didn't. You're here, I'm here—"

His smugness was irritating. "Where is she?" Josie asked.

"She and Ty went to St. Paul to see a picture show."

"They did not," Josie insisted. "Norma Rose would never…" Actually, the old Norma Rose wouldn't. The one that had emerged since Ty had arrived was different. She and Ty were always going places together. Still, Josie knew one thing for sure. "She would never leave guests unattended to."

"They are being attended to," he said. "By a dozen employees."

That wasn't exactly what she had meant. "Norma Rose—"

"Left Gloria in charge," Scooter whispered in her ear. "Which is why I'm here. And I'm not going anywhere. Not without you."

Josie's insides quivered, though it wasn't with dread.

"Come on." He tugged on her arm. "I'll let you eat something before we leave."

"Leave?"

Steering her down the hallway toward the kitchen, he said, "I need you to help me clean the raft and float it ashore. I don't want a boat to accidently run into it."

The idea of spending the day with Scooter was growing on her. As ridiculous as that was. It probably had something to do with the idea of facing Gloria today. That made her stomach ache. The other woman was sure to be mad about yesterday, and Gloria's wrath was a force to reckon with.

"What about Dac?" Josie asked. "Can't he help you?"

"Dac had a bit more to drink than he should have last night. His dad hauled him and his motorcycle home in their farm truck in the early hours of the morning."

"Really?" she asked, only to give herself a moment longer to think. If there was no one else to help Scooter, she should. It would be the right thing to do. However, it would make her think about all sorts of wrong things. Maybe she should just go back to bed.

"Yep. At least that's what Brock told me when he and Ginger came up to bed."

The thought that he'd already been in the hallway then made her feet stumble, but she set them straight before his stride was broken. "You were really on those chairs all night?" She truly hadn't believed him before, especially about her father giving him the pillow and blanket.

"Yep."

Tucking that knowledge aside for deeper consideration later, she asked, "Brock slept in Ginger's room?"

"Yes, although, at breakfast, your father promised he'd have the room painted before Brock and Ginger visit again."

His wink made her feet stumble again.

He caught her arm this time, and held it until they arrived at the kitchen. Pushing the door open, he made a sweeping bow. "After you, my lady."

Scooter had never been in the resort's kitchen, and the size of it was a bit intimidating. The three refrigerators that lined the back wall made the one he'd purchased for his mother last year look like an icebox. That refrigerator had cost him a pretty penny, and he couldn't rightly fathom how much each of these must have cost. Not to mention the two stoves and the cupboards and counters. He knew Moe, the assistant cook, well. He worked on the man's car, along with Silas's vehicle. Silas was the main cook and Moe explained to Josie that his boss had the day off as he ushered them to a small round table on the far side of the room.

"Sit down, sit down," Moe said. "I'll fix you both something to eat. It's been a while since breakfast. Not too many to cook for today. They all skedaddled. Doesn't look like there will be many for tonight, either. Not with everyone off in all directions."

Scooter sat and watched Josie's cheeks turn pink as Moe rattled on about all the girls getting married, swept off their feet by handsome gentlemen. The balding cook made it all sound like one of the fairy tales in the books Maize was always checking out from the library.

The man never stopped talking, but that didn't seem to interfere with his cooking. In no time he had bowls of potato soup, along with egg salad sandwiches, on the table.

"I had the soup simmering on the stove," Moe said.

"Thank you," Josie answered. "It looks delicious."

"I've never known you to sleep in so late," Moe said. "Putting on that party yesterday must have worn you plum out."

Josie's cheeks turned red again. Scooter tried to stop thinking about how cute she looked fresh out of her bath by spooning in a mouthful of soup. The soup was tasty, but not even the large chunks of bacon could distract his thoughts.

"That was quite a party," Moe said, sitting down in a chair. "Silas was beside himself. He worked for two days on just the cake. He wanted it to be perfect for Twyla." Moe propped his elbow on the table in order to set his chin in his palm. "Next it will be Norma Rose." Sighing, the cook added, "And then you."

Josie's spoon clattered against the side of her bowl, and for a moment, Scooter thought it was his. The way his hand had shook at the cook's words, it could have been.

"That won't be for a very long time, Moe," she said.

Moe lifted a brow before he shook his head. "I know your daddy hopes that. He'd be beside himself to lose all his girls in one summer. The man wouldn't know what to do with himself. I suspect he'd learn to live with it, though."

A heavy silence filled the room then, a silence only made thicker by the clink of their spoons scooping up soup. Moe was looking between the two of them, and much like Josie was doing, Scooter kept his gaze from meeting anyone else's.

By the time the meal was over, his stomach was acting as if he'd eaten a bowl of grasshoppers instead of the thick and delicious soup. Marriage was not something he contemplated. Especially not to Josie. That would be a far-fetched fairy tale. The Princess and the Grease Monkey. Although he figured he had enough money to pay for the lemon-scented perfume she'd sprayed on her wrists this morning—it had been the first thing that had hit him when he heard the door open earlier—he'd never make the kind of money her father made.

He'd gotten whiffs of her perfume in the past, but this morning, with his eyes closed, he'd examined the smell fully. Dissected the scent right down to wondering where she'd applied it. Her wrists, behind her earlobes, in the hollow of her neck...

Scooter shot to his feet, thanking Moe and asking Josie if she was ready in one breath. The fresh air would do him good. At least he hoped so. Marriage wasn't in the scheme of things and keeping her safe was where his focus needed to stay.

They exited the building through the side door, the very one she'd disappeared behind yesterday with Gloria. Norma Rose had asked the other woman to oversee the front desk, with some coaxing from Ty. Scooter and Ty had talked last night about the incidents. The fireball and the boathouse. Roger had been told about both and had appeared surprised. He'd said the fireworks show had been perfect. That he would never have known about the fire if he hadn't been told.

He was upset, too. That someone had been so close to harming his daughters. On his own property, no less. The conversation had taken place in the hallway upstairs, where Roger had given Scooter permission to sleep in the chairs. He'd assured Scooter that his men were on duty, but considering the number of guests filling the resort, they all agreed that one extra person on guard was a good idea.

Scooter had come within inches of telling Roger all he knew. Common sense, or perhaps his will to live, had held him back. While sitting in that chair last night, he'd mulled over his options, and come up with a plan. Josie wasn't going to stop going to Duluth until she had to. He was going to see to it that she had to.

"We'll take my motorcycle," he said, waving toward the parking lot.

She didn't say a word, but her grin sparked an inner fuse inside him. One that really hadn't needed to be lit.

The sun was straight overhead, sending down rays of heat that suggested today could be the hottest of the year so far. It had to be pushing eighty. He was already hot enough to burn toast. Had been ever since he'd heard Josie leave her bedroom. Imagining her soaking in a tub of water had taken over his mind.

"What about the stands you built?" she asked. "We can't carry them on your motorcycle."

"We don't have to," he said. "Bronco had them hauled up to the barn last night." The hours after she'd raced upstairs had been busy. Roger had ordered his men to comb the entire resort thoroughly upon hearing what had happened. No specific clues had been unearthed, or anyone identified, but by then a large number of partygoers had already left. Scooter had remained stoic and had stuck to his prankster theory. His gut told him Roger hadn't bought it, but when the man had remained silent on the subject, Scooter had, too.

They arrived at his motorcycle and after he got the engine running, Josie climbed on behind him like a natural. He shifted into gear and took off for the dock, his skin blistering beneath his clothes everywhere she touched him. Thankfully it was a short ride.

Scooter told Josie to wait on the dock while he pulled the boat out of the boathouse. The resort's boats were all dinghies, painted white with red trim, which made identifying the one on the water last night impossible. Just as frustrating was that several dinghies had petrol motors, all also identical.

He hopped in as soon as the boat hit the water and Josie caught the bow as it floated up to the dock. Once she was seated, he took up the oars.

Looking behind him at the boathouse, she said, "The doors have already been repaired."

He nodded. "Bronco saw to that last night, too."

She hung a hand over the side of the boat, skimming her fingers over the water. "A lot seems to have happened after I went to bed last night."

Scooter considered not answering, but since she had no way of escaping, other than if she dove in the water and swam to shore, he decided to take advantage of the moment. "So, what made you so mad last night?"

She leveled a dull stare on him.

"I'm serious. One minute…" He bit his tongue. That hadn't been how he'd meant to start out, reminding himself of things he'd never forget. Because he couldn't take it back, he waited until his silence had settled before he said, "The next you were mad as a gopher and running for the house."

Resting both hands next to her hips, palms flat on the bench seat, she let out a sigh. "No one knows who I am, Scooter. No one."

"In Duluth, you mean."

She turned, gracing him with a lovely profile as she stared out across the water.

"Plenty of people around here know who you are," he pointed out. "More than one could have seen you in Duluth any number of times."

Without turning, she said, "Maybe, but they wouldn't have recognized me. I'm careful."

In the hopes of making her understand, he attempted to tell her what she thought was a disguise was far from it. "Wearing pants and a shirt—"

"I wear those under other things."

"What other things?" he asked. "When I picked you up—"

"I'd already changed," she interrupted.

"How? When? In jail?"

"No, in my car." The frustration in her voice said she didn't want to tell him, but would in order to justify her actions. "I have several dresses. Old-fashioned ones I'm able to slip on and off quickly. Scarves with gray hair sewn in them, and a purse that everything fits into." Lifting her chin, she said, "I've walked past you and you never recognized me. I've had tea at your mother's table, with you in the kitchen."

His mother had women from the Ladies Aid Society over all the time. He never gave any of them a second look. Minus six or seven of them, they were all pushing eighty. Yet he knew them all, by name and look. The tingle that inched over his shoulders made him stare at her more intently. A second later he saw beyond the Josie he'd always thought he'd known. Disbelief had him blinking his eyes and shaking his head. It couldn't be, yet he asked, "Mrs. Weatherby?"

She shrugged.

As preposterous as it seemed, his mind was finding similarities. "You're Anita Weatherby?" He shook his head again. The glasses and stringy gray hair he could understand, but… "No one could make their face look that old. That wrinkled."

"I draw wrinkles on with a pencil."

"A pencil?"

"Yes and then cover them with rice powder."

He'd never closely scrutinized any of the women that graced his mother's kitchen, but he would in the future. Scanning Josie's face, he couldn't imagine she was Anita Weatherby, but add glasses, ugly gray hair and a colorful scarf and… "Wrinkles can't be drawn on," he insisted.

Josie's believe-me-or-not shrug twisted his thoughts. She'd almost had him—for a minute. He pulled in the oars to let the boat float up against the anchored raft. "Furthermore," he said smugly, "Anita Weatherby has lived on the far side of the lake, over by Hog Back Ridge with her sister, Colene Arneson, for years. Ever since their husbands died, prior to the war."

She stood up and looped the tie down around the post before turning his way. "Until three years ago when she moved to Missouri to live with her daughter."

"Exactly," he said. "And she didn't like it and moved ba—" His voice trailed off as Josie's grin increased.

"Moved back," Josie said with a twinkle in her eyes, "in with her sister Colene, who is ten years younger than Anita and very active in the Ladies Aid Society. As a matter of fact, Colene is one of the founding members."

"The real Anita Weatherby is still in Missouri, isn't she?" Scooter's mind was putting more than one piece of the puzzle together. "And there's an old road that leads from the resort to the back of the lake."

"To Hog Back Ridge," Josie said, climbing onto the platform. "However," she added, "Anita is ailing and rarely leaves the house these days."

"She doesn't have to," he said, climbing onto the platform beside her. "Gloria makes regular house calls to check on her health."

As if their conversation was as trivial as discussing the weather, Josie turned her attention to the charred bits of wood that yesterday had been barrels and crates full of fireworks.

"So, what are we going to do with this stuff?" she asked.

Scooter reached down and grabbed the bucket out of the boat. It was the same one he'd used to douse the flames last night. "We put the big pieces in here, and kick the ashes into the water," he said. However, his mind hadn't shifted far off topic. "It's not as ironclad as you think it is."

She'd already started picking up chunks of blackened wood. "What's not?"

Her back was to him, and she didn't turn around. "Your little scheme. When your father discovers—"

That had her spinning about. "You can't tell him, Scooter. You can't."

He told himself to ignore the pleading in her eyes, and her tone. It didn't do much good. In fact, it only made him think about last night. Holding her. Kissing her. That had been an idiotic thing to do—acting on the desires he'd had for years. It could only make things worse, and that he didn't need.

"It has to stop, Josie."

She tossed a chunk of wood into the bucket with enough force that the pail tipped over. They both bent down to retrieve it. The faint lemon scent that filled his nostrils added a degree or two to the temperature of his blood. He wouldn't give in to his desires again. Would *not*.

"I know I have to stop lying to my father, Scooter, but not until—"

He grasped her shoulder. "Until when, Josie? When you're taken by one of those ships? Sold overseas to some man's harem? That's what happens, you know. The girls who refuse to work at the docks are shipped out, never seen again."

"That doesn't happen anymore," she said. "There are too many border patrol officers checking for whiskey."

Bile rose in his throat. Maize had never said a word about what had happened to her. Refused to talk about it to this day. Scooter, however, had an imagination, and didn't like the things that formed in his mind when he thought of his sister's imprisonment. Even as short as it had been, she'd been hurt. Not in ways anyone could see, but inside, where she still kept it hidden. "Just because they aren't being shipped out doesn't mean they aren't being hurt. Doesn't mean they aren't being forced—"

"I know," Josie said, sinking down onto her knees. "Which is why I can't stop. Please, Scooter, don't try to make me. I have to finish what I started. I have to."

There were no tears in her eyes, but he could hear the sorrow in her voice and that made his throat turn raw. He

kneeled down and this time took her by the arms gently.
"You could get hurt or worse."

"Not if I'm careful. And I am." She shook her head.
"But there are others, and they are being hurt."

"Others?" In his mind, he'd put all the blame on Galen
Reynolds. It wasn't until he'd learned about Josie's trips to
Duluth that he'd considered the other women who hadn't
been as lucky as Maize. Not until Josie's call from jail,
after talking with that truck driver, had he started contemplating that perhaps the men Galen might have been
in cahoots with were still in Duluth.

She nodded. "And they need my help. I can't stop now."

He'd already concluded he'd do whatever it took to
make her stop. If that meant helping her complete what
she'd started—whatever that might be—then that's what
he'd do. "I won't tell your father, Josie, but only if you
let me help."

She glanced up at him. With her eyes full of caution,
and perhaps a hint of regret, she shook her head.

"It's your choice," he said. "You either tell me everything that's going on, or I tell your father."

Her eyelids fluttered shut. The single tear that slipped
out struck him harder than if she'd been sobbing. So did
her sigh.

"You can't help, Scooter," she whispered. "No one
can. Gloria would be furious to know I've told you as
much as I have."

He caught her beneath her chin, keeping her gaze
locked with his. "I don't give a damn about Gloria. She
never should have dragged you into this. But I do care
about you, Josie. No one will know that I'm helping you.
I promise."

The want in her eyes could have blinded him and the

desire to kiss her right then had him pulling up fortitude he didn't know he had. Keeping his lips from going where they wanted to go, from doing what they wanted to do, he repeated, "Just you and me. I promise."

Putting a touch of finality to his words, he let her loose and tossed a couple of chunks of wood into the pail as he stood. His mother had told him to let what had happened rest years ago, and stupidly, he had, mainly because Roger had started waging vengeance against Galen, and everyone had known who'd win that war.

"Scooter—"

He continued tossing burned wood in the bucket. She needed some time to weigh the consequences of the options laid out before her. "Let's get this cleaned up so I can pull up the anchors."

Josie didn't say anything, just started picking up the large pieces of wood, and in no time they had the area cleared of anything except ashes, which he kicked through the cracks between the wooden planks. With or without her information, he'd be investigating what was happening in Duluth.

"I'll put this in the boat and then get the anchors," he said, lifting up the bucket.

"How many anchors are there?"

"Two," he answered. "I wanted the platform to be as steady as possible."

"Are they tied to these ropes?" she asked, leaning over the left side of the raft, where he'd threaded anchor ropes through the large holes he'd drilled in the side boards.

"Yes, but they're heavy. I'll get them."

She shot him a glare. He chose to ignore it. After setting the pail in the boat, he went to the side of the raft opposite her, to pull up that anchor first. Made from a large chunk of old scrap iron he'd had lying around, the anchor was heavy and it took a hefty tug to break it loose from the sandy lake bed.

Hand over hand, he pulled up the rope until he was able to grasp the iron and set it on the platform. No longer held down, the barrel under the raft on that side rose in the water, making the raft rock.

A yelp had him turning around.

Backside in the air, Josie was hanging over the edge, pulling on the other anchor rope.

"I told you I'd get it," he said, rushing to her side of the raft. The fast shift of weight rocked the structure more. He tried to grab her, but wasn't fast enough. Her squeal ended with a splash.

Chapter Eight

Head first, Scooter jumped in, searching the spot where Josie had submerged. Her hands could be twisted in the rope, pulling her downward. Although the water was clear he couldn't see her, so he surfaced in order to dive lower.

"You fell in, too?"

He spun around. Josie held on to the raft with one hand, water dripping from her hair and eyelashes.

Her eyes widened and then she dove sideways. He watched as she retrieved his hat before it sank. Her movements were agile, her form sleek, confirming what he'd already known. Just like him, she'd been swimming in this lake her entire life.

A moment later, she plopped his hat on his head. He waited for the cascade of water to subside before reaching out and grabbing her waist. The desire to pull her close assaulted him again, along with the idea of kissing her. He was dead set against either of those things happening again, and hoisted her upright and then set her on the platform. Releasing her as soon as she was settled, he placed his hands on the wood beside her.

"No, I didn't fall in," he said. "I jumped. I didn't know if the anchor rope was wrapped around your hands."

She scooted backward and then stood, moving to the far side of the raft so it wouldn't topple over when he crawled out of the water. "Of course it wasn't wrapped around my hands. I know better than that."

The sun was shining down on her like a spotlight, allowing him to see right through her white top and the thin undershirt she had on beneath it. Regardless of the fact he was in water up to his armpits, fire shot through his veins. The way she had her hands on her hips emphasized the wet material over her breasts. His eyes refused to look away, so he closed them, but it did little more than burn the vision into his brain.

Hoisting himself onto the raft, he spun around to face the lake, and took his time dumping the water out of his boots as an excuse not to glance her way again.

"You don't need to keep trying to save me, Scooter. I'm completely capable of taking care of myself."

There were a dozen ways he could respond to that, but he chose silence. It was his best option. After removing his socks, he tucked them inside his boots, which he then tossed into the boat. Then he grabbed the anchor rope.

"So now you aren't talking to me?"

He shook his head and kept pulling on the rope.

"Ducky, Scooter, just ducky."

A grin tugged at his lips. She was too cute for her own good. "Maybe I just don't have anything to say," he said.

"That would be a first."

He grabbed the second anchor, made from another chunk of scrap iron, and set it on the platform. Set free, the raft, and the boat tied to it, started to drift. He should climb into the boat and tow the raft to shore and then head home. Get as far away from her as possible. That would be the smart thing to do. As much as he knew it couldn't happen again, he wanted to feel Josie in his arms again. Kiss her again.

"We're all sworn to secrecy."

Scooter turned around. She'd sat down, and he refrained from mentioning how black her wet britches would be from sitting in the layer of ash covering the wood. Her shoes were sitting beside her and her bare feet, her toes, were as cute as the rest of her. He bit the inside of his cheeks, trying to dissolve yet another bout of desire. His willpower wasn't easily found, so he dug deeper. She was Roger Nightingale's daughter, and Roger didn't like anyone sniffing around his daughters.

His traitorous mind chose that moment to point out that nothing bad had happened to Brock, or Forrest, or Ty Bradshaw. Telling himself that was like comparing a Ford to a Buick, so he forced his attention back to what she'd said. Secrecy. That was an understatement. He hadn't been able to crack much from his mother or Gloria. He'd considered asking Maize, but he couldn't do that to her. It had taken too long for the haunted dullness to leave her eyes. She still wasn't the person she'd been before that night, and he feared she might never be the same.

"Sworn to secrecy after Maize was taken," he ventured.

She nodded.

"How'd you get involved?"

Josie had no idea what made her want to tell him everything. Other than that she was at her wits' end. Scooter was relentless. Her only hope was to make him understand why she couldn't stop. Not right now. She didn't have to tell him everything, just enough to make him see things her way.

Water still dripped off his hair, off the hat she'd purposely plunked on his head without emptying. The smile that wanted to appear on her lips was stifled by the frustration inside her. His handsomeness had never affected her before, not like it was now. For a split second, when they'd been in the water together, she'd thought he might kiss her again. She hadn't just thought it. She'd wanted it to happen. That couldn't happen any more than he could help her. Last night had been a fluke. She'd been caught up in all that was happening around her. The kissing, the dancing, the companionship her sisters were all experiencing. She'd wanted that, too, and because Scooter was close at hand—had never left her side—she'd used him to experience it.

That was as good an excuse as any. She'd come up with that reasoning while sitting across from him in the kitchen, eating the lunch Moe had prepared for them. Now, though, she knew it had gone far enough. She had to put a cork in it. She had no desire to get married—not that kissing Scooter would lead to marriage. Moe's comment had been a startling revelation. People would now start questioning when she'd be getting married. She couldn't rule it out entirely, but it certainly wasn't going to be today, or this summer. Nor would it be with Scooter. When she finally fell in love, it would not be with a man who continuously threatened to tell her father about every little move she made.

In fact, her plan for the future put her far away from Scooter. From the resort and all the suffocating expectations that went along with being Roger Nightingale's daughter. She'd remain in close contact with her family, for she did love them, but she'd be doing more with her life than she ever could around here. She'd be saving lives.

"How'd you get involved?" Scooter repeated. He'd moved closer and was now sitting beside her with his long legs stretched out. His gaze went across the lake to the shore that they'd eventually drift to if neither one of them climbed in the boat and started paddling. "I know Gloria masterminded Maize's escape plan, but how'd you get dragged into it?"

"Maize told you I was there?" Josie snapped her mouth shut, realizing she was gaping. Everyone had been sworn to secrecy and she'd never, ever, have expected Maize to be the one to reveal anyone's involvement.

"No," he said. "Maize has never said a word about any of it. I discovered your involvement on my own."

"How?"

He let out a loud exhale before turning to look at her. "Unlike your father, I know it doesn't take that much gas to drive little old ladies to and from society meetings."

She pinched her lips together. Only Scooter would piece that together.

"Don't worry. No one else has figured it out, and I haven't told anyone."

She considered asking how he could be sure of that, but instead pointed out, "Except for Gloria and your mother. You've told both of them."

"Yes, I have."

"Why?"

"Because it's dangerous. Both Gloria and my mother need to know their lives are going to change drastically when your father discovers all that's happened. Gloria is going to end up homeless and my mother is going to put us all back in the poorhouse."

The shiver that rippled her insides had nothing to do with her wet clothing. In fact, sitting out here with the sun reflecting off the water was getting hot, even with damp clothes. The chill she felt was deep inside. She'd just been given an answer she hadn't known she was seeking. Scooter wasn't demanding that she stop going to Duluth because he was worried about her—he was worried about himself. Not everyone knew he slept in the upstairs of his gas station, but she did. And she knew why. The bootleggers who drove whiskey for her father filled their gas tanks late at night, or early in the morning, after their runs, and they all used Scooter's station. It was located four miles from town and was the ideal place for such late-night activities. However, one word from her father and they'd use a different station.

She couldn't fault him for looking out for himself, for his family, but deep down she had a sickening feeling, as if she'd hoped he'd been so insistent for a different reason.

"Your father will find out," Scooter said. "It's gone on long enough. Too long actually."

That couldn't be denied, and the fact settled within her. With her sisters married, she'd no longer be able to hide in their shadows. Her father would be keeping a much closer tab on her whereabouts. That was where the urgency inside her sprang from. If she could rescue those captive girls before Norma Rose got married, things would be settled enough that someone else could take over her trips to Duluth for a few weeks. Afterward, when everyone was settled back at the resort, she could announce her plan to move to Duluth.

Scooter was sure to be happy about that. He'd never have to worry about her calling him again. Or having to come to her rescue. She'd probably rarely see him, only if she chose to come home for one reason or another. He'd be too busy with his station to ever travel that far.

"Are you going to tell me or not?"

A sigh had built to mammoth proportions in her chest. After letting it out, she drew in a fresh breath and settled her gaze on the far shore of the lake. "I'll tell you what I can."

He lifted a brow.

She sighed again, and then launched into an explanation she hoped he'd accept. "For the most part, the shipping of girls stopped shortly after Maize was rescued. Congress passed several acts to prevent immigrants from entering the United States and that pretty much put a stop to Galen selling girls out of Duluth. That's when he started transporting them to California, claiming they worked for his film company. In reality, he was selling the girls to Mexico."

"That's when your father got involved."

She nodded. "For different reasons, but yes. Gloria's house had burned down, and she blamed Galen."

"As did many others," Scooter said. "It was right up Galen's alley. From the time Maize went to work serving drinks at the Plantation, she said Galen wanted her to sing at a nightclub in Duluth. Mother and I both said he was playing her, but she was convinced it was the real deal and she wouldn't listen."

The frustration in his tone said he'd been more affected by what had happened than she'd given credence to. "They met at the resort the next morning," she said. "Probably because they didn't want to be spotted together in town."

"Who met?"

"Gloria and your mother. The rest of the Ladies Aid

Society was there, too, but not at the same table. I served them brunch." Josie let her gaze wander back to the lake. "I think they had the idea to recruit one of us girls when they arrived. Ginger was too young, Norma Rose too stubborn, Twyla too…"

"Wild," Scooter stated.

"For lack of a better word, yes," Josie admitted.

"So they chose you."

She nodded.

"They probably had you in mind all along." His sigh hung in the air before he added, "You fit the bill perfectly."

Josie held her gaze, focusing on the tall oaks on the shore, how their leaves fluttered in the breeze, rather than how unsettled the gravity in his tone left her feeling.

"So what happened that day?" he asked. "The day Maize was rescued?"

"We found her and brought her home."

"I know that," he said dryly. "I want details."

He would just have to get details from someone else. She was done. Had to stop. The more she told him, the more she wanted to tell him, and that couldn't happen. There was no betting on what he'd do if she let it slip that Maize had been naked when they'd found her. No one ever made mention of that, but she remembered it pointedly. "We should get in the boat and tow this raft to shore," Josie said. "If we just keep floating we're going to end up on the other side of the lake."

"Yes, we will," he answered.

Josie waited for him to move first, not overly eager to return to the resort. Her gaze shifted to the island off to their left. A boat was pushed up on the beach, near a tent. Discontent like she'd never known rose up inside her. Twyla and Forrest were still on the island, celebrating their marriage. Ginger was visiting her new in-laws and Norma Rose and Ty were off having fun together. They were all content. All happy. And here she was...

"What happened that day, Josie?"

He wouldn't give up, nor would he row them back to shore, until she gave in. She knew how to row, and could easily climb into the boat and grab the oars, but she didn't want to. Her gaze was still on the island and she was recalling her conversation with Twyla shortly after her arrest. Twyla and Forrest had almost been kidnapped, a harrowing experience full of Tommy guns and fast cars, especially the way Twyla told it. Josie was remembering something else Twyla had said then. Her sister had said she wished Josie had someone like Forrest. Someone who would erase all of her fears, even while being shot at.

Perhaps that was when she'd started to wish for that exact same thing. Except she didn't need that. Didn't want that.

She did, however, want to release some of the weight dragging her down. Scooter had kept her secrets this long because he had just as much to lose as she did. Perhaps more. One word from her father and his business would be wiped out. She wasn't afraid of her father's wrath. Her fears came from not rescuing those young girls in time.

Father would forgive her, eventually, but he rarely forgave someone who put his daughters in danger. That was the reason Galen Reynolds was finally arrested. The charges against him had been for counterfeiting, but everyone knew Galen had been sent to jail so he'd never threaten Norma Rose again.

The dread inside her grew larger than ever. Scooter

could lose everything because of her. The weight of that
was more of a burden than she could carry.

"Josie?"

Pulling her eyes away from the island, she said, "We
left the resort that day as soon as brunch was over. Gloria,
your mother, a couple of other women from the society
and me. It was before noon. Once in Duluth, I walked
along the piers, waiting to be approached."

"You walked the piers? Alone?"

Ignoring the anger in his tone, she continued, "Once
I was propositioned—"

"Propositioned?"

Unable to ignore his shout, Josie shot a glare his way
and snapped, "Do you want to hear what happened or
not?" Her insides had become a tangled mess. Her life
was a tangled mess.

His glare was as sharp as hers, but he gave in. "Go on."

"I let the man lead me toward the warehouse. The
other women were hiding and watching. I knew they'd
follow." The confidence she'd gained that day, at how easily their plan had worked, renewed itself inside her. "All
went exactly as planned. As soon as he unlocked the door,
the rest of the women charged forward. The plan was for
me to run for the car. Colene was the driver and waiting
just around the corner. While I ran, Gloria, your mother
and the others found Maize. It wasn't too hard. The men
never expected a hoard of umbrella-wielding women to
charge at them, especially not in broad daylight. Colene
pulled the car around the corner and everyone ran across
the parking lot and climbed in." Pausing, she pointed out,
"We had Gloria's big Buick so there was plenty of room.
She won't be seen in a Ford, you know."

He nodded and asked, "What happened then?"

Josie scooted forward and lowered her bare feet into the water. "We drove home and never spoke about it again."

"When did you start making regular trips to Duluth?"

Josie held in another sigh. She'd opened a can of worms, and wasn't sure how to put the lid back on. "After Gloria's house burned down, she moved here to the resort, and started passing out condoms to the girls who rent out rooms during large parties. Some of them were from Duluth and wanted to take condoms back to other women they knew, especially after Gloria pointed out all the benefits. How they not only prevent pregnancy, but the spread of disease. Up until last year you still had to have a prescription to buy them and even now, most places only allow men to purchase them." Josie splashed her feet into the water, hoping it might help alleviate the sting in her cheeks. The subject usually didn't embarrass her, but discussing condoms with Scooter was different than discussing it with the ladies from the society or her sisters.

"And?"

She took a deep breath. "Gloria started purchasing cases of them and Colene and Hester Williams started making regular trips to Duluth to give them to the girls, but walking the piers and streets near the docks became too exhausting for them. They are both rather elderly."

"That's when you started dressing up as Anita Weatherby?"

She nodded. "It was Colene's idea."

"What happened then?" he asked.

"Nothing. I drove up there a couple of times a month at first, then weekly."

"Why?"

She shrugged. "Because it got me out of here. By then

Father was deep in his war with Galen and kept us all close to home, but because I was attending with Gloria, he let me go to the society meetings."

"That's a long drive," he said. "It takes over three hours to get to Duluth."

"I know. I'd leave around eight in the morning and be home in time for supper."

"So what changed?" he asked. "When did it become more than passing out condoms?"

"Shortly after Galen was arrested last fall, Francine Wilks moved to Duluth. She'd lived in St. Paul and New York before that. Francine has someone behind her, someone with a lot of power, because she's taken over the entire prostitution ring up there." Josie's cheeks were no longer burning. Her insides were now on fire because of the number of girls that had become involved since Francine had moved to Duluth. "Believe it or not, Scooter, she's worse than Galen Reynolds ever was."

"How so?"

"Girls are no longer being shipped in and out of Duluth, but the port is busier than ever with J. P. Morgan's US Steel company booming. In order to keep up with the demand, Francine found a new supply of girls."

Scooter was frowning. "I don't follow you. A new supply from where?"

"Francine is hauling in young girls from the reservations near there. No more than thirteen and fourteen years old. It's awful," Josie said. "And the law won't do anything about it."

"So you've set your mind to do something," he stated.

"Someone has to." Turning to face him, she explained, "We'd set up a secret code of sorts. If the girls asked me for two boxes, I knew either they or someone they knew wanted to escape. I'd give them one regular box and another box that contained a train ticket to Cloquet. There's a woman there who will transport the girls back to the reservation, or help them get a different job." Josie stopped herself from saying that's what she intended to do, set up another safe house, right in Duluth.

"And?"

"Somehow Francine learned about that," Josie said. "The day I was arrested, I'd asked a regular why no one had wanted two boxes for several weeks. She told me it was because Francine was keeping the new girls locked up in a warehouse. Wouldn't let anyone get close to them until they were *ready*."

"And you decided to try and rescue them by yourself."

"No," she said. "I just wanted to figure out which warehouse they were in, but one of Francine's men saw me. I ran to my car. He jumped in a car and started to chase me. I was afraid he'd catch me, so I drove past the police station, going as fast as I could, hoping I'd get arrested for speeding. And I did."

"So this guy saw you, he knows what you look like," Scooter said.

"No, I took off my Anita disguise before I started snooping around the warehouses and put on my young-boy clothes."

"Young-boy clothes?"

"Yes, I have a hat with brown hair sewn into it and a flannel shirt. I didn't take them off until I got inside the police station. The officers were surprised. It works as well as the Anita disguise does." Rehashing all the details aloud made her stomach churn. "It seemed like a good plan at the time, but when the officer stopped me, the man in the car just pulled over. Like he was waiting for them to let me drive away. That's when I said the gas pedal was stuck and I had to call you to come and get me."

Scooter's expression changed, went from frowning to—well, she couldn't quite describe the way his face grew distorted and his eyes darted around nervously.

A shiver raced up her spine. "What?"

"That fireball, being locked in the boathouse, that wasn't because they recognized you."

"I know," she said. "There was no way they could have. I was still in disguise."

"I wasn't," Scooter said solemnly. "They must have seen me working on your car on the side of the road, and they recognized me last night."

Josie's blood turned so cold goose bumps prickled her skin. She'd never considered that possibility. "No," she whispered. "No."

"Yes," Scooter said. "They probably watched me drive your car to the police station. They could even have followed us all the way back to my gas station." He bounded to his feet. "No wonder they were here last night."

Chapter Nine

Although he didn't know the man well, Scooter was happy to see Ty—and Norma Rose—climbing out of Ty's truck. Forrest had told him Ty used to be a private investigator. That's what had brought him to Minnesota. He'd hung that hat up before asking Norma Rose to marry him, but he still had connections. Ones that had helped Forrest solve the case against Galen Reynolds. Scooter hoped Ty might be inclined to help him. He had a feeling he was going to need it.

Pulling his motorcycle up to the front door of the resort, Scooter cut the engine. "You go on in and change your clothes," he told Josie.

"What are you going to do?" she asked.

"I'm going home to put on dry ones, too."

She climbed off the bike, but her steady stare said she didn't believe he was simply going home. He wasn't. But he wasn't about to tell her that.

Hand in hand, Ty and Norma Rose approached. "Did you two fall in the lake?" Norma Rose asked.

"Yes," Scooter answered. "Well, she fell in," he said, correcting himself. "I jumped in to save her."

"I didn't need to be saved," Josie said.

"What were you doing?" Norma Rose asked.

"Bringing in the raft we used last night."

"Was it salvageable?" Ty asked.

"Yes," Scooter answered. "Nothing more than a few surface burns. We pulled it ashore down by the first dock." Hoping the other man would catch his hint, he added, "I'll need some help and a truck to haul it to the barn."

"Let's go and do it now," Ty said. "It'll fit in the back of my truck."

"If you don't mind," Scooter said, trying to cover up his gratitude.

"I thought you were going home to change," Josie said, eyeing him guardedly.

"I am," he said. "This way I won't have to come back later."

She pinched her lips together and glowered. "Then I'll come with you and help." Nodding toward Norma Rose, she added, "We'll all go."

"No, we won't," Norma Rose said. "You need to go and change your clothes. Those pants will probably be stained forever. Besides, I want to talk to you."

"About what?" Josie asked.

"The resort." Norma Rose stretched up on her toes and kissed Ty's cheek. "See you later." Snagging her arm, she tugged Josie toward the door. "I'll put your pants in to soak while you change."

"I'll meet you at the dock," Scooter told Ty as Josie watched him over her shoulder. "I don't want to get your seat wet."

Ty nodded and walked toward his truck while Scooter started his bike and headed back toward the lake. The cycle was parked and he was standing next to the raft when Ty arrived. Waving both hands, Scooter guided Ty as he backed the truck down the hill, and then he placed a rock behind the back wheels so it wouldn't roll when Ty cut the engine.

As Ty climbed out of the truck, he said, "Norma Rose and I didn't go to a picture show. We did a little investigating instead."

"Investigating?" Scooter asked, making no move to start loading the raft.

"Yes, on Francine Wilks. I thought I recognized the name when Bronco mentioned it last night and wanted to check it out."

Scooter's throat went dry. "And?"

"And," Ty said as he leaned against the back of his truck, "when I was looking into Galen Reynolds's past, I discovered he was involved with the Eastman gang out of New York. Since the late 1800s, they've created quite an empire. An underground one. Prostitution, gambling, peddling opium. They also have droppers all across the nation. Some are little more than front men who aren't really accepted or protected by the gang. Galen was one of those. A middleman in their opium deals. The drugs were stored at the Plantation until runners picked it up. Galen never really had control of any of it. When Prohibition hit, the feds caught his shipments at the port of Duluth and the Eastman gang pretty much ousted him. He dipped his fingers in prostitution, importing and exporting some girls, but he was too greedy. Too many girls disappeared under his reign. From what I've seen of the Eastman gang, Galen's lucky he lived long enough to go to trial for his counterfeiting. If the gang's big boys had discovered what he'd been doing, they'd have filled him with lead long before he was arrested."

Scooter was listening, but also trying to find a way to interrupt. Galen Reynolds's past was of no concern to him.

"You're wondering why I'm telling you all this," Ty said.

"Yes, I am," Scooter agreed.

"One of the founding men of the Eastman gang was Ike Eastman. He married a woman named Patricia Wilks, and brought her entire family into his operation."

"Wilks," Scooter said, "as in Francine Wilks."

"Yes," Ty answered. "From what I can figure out, she's a great-niece and well-established in the family. Francine's been working her way west the past few years. Detroit, Milwaukee, Chicago, St. Paul. Setting up prostitution rings, solid ones, before moving on to the next city and still making a portion of every dollar those rings bring in. Francine is not like Galen. She's the real McCoy, with an entire establishment behind her. A force to reckon with."

Scooter let out a low whistle before he asked, "Have you told Roger any of this?"

"No," Ty said. "I just confirmed it all while Norma Rose and I were in St. Paul today."

Scooter planted both elbows on the box of Ty's truck and rubbed his forehead with his palms. Things couldn't get a whole lot worse than this. He released the air he'd been holding in and rubbed his forehead harder.

"What is it?" Ty asked.

Scooter sighed and then started talking. He began with Maize's disappearance and ended with Josie's arrest. When he finished, this time Ty was the one who whistled.

"Roger doesn't know about any of this?"

"Not that I know of," Scooter said.

Ty was shaking his head. "He must not know. He'd have mentioned it, and he'd have stopped Josie's involvement long ago." Pacing the ground near the back of the truck, Ty continued, "I knew about the rubbers in Josie's closet. Norma Rose told me. She believes Josie just stores them there for Gloria Kasper to pass out to the girls who rent rooms on the third floor."

"Does Roger know about them?" Scooter asked. "The rubbers?"

"That they are in Josie's room?"

He nodded.

Looking shocked, Ty asked, "What do you think?"

Scooter's spine quivered. "No."

Ty nodded. "He'd have put a stop to that, too." Letting out another whistle, Ty added, "What was Gloria Kasper thinking? Dragging Josie into it like that? The woman must have a death wish."

Scooter wondered if he also had a death wish. He could hope Roger bumped him off in a quick and smooth fashion, but considering how long he'd known what was going on, Roger would most likely make him suffer. Long and hard.

Ty must have had somewhat similar thoughts because he'd stopped pacing and the look in his eyes was sorrowful. "I'd hate to be in your shoes, Scooter."

Rubbing his head again, which was pounding, Scooter answered, "They aren't very comfortable. I'll tell you that."

"Will you quit staring out the window?"

Josie spun around. "I'm just wondering what is taking Scooter and Ty so long."

"It hasn't been that long." Norma Rose leaned back in her chair on the other side of the desk. "You haven't heard a word I've said, have you?"

Josie opened her mouth to say yes, but if Norma Rose asked what she'd heard, she wouldn't have an answer. She hadn't been listening. Her mind had been on Scooter. He'd made her promise not to mention what they'd figured out to Gloria. Josie hadn't planned on it—then. Now she was contemplating it. Scooter could be in real danger. As much danger as those poor girls locked in the warehouse.

"Josie?"

Snapping her head up, she asked, "What?"

"What is wrong with you? It's not like you to be so preoccupied."

"I'm not preoccupied," Josie said. Searching for an explanation, which wasn't easy, she added, "I'm just worried about—"

"Who threw that fireball at the raft last night?" Norma Rose asked. "Well, don't worry. Ty's looking into it."

Every muscle in Josie's body went stiff. "There's no need for Ty to be investigating it. I'm sure it was just some pranksters."

Norma Rose sighed. "If you're sure of that, why are you worried?"

This was exactly why Josie had chosen to remain silent for so many years. It was way too easy to talk herself into a corner when it came to her family. Fortunately, she had heard a word or two her sister had said earlier. "Tell me again what you are suggesting when it comes to Maize?"

Norma Rose frowned, but then leaned forward and pointed to the calendar on her desk. "Ty and I are going to be gone for two weeks. Now, I know Twyla said she'd come and help, but I believe she's going to be very busy at the Plantation. I was thinking we could hire Maize to help you. She could bring Jonas with her. A boy his age will find all sorts of things to keep him busy out here, fishing and swimming. All the things we used to do as kids. Uncle Dave suggested it yesterday, and after seeing Maize last night, I think she'd do a good job. I didn't mention anything to her, because I wanted to ask you first."

Thankful the conversation didn't require much thought on her part, Josie nodded. "That sounds fine to me."

"I know how important your Ladies Aid meetings are to you, and I don't want you to have to miss them while I'm gone. With Maize here, you won't have to."

Josie held in her sigh. "I said it sounds fine."

"I was thinking I'd ask her to start this week, if she's interested," Norma Rose continued, as if Josie hadn't spoken. "That way she can shadow me for several days. Learn all the ins and outs and…"

Careful that her sister didn't catch the way she glanced toward the window out of the corner of her eye, Josie leaned back in her chair and let Norma Rose go on. She was bound to, whether Josie spoke or not. Which was fine, as it gave Josie free rein to wonder what was taking Scooter and Ty so long. All they had to do was load up the raft. It wasn't even that heavy. Well, it was for her, but not for two strong men. She feared but doubted Scooter would tell Ty anything about her trips. He'd held his silence for this long. Then again, he hadn't been as involved then as he was now. All because of her.

Josie's thoughts were completely twisted among themselves when the office door opened. "Where's Scooter?" she asked, as Ty entered the room.

"He went home," Ty answered. Turning to Norma Rose, he said, "Your father just arrived. So did Ginger and Brock, along with his family. And I saw a boat coming across the lake, so I'm assuming it's Twyla and Forrest. You might want to let Moe know they'll all be here for supper."

"That will be nice," Norma Rose said. "We can have a family dinner one last time before everyone goes their separate ways."

Glad to have an excuse to leave the room, Josie stood. "I'll go and let Moe know."

"Tell him to add a plate for Scooter, too," Ty said. "I invited him to join us."

Josie flinched. She wanted to talk to Scooter, but didn't need him talking to the entire family.

And that was precisely what happened. She'd barely had a chance tell Moe who'd be there for dinner and change her clothes before the entire family, plus Scooter, were gathered on the balcony raving about the party the night before, including Scooter's fireworks, while eating Moe's fare.

Twyla's animated description of watching the fireworks from Forrest's airplane dominated the conversation for an enormous amount of time. Josie kept glancing at Scooter, who was at the other end of the table, next to her father. The two of them had had a brief but deep discussion that left her hands trembling, especially when they both looked her way.

Her mind was trembling, too, and for the life of her, she couldn't come up with an excuse to leave the table. The subject had turned to Babe Ruth and went on forever. In fact, it seemed everyone was gathered around the table for hours.

When Brock's mother said it was time for them to leave, Josie all but leaped to her feet. Scooter did, too, but in order to offer to help Brock load up the wheelchair. He walked past her without so much as a sideways glance.

Josie followed everyone as far as the front door, where Twyla once again dominated the conversation, talking about how she'd start moving her things to the Plantation the following day.

Twyla was still talking when Forrest led her out the front door. The familiar sound that hit Josie's ears should have made her happy, but it didn't. Neither did seeing the taillight of Scooter's motorbike as he rode it down the driveway.

Ginger and Brock said good-night and headed for the stairs. Norma Rose and Ty said they were going to take a walk before turning in, and Josie spun around, ready to retreat to her own room, when a powerful sense of unease rippled through her.

Her father's hand fell on her shoulder. "I need to talk to you, Josie-girl."

"Oh," she said, almost choking on a solid lump in her throat. "About what?"

"You and Scooter—"

Josie's ears started to ring and the room threatened to spin. She knew it. Knew there'd come a time when he'd betray her.

"—aren't going to be able to pick out your new car tomorrow. Big Al informed me last night he'd have a new shipment coming in next week. He wants you to wait, and I agreed. It would give you several more to choose from."

A car. Really? She'd almost fainted because of a car? She didn't even want a new one.

"I'm sorry to disappoint you. I've already told Scooter.

He said he'd take you over there as soon as I hear from Big Al."

Her mind was still going in other directions, none of which included a car—old or new. Scooter hadn't told her father. Just like he'd promised. That caused even more confusion inside her.

"It'll be sad to see Ginger leave tomorrow," her father said. "It's been nice having her home. But she and Brock are doing well down in Chicago. I'm happy for them."

"Me, too," she said.

"And for Twyla and Forrest," he said. "Your sister will soon have the Plantation buzzing again, and Forrest will get his airmail contract. I'm sure of that."

More like he'd make sure of it, Josie thought, but she merely nodded. Her ability to make small talk was gone. Scooter had taken over her mind.

"Things sure have changed around here," her father said. "Quickly."

"That's how change is," she muttered. "Doesn't even give us time to contemplate what's happening."

He grinned. "You're right there." Giving her shoulder a squeeze, he said, "You're so much like your mother, Josie. So levelheaded and rational. The opposite of a couple of your sisters."

The lump in her throat was back.

"I appreciate that, darling. I've never had to worry about you."

Dread, or perhaps shame, wouldn't let her ramble down that road. "It's late, Daddy. I'm going to turn in." As unfathomable emotions bubbled up inside her, she stretched up on her toes to kiss his cheek. "I love you."

"I love you, too, Josie-girl," he said. "Good night."

"Night."

She was almost at the ballroom when he asked, "Oh, what do you think about Norma Rose's idea of hiring Maize Blackburn? The poor girl hasn't had it easy since her husband died. Or since that debacle with Galen Reynolds."

Squeezing her hands into fists to stop them from shaking, she dredged up a smile. "I think it's a fine idea." Then in great need of escape, she repeated, "Night."

Her flight up the stairs was swift, but as soon as she shut her bedroom door, Josie realized there was no escaping. Not for her. There might never be.

Chapter Ten

Tuesday morning wasn't any better than Monday morning had been. Scooter was still at a loss. He'd never been this hopeless before, not even when his father had died and he'd found himself responsible for his family. Knowing what had to be done, he'd dug his heels in and went to work. Sleep had been nonexistent for a time. He'd delivered groceries during the day and repaired any and all types of vehicles at night. From bicycles and motorcycles to automobiles. It had taken a long time to build up a customer base large enough for him to quit the grocery store, and a bit longer before he'd saved enough to buy his first gas pump.

All the time his friends had been going to school and visiting the amusement park on weekends, he'd been working. And saving. He'd been tired, exhausted at times, but never scared. Hardly even worried. Deep down he'd known it would all come together and that someday he wouldn't have to watch his pockets empty out at the first of every month.

It had worked out and he no longer fretted when it was time to tear off another page of the calendar. He wasn't flush with money, but his family was clothed, fed, had a roof over their heads and there was still money in the bank at the end of every month for rainy days.

Flipping the sign hanging on the door of his gas station from Closed to Open, Scooter stared through the glass, not really looking at anything in particular. The sun was shining. The sky was blue. The train whistle sounded as usual. A normal day.

Except everything was not normal. He had an overwhelming desire to punch something.

Scooter unlocked the door and pushed it open. For the first time in his life, hard work, long days and short nights weren't going to be enough. Furthermore, he was scared. And he didn't like it.

He'd spent half the night trying to come up with a plan to rescue those girls in Duluth, which would also put a stop to Josie's trips, but he knew nothing about going up against mobsters. Ty had told him to hang tight for a couple of days, give him time to investigate a bit more, and that left Scooter feeling as if he was sitting on a gas can in the middle of a ring of fire.

Scooter grabbed the bucket he used to wash windows on customers' cars and carried it to the water spigot to fill it for the day. He'd just wet the rags he hung to dry each night when a car pulled into the station.

He filled the gas tank, checked the oil and tires, washed the windows and made small talk with the owner, then did the same with the next car, too. Customers pulled in regularly, as was customary, for the next hour or so. Willard Ralstad had just driven away in his old Model T when Dac Lester pulled up in his one-ton stock-hauling truck that doubled as his shine runner. Yellow and black, the GMC was a brute of a vehicle, with a box longer and taller than all others around. The painted wooden slats on the sides were nailed close together. Nothing but a hump of hair could be seen of the big black bull Dac hauled with him everywhere he went.

Scooter cranked up the gas pump again, preparing it to fill the stock truck, when the phone in his station rang.

As Dac cut the truck's engine, he leaned out of the window. "Go ahead and answer that, I'll get the gas."

Scooter acknowledged Dac with a wave before jogging through the door he'd propped open. The phone hung on the wall next to a set of shelves full of oil cans. He rested one arm on the top shelf while grabbing the earpiece and speaking into the mouthpiece attached to the wooden base. "Scooter here."

"Scooter, it's Maize."

He grinned. Norma Rose had called yesterday and offered Maize a job working at the resort.

"Shouldn't you be working, not talking on the phone?" he asked teasingly. Deep down, he was glad she'd accepted the opportunity. Maize had rarely left the house for the past three years, and she had been very excited when she'd driven away this morning.

"I thought you'd want to know something," she said.

The concern in her tone had him standing upright. "What? What is it?"

"Dave's car is missing."

"Where's Dave?"

"He's here, but no one else is. Norma Rose and Ty took a load of things to Twyla, and Roger went with them."

Scooter had noticed Ty's truck go by earlier and assumed the load in the back had been for Twyla. "Where's Josie?"

There was a noticeable pause before Maize said, "At her Ladies Aid meeting."

Scooter cursed. He hadn't told Ty to find a way to make Josie stay at home. He hadn't thought it was necessary. The tingling of his spine told him all he needed to know, yet he asked, "Is her car there?"

"Yes," Maize said. "It's in the garage. Dave says it won't start."

Scooter cursed again under his breath before he said, "Let me talk to Dave."

A second later, he heard the man say, "Hey, Scooter."

"When did your car come up missing?" Scooter wanted to tell Dave to start taking the keys out of his car. Twyla had stolen it a couple of weeks ago. He'd been the one to call Forrest that morning and tell him Twyla was heading to town. But a car without keys wouldn't have stopped Josie.

"I just noticed it was gone a short time ago," Dave said. "I was out late last night and slept in this morning. I've gotta be back down in St. Paul in an hour."

Josie had been the first thing Scooter had thought of this morning, but that wasn't unusual. He'd realized it was a Tuesday, too—Josie's day for Ladies Aid meetings—but also recalled he'd never reconnected the ignition wire on her car. "You can take Josie's car," he growled into the phone.

"It won't start."

Scooter proceeded to tell Dave how to reconnect the wire and then hung up. Kicking the brick away that propped open the main door, he turned the sign to Closed and then locked the door, exiting the building through the repair bay door.

Dac eyed him curiously as he rounded the building. "Closed? Why?"

"I think I need your help." Scooter's mind was going a hundred miles an hour. In a circle.

"You think?"

"Hold on a second." Scooter tried to focus, to come up with a plan to get Josie out of Duluth, alive, but wasn't having much luck. He didn't have time to waste, either. The sick feeling in his gut said she could be in trouble. Serious trouble. "Yeah, I need your help," he said. "We need to go Duluth."

"Right now?" Dac asked.

"Yes, right now," Scooter snapped.

"Okay. What for?"

"Open your tailgate so I can load my motorcycle in the back, and I'll explain on the way." Turning to retrieve his bike, Scooter spun back around. "Nobody, and I mean nobody, can know about this."

Eyes wider than normal, Dac nodded. "All right."

As always, when she rolled into the outskirts of Duluth, Josie pulled into a fueling station. The young man that appeared at her window looked nothing like Scooter, yet he was on her mind. He had been ever since she'd left home. All night actually. All day yesterday, too. He'd told her not to go, but not making her regular run would look suspicious. She'd made other runs since getting arrested and they'd gone just fine. Today would, too. In fact, today would be better. She would not leave until she'd learned something significant.

The attendant took her money for the gas and she drove to the back of the station building. Grabbing one of the two large bags from the seat beside her, she climbed out of the car and entered the powder room. A few minutes later, dressed as Anita Weatherby, she opened the door a crack to make sure no one was around before she hurried to the car. As quickly as possible, but not so fast it would draw attention, she drove around the building and back onto the road.

Traffic always lined the streets in Duluth, and the steep hills made her nervous, even after all the times she'd successfully maneuvered them. In truth, she was edgy today. Her stomach had been churning since she'd stolen Dave's car. With Twyla living at the Plantation, there was no option to swap vehicles. Norma Rose never loaned her car out to anyone, and Josie certainly didn't have the courage to take her father's. She had considered taking the one that had been Ginger's, but it hadn't been driven since Ginger had run away and she couldn't take the chance it wasn't in good running condition.

Dave's car was. He had Scooter check it regularly.

Turning the final corner that would take her to the dock area, she drew in a deep breath in an attempt to quell her quivering insides. This was no different to any other Tuesday.

The US Steel parking lot was always the busiest. Hoping Dave's Chevy would blend in with all the other cars, she chose that lot to park in. Maneuvering the Chevy between a Buick and Model T, she made note of the other vehicles to help her find the car again later.

Lifting her supply bag off the seat, she tucked the other one that had held her disguise under the passenger seat, since there was no backseat like in her car. She left Dave's pile of stuff—a shirt and several brochures—on the seat. Removing the key from the ignition, she climbed out. After she dropped the key in the deep pocket of her long paisley print skirt, she shut the door and headed across the gravel parking lot. It was a long walk to the area the girls knew she'd be at, and she used the time to scan the area. The warehouse she'd tried peeking into was over near the stockyards, a farther distance yet, but that wasn't to say any one of the buildings wasn't being used to hide the young girls.

The docks were noisy. Ships blew their horns as they floated beneath the huge bridge connecting Duluth to Superior, Wisconsin, gulls screeched and men yelled instructions. She heard the buzz of saw blades from the lumberyard, cattle mooing, trucks making deliveries, train whistles, the hissing of steam and other sounds mingling in with all the rest. The area was a hub of activity.

No matter how many visits she made, the smells of the docks still assaulted her. They were as prevalent as the noises and, to her, more overwhelming. Josie kept her head down, never making eye contact with anyone, yet stayed alert as she made her way to the long pier that visitors to the area liked to frequent. Crewmen from the ships used this long dock, too, but mainly to connect with the many prostitutes that walked the boards day and night. The port was busy with boats arriving and departing around the clock.

The thud of heels that echoed behind hers as she stepped onto the wood confirmed there was someone behind her. Pulling her face into a tight frown, Josie stepped to the side and waved an arm.

"Go on, you're much younger than me," she said in her best old-woman voice. "I don't need you stepping on my heels."

"Excuse me, ma'am," the sailor said, hurrying past.

Josie made her way halfway down the pier, where there was a bench near the shore-side railing. There, she settled herself on the seat and dug a loaf of bread out of her bag. In less than a minute, a young woman sat down next to her—a familiar one who'd visited her before. Unfortunately it was one who never said a word.

The woman took off one shoe as if her foot hurt. The signal for one box.

Josie took a small box out of her bag and set it on the bench between them. The woman put her shoe back on, slid the box into her pocket and walked away.

This happened several times within the next hour or so. When an older woman, not of great age but older than most of the prostitutes, sat down next to her, the hair on Josie's arms quivered. The woman wasn't familiar. She wasn't dressed like a tourist, either.

Going with her gut instinct, Josie tossed the final few pieces of her loaf of bread over the rail to the gulls and then picked up her bag as she stood. The woman stood, too, and before Josie could take a step the other woman latched on to her arm.

"That's right," the woman hissed. "We are going to take a walk. Real slow so we don't draw attention."

Scooter was second-guessing his plan, and cursing himself for not gathering more information before he and Dac had headed to Duluth. He'd never visited the shipyards, and had no idea the area was this large. Having unloaded his motorcycle near the stockyards, he'd zipped in and out of half a dozen parking areas, spotting several blue Chevys, none of which turned out to be Dave's.

Warehouses went on for what seemed like miles, and he hadn't even reached US Steel's property. That alone was massive. He had no idea which dock Josie used to pass out her condoms. She hadn't been at the three he'd already jogged up and down. Changing his tactics, he'd decided to find the car first, figuring that at least would tell him she was in close proximity.

He headed for the last lot. Working his way back might be his best bet. Maneuvering around and through the automobiles, his heart skipped a beat at the sight of a blue Chevy. He'd recently started selling tires at his shop, and recognizing the ones he'd put on Dave's car a short time ago was all the proof he needed, yet he rode closer, hoping, yet doubting, Josie would be in the car.

She wasn't, but a man was in the Buick next to it. It was a Master Six model touring car, dark green with gold trim, including the wheel spokes. The car was a beauty, and Scooter wouldn't have minded looking under her hood, if he had been in his normal state of mind. Right now, cars, although his one true love, weren't foremost in his thoughts. As unusual as that was.

The man climbed out of the Buick to stand beside the passenger side of Dave's car as Scooter stopped near the front bumper. Though tall and broad, the man was older, perhaps middle-aged, judging by the graying of his short sideburns. The rest of his hair was as dark brown as the three-piece gold-pinstriped suit he had on.

Scooter cut the engine on his motorcycle. "You see the driver of this Chevy?"

Leaning back against the side of his Buick, the man asked, "Who wants to know?"

If he'd gotten a look at the person who'd thrown the fireball or whoever had locked him and Josie in the boathouse, he'd know if this man was a foe or just a nosy stranger. As it was, all he had were his gut instincts. This man had been sitting next to Dave's Chevy for a reason. "I'm just looking for a friend, mister," Scooter said.

The man glanced at the Chevy. "There's a brochure sitting on the seat of this car. It's from Nightingale's Resort in White Bear Lake."

"So?" Scooter asked. "What's it to you?"

"Just curious," the man said. "I knew a woman named Nightingale." After a sigh, he added, "Once."

The pit of Scooter's stomach turned cold. "Once?"

"Years ago," the man said. "Her name was Rose." Letting out a longer more wistful sigh, the man unfolded his arms and walked forward. Stretching out a hand, he said, "Clyde Odell."

"Eric Wilson," Scooter replied, before he had time to wonder if he should have used an alias.

"I met her out east, years and years ago."

Scooter shook his head. "That wouldn't be the same Rose Nightingale," he said. "Not as the one related to Nightingale's Resort."

"Why do you say that?" Clyde asked. "The one I knew was from Minnesota. White Bear Lake, Minnesota."

"Could be more than one," Scooter said. "But the Rose Nightingale I knew never went out east."

Clyde was rubbing his chin. "She died several years ago, during the flu epidemic."

"The one I knew did," Scooter said, growing curious as to who this man might be. "And I know for a fact she never left Minnesota."

"How do you know that? She'd have been a lot older than you."

"Old enough to be my mother."

Clyde's eyes nearly popped right out of his head.

"Rose and my mother were best friends their entire lives," Scooter said, a bit startled by the look on Clyde's face…a face that looked almost familiar. "They grew up next door to each other. What one did, the other did. Trust me, my mother would have talked about Rose going out east if that had ever happened."

"Tiny, about this tall—" Clyde held his hand next to his shoulder "—with blond hair and brown eyes?"

"Blue eyes," Scooter said. "Sky blue, just like her daughters'." Brought back to the mission at hand, he asked again, "You see the driver of this vehicle?"

Clyde was now frowning, but he nodded. "I sure did. I was wondering why someone would park in this lot when they clearly didn't have any business with US Steel."

"How would you know that?"

"It's my job to know that. I'm the new manager. Just arrived last week. I've worked for J.P. for years. Mainly out east, but when things weren't going as smoothly as they should here, J.P. sent me to see why."

"J. P. Morgan," Scooter said, to clarify. One of the richest men in the nation. The man had become an icon, who'd risen to power by eliminating the competition. Single-handedly, he'd created a vastly powerful empire when he'd bought Carnegie Steel Company for four hundred and eighty million dollars, and rumor had it he'd have paid more if need be.

"Yes, Mr. Morgan himself."

Scooter couldn't find it in himself to believe J. P. Morgan or Clyde Odell were connected with the likes of Francine Wilks, so he gave the man a nod. "I wish you well, Mr. Odell. I need to find the driver of this Chevy. Would you happen to know which direction they went?"

Clyde spread his feet a bit wider, like a boxer taking his stance as his face turned hard. "I hope you, Mr. Wilson, and that old lady that climbed out of this car aren't involved in my dock workers being rolled."

Scooter shifted the weight of the bike, giving his foot easy access to the kick starter. He wasn't afraid of a fight, but getting in a brawl with a dock worker was not on his agenda today. "Rolled?"

"Yes, rolled." Clyde popped the knuckles of one hand. "There's a ring of thieves liquoring up my dock hands, plying them with whores and robbing them blind when they pass out. I'm here to put a stop to it."

"Any idea who's behind it?" Scooter asked, already convinced of the culprit himself.

"Oh, I know who's behind it," Clyde said, "and I know who's behind her."

Scooter took a chance. "Francine Wilks."

Clyde merely lifted a brow.

"I'm not working with her," Scooter said. "And neither is the woman who climbed out of this car. She's not an old lady, she's a young girl, one Francine is after."

A surprised look crossed Clyde's face, but he hid it quickly, as if not quite believing what Scooter had said.

Unable to think of anything to corroborate his story, Scooter said, "I've got to find her before Francine does."

"Why?"

"Why?" Scooter almost shouted. Shaking his head, he said, "Josie, the girl I'm after, is trying to stop Francine from kidnapping Indian girls and putting them to work."

Clyde let out an expletive. "Francine's as nasty and evil as the rest of her family." He waved a hand toward the lakeshore. "The girl you're looking for is on the second pier, the big one, sitting on a bench."

Scooter kicked the starter pedal. As he squeezed the throttle, something else crossed his mind, a flash of a memory that was insignificant, yet perhaps because the man had been helpful, Scooter felt inclined to say, "The only woman from White Bear Lake my mother ever talked about going east was Karen Reynolds. She does have blond hair and brown eyes."

The gravel lot was rutted and he bounced left and right, but never let off the gas. He took a shortcut through the weeds separating the next lot from the shoreline, and almost laid the motorbike on the ground when he had to swerve around a concrete barrier that seemed to come out of nowhere. Righting the bike, and keeping his head lowered to keep his eyes from being stung by the wind his speed was creating, he kept his focus on the second pier, which was still some distance ahead.

When he saw a tall woman leading a short, older one off the walkway, he squeezed the throttle harder, frustrated that he was already giving the bike all the gas he could.

Chapter Eleven

Focused on trying to come up with a way to escape, at first Josie didn't recognize a new sound joining all the others. When she did, she glanced up and her heart soared. Scooter was speeding toward her on his motorcycle. She had to blink twice to make sure she wasn't seeing things.

She wasn't—in a few more yards he'd run them over.

Gravel flew in all directions as the motorcycle spun around directly in front of her.

"Get on!" Scooter shouted.

The hold on her arm was gone. Maybe she'd pulled away, or maybe the other woman had fled. Josie didn't take time to question either possibility, just leaped on the bike behind Scooter. Wrapping her arms around his waist, not caring that she had to drop her bag in order to do so, she planted her feet on top of his and plastered her body as close to his as humanly possible.

The motorcycle was already racing forward again. Josie peeked over her shoulder. Several men, and the woman who had grabbed her, were running after them. "Faster!" she shouted to Scooter. "Faster!"

"Just hold on," he shouted in return. "Don't let go for anything."

Burying her face against his back, she answered, "I won't!" She wouldn't, either. During the short time the woman had a hold of her arm she'd wished Scooter had known where she'd gone. He was the only one she could imagine rescuing her.

Afraid of what she might see, yet unable not to look, Josie quickly glanced over her shoulder. A car was now speeding across the parking area. "They're coming," she shouted. "In a car. They're coming after us."

"I know," Scooter answered. "Don't let go."

Josie would have clung on to him tighter, but was already holding on as firmly as possible. When he leaned slightly, she leaned with him and the motorcycle shot onto the street. Horns honked and her teeth rattled as the tires thudded over the rough road.

"I told you to stay at home!" Scooter shouted above the ruckus.

"I couldn't!" Her shout was slightly muffled by the back of his shirt billowing against her face. "Those girls have to be rescued!"

"Not by you they don't! Neither can you save the next group Francine kidnaps. She can kidnap them a great deal faster than you can rescue them."

Josie wanted to tell him that wasn't true, but it was. It was a fact she hadn't wanted to face. "So I'm just supposed to forget about them?"

"No," he shouted, "but I told you I'd help."

Scooter leaned the other way, and she did, too. With more horns honking, they took another corner. The motorcycle shot up the hill faster than any car she'd ever ridden in. At the top, they turned again, onto another side street.

The ride continued like that. Up hills, down hills, around left and right turns, passing other vehicles at what seemed to be lightning speed. Josie grew completely disoriented. She had no idea if they were heading north, east, south or west. Not that it mattered. They'd soon be changing direction again. Lifting her head might have helped, but she was afraid to look. The sound of all the traffic was enough, and she didn't want to know if they were still being followed. She hoped not. There was no telling where Francine Wilks had been going to take her, but she had an idea it wouldn't have been good.

Despite all that, Josie was hoping Scooter wasn't going anywhere near the police station. If he got arrested for speeding, there would be no one to call. Other than her family. And that would be disastrous. For everyone.

The motorcycle was going downhill again, quite rapidly. If they hit a bump, she could very well fly right over Scooter's head. Of course that wasn't likely. He hadn't hit any yet, and she held his waist so tightly her arms were growing numb.

His speed slowed considerably. The bouncing and jarring suggested it was because of the roadway, and the stench made her lift her head. Peering over Scooter's shoulder, her heart practically buckled in her chest. They were back at the docks—in the stockyard.

"What are we doing here?" she asked.

"Just hold on," he said, leaning to the left again.

She leaned, too, and waited until they'd made the corner before she stressed, "I am!"

Mud covered the roads. She could imagine why it

was there, and it wasn't because it had rained anytime lately. Her body had started to read Scooter's slightest shift, and it was almost as if they were one, the way she instinctively leaned, to the right this time, as he took a corner around a large wooden pen.

A truck parked in the roadway made her shout, "Watch out!"

"Just hold on," Scooter said again.

Their speed slowed, but he was still heading directly for the back of the truck. "Scooter, there's a truck!"

"I know!"

The motorcycle shot forward again with a jolt and flew right up the long tailgate of the truck...where a huge bull stood.

The motorcycle came to an abrupt stop. "Jump off," Scooter said.

Josie got off on the side near the truck's sidewall, and spun around to dash down the ramp, but it was already slamming shut. Turning back around and purposefully not looking toward the bull, which took up a large portion of the truck bed, she saw Scooter covering the bike with a tarp.

"What—"

"Get down," he said, "and hold on."

"To what?"

He nodded toward the bull. The truck jolted forward and Josie stumbled.

Her natural reaction to save herself from falling made her reach for something to hold on to. The hard and lifeless form of the bull shocked her more than warm flesh would have.

"Get down," Scooter repeated, pulling her down to the floorboards.

"It's not real," she said.

"It's very real," Scooter said. "They're out for blood."

"I meant the bull," she said.

"Humphrey," Scooter said. "He's real, all right. Just no longer living."

Josie shifted, unfolding her legs from where she'd landed on her knees, and settled back on the floorboards. "Since when?"

"Last year." Also on his knees, Scooter had spun around and was lifting a corner of the tarp as if checking on his motorcycle. After pulling out a few strands of straw, he tucked the corner of the tarp under the back tire. Turning toward her, he said, "I don't want the muffler setting anything on fire."

Josie couldn't get her mind off the bull. It was all there. A massive black body, four legs, a head, complete with eyes, a tail and other things she tried to not look at. "He looks just like he did when he was alive."

"Dac had him stuffed."

"Why?"

"Because no one's ever searched his truck for booze with Humphrey in the back." Scooter stretched underneath the bull and pushed aside a thin layer of straw. "Which reminds me, if I tell you, climb through here." He'd lifted a board up a couple of inches.

"I'll fall beneath the truck," she said, briefly glancing toward the dark space.

He lowered the board and the bouncing of the truck shifted the straw back into place. "No, you won't. It's a hidden cavity. It's where Dac hides the shine he runs for your father."

"Dac runs shine for my father?"

"Everyone runs shine for your father."

It would be impossible for her to know all of the boot-leggers driving for her father, but she hadn't suspected Dac. "Do you?"

"No," Scooter said, crawling beneath the bull's belly. "I stay busy enough keeping their cars fuelled up. That's my bread and butter."

He was between the bull's back legs, peering out the little square hole that Humphrey's tail stuck out of. Josie had more questions about that—the stuffed bull—and about Scooter not running shine, but instead asked, "What are you doing?"

"Checking to see if we are being followed. I think we lost them, but nothing's guaranteed."

Above the rumbling and rattling of the truck, other vehicles could be heard. She'd like to check if they were being followed, but was not about to crawl between the bull's legs. "And?"

"And what?"

"Are we being followed?"

"There's too much traffic to tell." He backed out from beneath Humphrey and then crawled over to sit down beside her.

His nearness made her heart do funny things, which was rather ironic after she'd been glued to his back for miles on end. Maybe it was the way he was looking at her right now. The glimmer in his eyes made her throat grow thick and sticky. Her lips grew dry, too, and she had to lick them.

Scooter's eyes darted away from her. "You got clothes on under that dress?" he asked, now looking at her skirt.

"Yes."

"Then take it off. The scarf, too."

She'd forgotten about her disguise. Pulling off the

scarf, she said, "You wouldn't have recognized me if I hadn't told you about my Anita clothes."

The brief gaze he sent her way was full of scorn. "I'd have recognized you. Dirty face and all."

"It's not dirt."

He shrugged. "You got a way to wash it off?"

"Yes. I'm always prepared."

He sneered and shook his head.

Josie sneered in return. She was glad he'd rescued her, but could do without his attitude. Digging in her pocket for the small container of face cream and the handkerchief she always carried, she discovered something else. "Oh, no."

He snapped his head in both directions. "What?"

Josie pulled out the key. "Uncle Dave's car. I have to go back and get it."

"We are not going back for Dave's car."

"I have to. I can't go home without it." A shiver rippled from her head to her toes. "If my father finds out..." She couldn't finish the thought aloud. It was bad enough just thinking about the repercussions of her father discovering she'd been at the docks. Grabbing Scooter's arm, she pleaded, "We have to go back."

"No, Josie."

"Don't you see?" she asked. "He'll know you saved me. He'll—"

"I know exactly what he'll do," Scooter said, "and it's too late to worry about that now."

Josie wasn't willing to accept that. "No, it's not. If we get Dave's car back, he'll never know. Dac won't tell, you won't tell. I won't tell." He was shaking his head and Josie dug deeper, searching for a way to make him understand. "Think about your mother," she said. "About

Maize and Jonas. What will happen to them if…" Her throat swelled completely shut.

Scooter grabbed the key out of her hand as he let out a curse. "Get out of that disguise."

"So we'll go back?" she asked hopefully.

"No," he said. "But I'll figure out a way to get Dave's car. You get out of that dress and clean your face."

"We could—"

"Josie."

The warning in his voice had her lips snapping shut, which was just as well, as she really didn't have any idea of what they could do. She was hoping something would pop into her head. He was rubbing his chin, as if thinking hard. She sincerely hoped whatever plan he was contemplating was a good one.

Scooter turned away as Josie shifted onto her knees and started unbuttoning the top of her dress. He didn't need to watch that. His mind was already bouncing in too many directions at the same time. She may not have noticed the men who took chase after them, but he had. They'd been packing heat. Going back to face those guns would be suicide. They could be following them right now. He'd taken the motorcycle down every narrow alleyway they'd come across, knowing the bigger car on their tail wouldn't fit, but still had no way of knowing if the men had caught up with them again or not.

Thank goodness Dac had been waiting exactly as planned, truck running and on hand to close the back as soon as they'd raced up the ramp. Dac also said he knew a back way south into Cloquet and was pretty convinced he'd be able to ditch anyone who might try to follow them.

On the way north, Scooter hadn't meant to share everything he had, but in the end he was confident he'd chosen the right person to help him find Josie. And that fact also made everything worse. Dac had as much to lose by angering Roger Nightingale as he did.

He wasn't overly concerned about losing his business. He could start over, but Dac's family couldn't, and Maize would lose her new job, too. His only option was to clean up this entire mess, every little detail, before telling Roger all about it. That he was going to do. Tell Roger. It would be the only way to assure Josie's Duluth days were over.

She was wiping off the white cream she'd spread all over her face with an embroidered hanky, and this time he couldn't pull his eyes away. The pencil lines she'd drawn on her face had made her look old. If he hadn't known what to look for, he wouldn't have been convinced that was her back at the dock. Of course, the way she'd been dragged along by the other woman had been a dead giveaway.

The rumble of the tires echoed beneath them and Scooter cleared his mind to listen more closely. There was no sound of any other traffic now. He pushed off the floor and carefully eased his head over the side rails. They'd just crossed a little bridge and trees lined the curving road on both sides—thick trees with underbrush so overgrown no one could hide in them.

He sat back down, knowing Dac would pull over soon.

Josie folded her dress and added it to the neat stack she'd created out of her sweater and scarf before she looked up at him. Scooter cursed himself deep down inside, where he hoped it would do some good. He should not have the feelings he had for her. No good could ever come of them. He'd known that for years, and up until recently, he'd been able to keep everything well concealed. Roger Nightingale's anger over these recent events could be deadly.

Although he doubted the man would go that far—even though the involvement of one of his daughters tipped the scale considerably—Scooter had long ago accepted the fact the man would never consider a grease monkey good enough to marry one of his daughters.

Roger maintained a friendly relationship with everyone in White Bear Lake, but he'd also let it be known his daughters were one step down from royalty, and would be treated as such. Scooter had to agree with that. That's how he knew he'd forever be out of Josie's league.

When this was all over, he didn't doubt the entire family would disassociate themselves from anything that had to do with Scooter and his family. Maize's hope of her job at the resort growing into something more would be shattered. His mother would no longer be accepted in the Bald Eagle Ladies Aid Society—that, he could live with, but she wouldn't take it lightly. Even Jonas, as young as he was, would be affected. He'd be shunned. Anyone who went against the Nightingales was looked down upon. Everyone in the entire area knew their livelihoods were due to Roger's success and the way he expanded his good fortune to include all of their businesses. Their families.

As much as all of that was true, none of it mattered to him, leastwise not as much as never seeing Josie again. That would be hard to live with.

She was looking up at him with those big blue eyes. Not saying a word, just looking at him as if she expected him to have all the answers to her woes. He wished he did. And he hadn't needed to see those pencil marks she'd now wiped away. They'd proven to him just how adorable she'd be even years from now, when her youth started to wane and age crept up on her. She'd still be beautiful. Still be full of a spark that would keep her and those around her young and kicking up their heels.

Her eyes would never lose their shine. They'd still sparkle and twinkle... Something snapped in his mind then. Her eyes. Blue, not brown. Clyde Odell. The man wanted to take down Francine, and with the backing of J. P. Morgan, he could.

Scooter was in the midst of trying to piece things together when the truck rolled to a complete stop.

Dac's door opened, and a moment later, the way his head popped up over the high side rails said he stood on the cab's running board. "How y'all doing back there?"

"Fine." Scooter stood and helped Josie to her feet before he squeezed between the side rail and his tarp-covered motorcycle so he could ask Dac a question. "You know anywhere around here that has a phone?" He considered whispering, but Dac wouldn't have been able to hear over the truck's engine, and keeping Josie from hearing would have been a moot point. She was pressed up against his back, once again making his skin tingle.

"Yeah, there's a place where I drop loads up the road," Dac said. "It's a roadhouse, but I'd never advise eating at it. That's just their cover."

"But they have a phone?" Scooter asked.

"Yes, they have a phone," Dac replied. "Who you gonna call?"

"US Steel," Scooter half mumbled. He wasn't sure

Clyde would help, but couldn't come up with anything else. Slapping the wooden rail, he said, "Drive, Dac."

The man nodded and disappeared. Scooter spun around and took Josie's arm. "Sit down," he said. "Dac's known for missing first gear."

Just as he'd warned her, the truck coughed and jerked before the wheels turned fast enough to catch up with the engine. The ride grew smoother, but not much considering the rough road.

"Why are you going to call US Steel?" Josie asked.

"Because that's where Dave's car is."

The relief that crossed her face jolted his heart rougher than Dac's driving shook the truck. So did the way she wrapped her arms around his neck.

"Thank you, Scooter," she said, her face buried into the front of his shoulder. "Thank you."

He wasn't nearly as excited, or relieved, as she seemed to be, yet he didn't have the heart to tell her his plan didn't have a whole lot of meat behind it. Grasping her shoulders, he separated them slightly. Her arms were still around his neck, and the idea of kissing her overcame his thoughts for several long seconds. Memories of doing just that had his heart rate climbing and he battled against his good sense like a first class soldier.

His willpower stood strong. He should thank his lucky stars for that, but he couldn't seem to feel relieved. Kissing her was just too memorable. Too fascinating and wonderful and—Scooter cut short his thoughts.

"You are going to do exactly as I say from here on, Josie," he said sternly. The twisting going on inside him was putting more pressure on his will. So were her woeful eyes. "No arguing," he went on. "No questions and no buts. You just listen and obey."

She frowned slightly. "But—"

"I said no buts." He set her farther away from him, breaking her hold on his neck. Once she was firmly planted on the truck bed, he let her go.

"Who are you going to call at US Steel?"

He scrounged up a deep scowl, even when part of him wanted to smile. Asking for no questions from Josie was like asking a bird not to fly. "Just you never mind," he said. "The less you know the better off we'll all be."

"We are in this together, you know."

"How could I forget?"

She pinched her lips together, then opened them, then closed them again. The *humph* she let out told him she had several questions and rebuttals, but was obeying by holding them in. The desire to laugh, or at least chuckle, rose up inside him. He had to turn away and tell himself several times that none of what was happening was a laughing matter.

Thankfully it wasn't much later when Dac turned off the road. Scooter's mind, even while it was conjuring up what he'd say to Clyde Odell, was questioning exactly why he couldn't kiss Josie again. Just once.

The truck stopped and Dac's head appeared over the top rail. "Phone booth is on the side of the building."

Scooter scanned the very run-down building and completely empty lot. "You sure it works? The place looks deserted."

"It is during the day," Dac said. "And yes, the phone works."

Although he had a general idea of their location, Scooter asked, "Where are we?"

"About five miles north of Cloquet. This road goes past the back of town. Near B. S. John's old place."

Scooter stepped up onto the seat of his motorcycle. Before using his arms to hoist himself over the side rail, he turned to Josie. "You stay put."

"Dac just said the place is deserted."

"I don't care. Someone could still be following us. Now stay put."

Her shoulders drooped, but she nodded.

Scooter climbed onto the cab of the truck and then down the driver's side. "Keep the engine running," he told Dac. "Just in case."

He dug change out of his pocket as he ran. The phone inside the wooden booth looked brand-new. Dropping in a dime, he waited for an operator, and let out a tiny whoop inside when a voice came on the other end. Scooter asked for the US Steel shipyard, and when a voice answered on the other end, he asked for Clyde Odell.

His toe was tapping a steady beat by the time the voice came over the line. "Odell here."

"Mr. Odell, this is Eric Wilson, we met earlier today in—"

"Are you and your girlfriend safe?"

Scooter stopped shy of saying Josie wasn't his girlfriend. "Yes."

"I saw you snatch her out of Francine's hold. I also tried to cut them off to stop them following you, but I wasn't fast enough."

"Thanks," Scooter said. He hadn't witnessed Clyde's actions but didn't doubt the man's word, and that gave him hope. "I gotta get that blue Chevy out of your parking lot."

"Yes, you do," Clyde answered. "Francine's boys are watching it, ready to swoop down like a hawk on a field mouse."

"That's what I was afraid of."

"Where are you?"

Scooter chose a vague answer. "South of town."

"Somewhere hidden, where we can meet up? I'll bring you the Chevy."

He wanted to trust his gut instincts, but the man seemed almost too willing to help. "I know a place we can meet up, a secluded one, but we've got the keys."

Clyde laughed. "I'm from New York. I know how to start a car without a key."

Scooter was giving himself a moment to decide if he should trust the man or not, when Clyde spoke again.

"No one will follow me. I'll make sure of that." After a short pause, Clyde asked, "If you're wondering if you can trust me, all I have is my word that you can. If you're wondering why I'm willing to help, well, besides the fact my boss wants Francine Wilks and her henchmen shut down, you have something I want."

Of their own accord Scooter's eyes shot toward Dac's truck. Josie must have been standing on the seat of his motorcycle to be tall enough to be leaning on the top boards of the rails, talking with Dac. Curse her. She could fall and break a leg.

"It's not your girlfriend, if that's what you're thinking," Clyde said.

"Then what is it?" Scooter asked.

"Information."

"What kind of information?"

"You'll find out as soon as I get there," Clyde said. "Now where do I bring the Chevy?"

He made the decision to trust the man, even if he doubted he had any information the man could want, but Scooter pointed out, "I can't give you a ride back."

"I'll arrange that. Just tell me where to meet you."

Not sure how familiar the man was with the area, Scooter explained, "There's a town about twenty miles south of Duluth named Cloquet, and about half a mile on the south side of town is a road that goes east. Take that one mile and turn south again..." After giving complete directions on how to get to B. S. John's scrap yard, Scooter said, "We'll be behind the barn."

"Good enough. I'll be there in an hour."

As he hung up the phone, it dawned on Scooter that Clyde most likely wanted all the information he could gather about Francine. The man probably figured Josie had that information. He was right, but getting it out of her would be another story.

Scooter left the phone booth and met Dac halfway across the yard.

"What's the plan now?" Dac asked.

"We go to B. S. John's." Scooter had done business with the man for years. Whenever anyone wanted to get rid of an old car, they called John. The man had a farm field full of everything from tractors to trucks, from horse-drawn wagons to motorbikes. He sold parts off every one of them for twice what they were worth, unless you knew him well. Even then he tried to convince you that his parts were worth more than anyone else's. That was how he became known as B. S. John instead of just John.

"What for?" Dac asked.

"Someone I know is delivering Dave's Chevy to us there."

Dac looked a bit surprised, but didn't comment. Instead he said, "You and Josie might as well ride up front. No one is going to see us between here and there."

If anyone had been following them, they'd have caught up with them by now, so Scooter agreed. He was about to tell Dac to open the tailgate for Josie to get out when a yelp had him spinning around.

Chapter Twelve

Josie was sure she was going to fall and most likely break something in the process—an arm or leg, or both. Scooter had climbed over the side so easily she'd assumed she could, too. Then again, his shirt was tucked in. Hers hadn't been and was now stuck on a nail. There was nothing for her feet to catch and steady herself on, and she'd tried holding on with one hand in order to unhook the cloth with the other. That hadn't worked.

When firm hands grasped her dangling legs, she knew without looking down who held her. "My shirt's stuck."

"I can tell," he said dryly.

She glanced down to give Scooter a glare when she realized her shirt was not only stuck, but her entire stomach was also uncovered.

"Oh." She squirmed, trying to pull herself up enough to get her skin covered.

Scooter hoisted her upward so quickly the shirt came loose along with her hands. He turned around. Rather than letting her down, he lowered her so she was sitting on one of his shoulders.

Heat blazed across her cheeks. "Put me down."

"I will," he said. "Inside the truck." As he marched around the vehicle, he asked, "Can't you stay out of trouble for thirty seconds?"

"I wasn't in trouble," she argued.

"You weren't?" he asked. "You were hanging by your shirt for the fun of it?"

Blowing out a heavy breath of frustration, she glanced down at the small rip in her blouse. At least it was repairable. Unlike the humiliation of him having to come to her rescue again. It was thrilling, the way he showed up right in the nick of time, but it was also becoming a bit embarrassing.

Scooter opened the door with one hand and more or less plopped her on the truck's seat with the other. He'd bent down, too, so she sort of slid off his shoulder. She hadn't realized just how broad his shoulders were until now, and she took another look a moment later, when both he and Dac climbed in the truck, sandwiching her between the two of them.

Settling in, she squirmed enough to shift her legs out of the way of the shifter that stuck out of the floorboards and then looked over at Scooter. "Are we going to get Dave's Chevy now?"

He barely glanced her way. "The 'no questions' order still stands."

Josie wanted to scream. She'd prided herself on her ability to keep her mouth shut her entire life, but when it came to him, her lips didn't want to stay still. Her lips were thinking of other things, too. A couple times today she'd thought Scooter was going to kiss her. At least she'd hoped so. Her entire being had wanted that to happen again. It hadn't. Not once. She told herself not to obsess over it. There were enough other things happening to occupy her mind for the next two years or longer.

Scooter was deeply involved in all that was happening, too. Maybe that's why her focus kept getting pulled back to him. She'd never been so aware of him before, or of anyone, for that matter. It was as if she'd become overly sensitive where he was concerned. Perhaps it was because she'd become indebted to him. Or maybe because she understood her actions had put his livelihood on the line.

Guilt was a terrible feeling. One she'd never felt before. Not like this.

Neither Dac nor Scooter was talking, and the silence grew oppressive. She tried watching the road, and then closing her eyes. Talking to herself didn't help, either, even when she told herself that once they got Dave's car they could return home safe and sound and no one would be any the wiser about what had actually happened today.

That really didn't help. It was purely a lie. There would be repercussions after today's events. Serious ones. She was no closer to rescuing those girls, either, which was what today's trip was supposed to achieve.

"Where do you want me to park?" Dac asked.

The yard they'd pulled into was lined with cars. Old ones with doors, hoods and windshields missing.

"Behind the barn," Scooter said. "John has a shop back there he's usually in."

As Dac followed the road—two well-worn tracks separated by a short crop of grass—Josie turned to Scooter. "What are we doing here?"

He grinned and shook his head.

She huffed out a breath and crossed her arms. Fine. She could be silent when she wanted to be. He'd soon learn that. She might never speak to him again. Ever.

Josie held her stance. When Scooter introduced her to an older man with a ruddy nose and cheeks, wearing the greasiest overalls she'd ever seen, she merely nodded.

The three men, Scooter, Dac and the one she'd been told was named John, started talking about cars and car parts, tires, oil and gas. To her utter surprise, Scooter handed the man some money and then they started walking toward a field so full of cars it looked as if they'd been planted there in rows, like farmers did planted corn in the spring. She followed, listening as Scooter explained he needed a radiator. The man named John claimed he had one, but it had to be removed.

Biting her tongue as she trailed through the tall grass, Josie grew exasperated. Now was not the time to be scrounging around for automobile parts, no matter whether Scooter needed them or not. They had to get Dave's car and get home. She didn't know the exact time, but it had to be midafternoon, which would leave only a few hours before she needed to be seated at the family table or her father would send men out looking for her.

Gloria would have a thing or two to say, too. Last night she'd told Josie her trip to Duluth today was canceled, which was part of the reason she'd taken Dave's car that morning. She'd crept away before Gloria could find her.

Nothing, not a single part of her day, had gone as planned.

The men had stopped at a car. Scooter lifted the hood and Dac held it open as John pulled tools out of his many pockets. The men continued chatting as if all was right as rain, while Scooter used the tools to remove the radiator. Then they all started walking back toward the barn with Scooter carrying the part.

When she didn't immediately follow, he stopped to

wait for her. Thankful he was paying that much attention to her, she hurried to his side. "What are you doing?" she whispered.

Shrugging, he said, "Killing time."

"We don't have time to kill," she insisted. "We have to get Dave's car and head home."

"Did you forget the rules?"

"Rules, schmules," she spluttered.

He grinned. "We'll have Dave's car in no time."

"How?"

He merely lifted an eyebrow.

She glared and waved a hand. "This isn't getting Dave's car."

"Trust me," he said. "And don't forget the rules." Shaking his head, he whispered, "You were doing such a good job."

"A good job of what?"

He grinned. "Being quiet."

Heavens but she wanted to kick him in the shin.

He laughed loud enough that the other men turned around. "Field mouse," Scooter said.

The men nodded and carried on walking.

Josie searched the ground. "I didn't see a mouse."

He grinned. It dawned on her he'd used the mouse as the reason he'd laughed.

"You aren't funny," she said. "Furthermore, I'm not afraid of mice."

"I never said you were," he answered. "Or that I was funny."

She marched along beside him, back straight, and told herself she would refuse to answer.

"But you are."

Unable to stop herself, she asked, "I'm what?"

"Funny."

She rolled her eyes skyward.

"Looking like that, with your nose up in the air and acting all hoity-toity."

"Funny-looking? Hoity-toity?" She huffed out a breath. "Think what you want, I've never acted hoity-toity in my life, but I do seem to be the only one who remembers what happened today. What could happen if we don't get Dave's car and get home soon."

Scooter hadn't forgotten anything, nor did he really think she was funny-looking. Adorable was more like it. All puffed out like a mother hen defending her brood against something twice her size. He was just trying to keep himself from thinking about things like that. How adorable she was. How her eyes snapped open and her lips pursed when she was mad. Just the act of her striding along beside him had his blood pounding in his veins.

Josie had never gotten under his skin like this. Then again, he'd always refrained from spending too much time in her company, knowing full well there would come a day when he wouldn't be able to keep his hands to himself.

Today would not be that day.

The rumble of a big engine vibrated in his eardrums. Scooter turned toward the road. The truck was huge, and so were the white letters painted on the side of the barrel-rack body of the trailer it was pulling. The name US Steel covered the iron-plated sides. If he'd been a praying type of man, he'd have thanked the Lord for stepping in at this precise moment. As a matter of fact, he went ahead and sent up that little prayer of gratitude. Then he turned to Josie.

"Remember the rules."

She opened her mouth.

"If you don't, I'll paddle your backside."

Her startled expression was laughable. He just wasn't in a laughing mood. His radiator tale had worked to kill time while waiting for Clyde, but the man's arrival would spike John's curiosity, and a viable excuse as to why Dave Sutton's Chevy was being delivered to him wouldn't form in his head.

"Don't think I won't," he warned Josie. "Not for a minute."

Her eyes were on the truck, which was now slowing down to pull into John's yard. "Uncle Dave's car is in that truck, isn't it?"

"Yes, but John doesn't need to know why."

She sighed. "I know that, Scooter. Good heavens, I'm not a dumb Dora."

He didn't bother responding to that. She wasn't a dimwit, but right now, he wasn't going to agree with her. "Just stay quiet, Josie, no matter what is said."

The wheels were spinning inside her little head. The way she gnawed on her bottom lip told him so.

"Promise me, Josie," he said sternly. "No matter what I say, you stay quiet."

She glanced from the truck to him. "Fine. I promise."

"Good. I'd appreciate it if you'd stay by Dac's truck."

She made no promise a second time, and he didn't push her for it.

Scooter carried the radiator to Dac's truck and then walked over to show the driver where to park the big rig. John moseyed closer, his eyes gleaming. The truck was a sight to see. Brand-new, with a stylish square cab so high off the ground a side step was mounted below the door. The apple-red paint probably still smelled factory fresh.

"Dave Sutton's Chevy was left in Duluth," Scooter told John "A man I know at US Steel offered to meet me here. They had a truck already going this way." He wasn't sure how much he had to tell the man to make it sound believable.

"Peddling some whiskey up in these woods, was he?" John asked.

Scooter didn't agree or disagree, and didn't want to further his lie, either. "Good thing there's a southbound train," he said, leaving it up to John to make his own assumptions. As Clyde Odell climbed out of the truck's passenger door, he added, "I'll be back in a minute."

John followed, and so did Dac, to whom Scooter tossed the key he'd taken out of his pocket. Surprisingly Josie stayed back. He'd expected her to follow on his heels. Dac and John stopped to talk to the driver while Scooter walked around the front of the big rig, admiring it.

"Don't worry," Clyde said, meeting him near the headlight mounted on the passenger side of the front bumper. "No one saw us and Howard won't say a thing. Not to anyone."

Scooter nodded. "I don't have a lot of cash on me, but I'll send—"

"There's no delivery charge," Clyde said. "Not in money."

"What do you want to know?"

With a slight gesture of his head in Josie's direction, Clyde said, "First, I need to know what's behind your girlfriend and Francine Wilks."

The man had helped him twice today, finding Josie and delivering Dave's car. If he could also help stop Francine, Scooter would promise him free gas for the rest of his life. Trying to keep the story short was the hard part. He chose to start with Maize and how Galen Reynolds had taken her to Duluth, then he shared how Josie had got involved and how she'd been providing condoms to the girls on the docks for the past couple of years, including what she'd seen the day she'd been arrested. Next, he quickly covered what had happened last weekend and what Ty had told him about Francine.

Clyde listened the entire time, nodding once in a while and glancing toward Josie several times. When Scooter ended his tale, Clyde said, "You left out the part about her being Roger Nightingale's daughter."

Scooter nodded and then shrugged. "Because you already know."

Clyde grinned.

Oddly enough, Scooter was reminded of Forrest.

"I do now," Clyde said. "My driver, Howard, is a local man. He saw the resort brochures, and knew that was Dave Sutton's Chevy." Clyde leaned a hand on the truck's bumper. "Nightingale has no idea what his daughter is involved in, has he?"

Scooter shook his head.

"And you're trying to keep it that way."

"I have to," Scooter admitted. "There are others who could be hurt. Once I've figured out a way to put a stop to Francine chasing Josie, I'll tell Roger everything, and accept the consequences."

"I don't doubt you will," Clyde said. "I sense you're a man of your word. I also trust you can keep a secret when it needs to be kept."

Scooter wasn't sure how to take that statement.

Clyde gestured toward the field full of cars, and

started walking that way. Scooter followed. They stopped far enough away that they could see everyone—Josie near Dac's truck, as well as Dac and John, all watching the driver now unloading Dave's car from the long trailer behind the big rig.

"Someday, Eric, you'll realize the right people come into our lives when the time is right, that things happen exactly when they are supposed to. Usually we're too impatient to wait for that time. We want everything now, not later."

Scooter's spine tingled as Clyde's gaze once again found Josie.

"I told you earlier today I once knew a woman from Minnesota," Clyde said. "I thought her name was Rose Nightingale, but I could have been wrong. You mentioned another woman who had gone to New York. I need to know everything you know about her."

Scooter wasn't surprised when his instincts wanted to know why this man wanted to know about Karen Reynolds. The only thing he could think of was her husband, Galen. If Clyde had been involved in any of Galen's dealings, Scooter didn't want anything to do with him.

"While you're thinking," Clyde said, "I'll mention that I talked to the chief of police in Duluth today. There'll be a raid on Francine's business."

"When?"

"The chief will call me back with the details."

Scooter shook his head. "Don't hold your breath. The police don't care about some young Indian girls." It was common knowledge that most didn't consider the folks on the reservations equals. That whatever happened to them was of little concern.

"They do if they believe J. P. Morgan has Indian blood running through his veins."

"He does?" Scooter asked. He'd never met the man, but everyone had heard of him.

"He might," Clyde said. "Who knows what any of us might find if we chase our roots back far enough. The bottom line is that US Steel puts a lot of money in the pockets of Duluth citizens. If the company was to go somewhere else, the town would feel the loss. If you were the chief of police, who would you be more interested in keeping happy? A multimillion-dollar company or a few criminal citizens who believe others are beneath them?"

Clyde didn't stop there. "I grew up in the slums of New York. The poorest of the poor. I know what it's like to have others believe you're inferior. If there is a warehouse full of young girls, which I believe there is, they need to be returned to their families. And I'll cherish being the man to railroad Francine back to New York. That neighborhood I grew up in was ruled by the Eastman gang. I had friends, family, die at their hands."

Scooter had been following the man's every word. "So that's why you want to know about Karen Reynolds. Because of her husband. Galen."

Clyde's eyes narrowed in a thoughtful way. "What about him?"

"He was associated with the Eastman gang," Scooter responded.

"Was or is?"

"Was. He's in prison in California right now, Roger Nightingale saw to that. Forrest Reynolds made sure he'll never get out."

"Who's Forrest?"

"Karen's son." Forrest had learned a few years ago

that Galen wasn't his father, and Scooter respected his friend's wish to not be called Galen's son.

"How old is he?"

"About my age," Scooter said, although Forrest was three years older. "Midtwenties."

"Tell me about Karen. When did she go to New York?" Clyde asked.

"My mother could tell you more," Scooter admitted. "All I know is the bits and pieces I've heard. Karen's father owned the Plantation nightclub and was the richest man in the area for a time. He built the amusement park next to the nightclub when the resorts in the area were thriving. He also sent both of his daughters to school out in New York. When Karen returned..." Scooter shrugged, he really didn't know all the details. "She might have already been married to Galen, or it happened shortly afterward. He was from New York. Karen's father died a couple of years later and Galen took over running the nightclub. It became a playground for gangsters. For years. If it was illegal, you could bet Galen was involved in it."

"Your mother and Karen were friends?" Clyde asked.

Scooter shook his head. "Yes and no. My mother claims they were friends before Karen went to New York, but afterward, after Karen married Galen, he wouldn't let her have any friends. Other than Rose Nightingale. Roger had something to do with that. I don't know what, but Forrest practically lived at the Nightingales' home when he wasn't down in the city at an all-boys school."

"Where are Karen and her son, Forrest, now?"

Scooter was starting to wonder if he'd said too much, but it was all common knowledge. "They live at the Plantation in White Bear Lake."

"I was so close," Clyde muttered.

"Excuse me?" Scooter said.

Clyde waved a hand. "Nothing. Well, it is something, but I have to deal with Francine first, then I'll tell you. You have a phone?"

"Yes, Scooter's Garage in White Bear Lake."

"I'll call you tomorrow with an update." Clyde held out a hand. "You have no idea how much I appreciate meeting you, Eric. But someday you will. I promise you."

"I appreciate meeting you, too, Clyde," Scooter said, accepting the man's firm handshake. "I'm indebted for all you've done for me today."

"Then we're even." Gesturing toward Josie, Clyde added, "Now you best get Roger Nightingale's daughter home. No one followed us and no one will follow you. I made sure of it. I will call you tomorrow."

Josie watched as Scooter and the man shook hands and then walked away from each other. The man went to the truck and Scooter strode toward her. She'd give anything to have been a field mouse hiding in the tall grass and listening to what they'd said to one another. It seemed to be a very serious conversation, yet they were both smiling by the end.

The stranger, who seemed oddly familiar, waved to her as he climbed into the passenger side of the big truck. She waved back at him and the driver, who started up the truck.

"Get in Dave's car," Scooter told her. "I'll drive you home."

"What was…who…" Recalling her promise and catching the way John looked at her, she flipped her question around and whispered, "What about your motorcycle?"

"Dac will drop it off for me," Scooter whispered in return, picking up the car radiator. Then, loud enough for John to hear, he told Dac, "Drop this off at the station for me, will you? Along with my stuff in the back. I'll catch a ride home from the resort with Maize."

"Sure thing," Dac said.

Scooter then shook John's hand. "Always a pleasure doing business with you. Catch you again soon."

The man replied and waved to all of them once they'd climbed in their vehicles, Dac in his truck, she and Scooter in Dave's Chevy.

"Who was that man?" she asked as soon as they started down the driveway.

"Why?"

"Because he looks familiar to me," she said, wondering if she'd seen him on the docks in Duluth at some point.

"You don't know him," Scooter said. "He just moved here from out east."

"How do you know that?"

He slowed to make the corner. "What happened to your promise?"

"What promise?"

"The one to remain quiet?"

"I completed it," she said. "It no longer applies."

His sideways glance contained a glimmer of a grin. She smiled, too. She couldn't help it. Her heart skipped several beats, too.

"He works for US Steel," Scooter said.

"Who?"

"The man who brought us Dave's car."

Bringing her mind around full circle, she asked, "How do you know him?"

"I met him while looking for you this morning."

"You just met him this morning?" That seemed unbelievable.

"Yep."

He was frowning now, and looking awfully thoughtful.

"What aren't you telling me?" she asked.

"Nothing you need to know," he said. "Not right now."

They'd arrived at the highway, and had to wait for a break in the traffic to pull out. Dac was right behind them. Skipping over Scooter's answer for a moment, she asked, "Is it safe to take this road home? What if someone is watching for us? For Dave's car or Dac's truck?"

"We'll be fine," he said, pulling onto the road.

"How can you be sure?"

"I just am," he said. "I just am."

A shiver tickled her spine at the way he repeated himself. For all her questions, she knew less now than she had before. These were things she needed to know. At least that's what her insides said. "Scooter?" she asked.

"What?"

"What don't I need to know right now?"

Chapter Thirteen

Scooter still hadn't answered her question and they were driving over the railroad tracks on the road to the resort. She'd asked more than once and finally had decided she could hold out as long as he could.

He turned and drove through the parking area of the Bald Eagle Lake depot.

"Where are you going now?" she asked.

"Taking the bootlegger's road into the back of the resort so no one sees us driving in with Dave's car."

"Oh."

"Forgot that little piece, did you?" he asked smugly.

"No, I haven't forgotten anything."

"Good," he said. "And don't."

"Don't what?"

"Don't forget what happened today. Don't steal Dave's car, or anyone else's, and head to Duluth by yourself. Don't even step off your father's property until I say you can."

Tired of being treated like a misbehaving child, she growled under her breath before saying, "For one thing, it's no longer my father's property. He signed it over to us girls a few weeks ago. Plus, I can go where I want, when I want, and you can't do anything about it."

He hit the brakes so hard she almost flew into the window. Would have if she hadn't caught herself.

"I can't keep chasing after you, Josie," he said. "I have a business to run. A family to feed."

"I know you do, and I never asked you to chase after me," she spluttered. Her insides stung, which fueled her anger. "You took that all upon yourself. Don't start blaming me now."

"I wouldn't have had to take it upon myself if you'd been at home where you belong," he said. "Why can't you be more like your sisters?"

That question stung worse than he could ever know. "More like my sisters?"

"Yes, none of them are out trying to save the world. They are at home where they belong, running the resort."

"For your information, none of them are home where they belong," she all but shouted. Tears were burning the backs of her eyes now. She never cried. Never. And she wouldn't start now because of him. "Ginger is in Chicago. Chicago, and married to Brock. Most certainly not home and not running the resort. Twyla is living in town, married to Forrest. Again, not home and not running the resort. In two weeks, Norma Rose will be married to Ty and on her honeymoon at Niagara Falls. A thousand miles from home. So who, Scooter, does that leave at home running the resort? Let me tell you who. Me. Me, the only sister home where she belongs." She stopped before she could say she was the one who didn't want to be there.

"Josie."

The softness of his tone did more damage than his

snarky tone had before. A tear broke loose. She swiped it off her cheek.

"I didn't mean right now, I meant before," he said. "When they were all home and you were the only one running around. The one I worried about making it back home before your father caught you."

She grasped the Chevy's door handle. He grabbed it before she could open the door. Closing her eyes to prevent any more tears from falling, she drew a deep breath. "I'll walk from here."

"No, you won't," he said. "You'll stay right where you are until I park this car in front of Dave's cabin."

The road was only a couple of miles long, and she could easily walk it, but knowing Scooter, he'd follow her. She let go of the door handle. "Fine." The faster she got away from him, the better. If that meant riding the last two miles, so be it. Then, after she climbed out of this car, she'd never set eyes on him again. Ever. At least not on purpose.

Her entire life she'd tried not to be like her sisters because she wasn't. She was her own person. Not Norma Rose and Twyla's little sister. Not Ginger's older sister. Not Roger Nightingale's daughter. Yet that was who she'd always been. Someone's something. Someone who had never quite fit in anywhere.

Her stomach bubbled as Scooter started driving again. Not even while passing out condoms on the docks had she been herself. She'd always had to wear a disguise. It was time for all of that to change.

"I'm sorry, Josie," Scooter said. "I didn't mean that like it sounded. Just please don't leave the resort. Not by yourself. If you need to go someplace, call me and I'll take you."

She could have pointed out he had a business to run, or that there was nowhere she needed to go. He knew all that anyway. But that wasn't why she chose not to talk. She was once again remembering what she'd learned long ago. Sometimes words were simply a waste. A complete waste.

"So now I get the silent treatment," he said.

She turned her gaze to look out the side window, and blinked away a few more tears threatening to fall. One other thing was settling in her mind. Scooter had always acknowledged her as herself and often pointed out things that made her unique. It was all a farce. All the time he'd wished she'd been more like her sisters.

As soon as he parked the car in front of Dave's cabin, she grabbed the bag off the floor and opened the door. When she'd reached the back of the car, he caught her by one arm.

"Josie, I'll explain everything when I can, but until then, please, don't leave the resort."

She kept her eyes off his face. There was too much sincerity in his tone.

"Please?"

"Fine," she said, irritated by how easily he could make her break her silence. No one else could.

"Thank you."

His lips touched her forehead and her knees almost buckled. She had to press her feet into the ground and hold her breath to keep from collapsing.

"I'll call you," he said. "I promise."

When he let go of her arm, she turned and made a rather awkward, but hurried, dash for the resort, cutting through the trees rather than taking the extra time to walk to the pathway.

She entered the side door and hurried up the back stair-

way. Thankfully her path remained free of distractions—
she had enough internal ones—all the way to her bedroom. There she tossed her bag on the floor and dropped
onto the bed.

Not prone to moping or questioning why nothing ever
turned out how she wanted it to, she didn't stay on the
bed long. It wouldn't do any good, and the clock said
she'd be expected at the dinner table soon. Grabbing a
dress out of the closet, she left her room for the bathroom down the hall.

A quick wash and change of clothes didn't help much.
It might if she was more like her sisters. Fashion, makeup,
shoes, jewelry and glossy magazines. All those things
made her sisters happy. She couldn't care less about any
of them. She couldn't care less as to what Scooter Wilson thought, either.

An eerie sensation had Josie lifting her head to meet
her own gaze in the mirror above the sink. Though her
reflection looked the same as always, she might as well
have been looking at a stranger. A brooding stranger. The
likeness in the mirror was challenging her, telling her to
think again. The mere fact she claimed she didn't care
what Scooter thought told her she did care. If she didn't,
she wouldn't be standing there trying to convince herself
that she didn't. Slightly taken aback, she shook her head.

The next truth that hit her made her close her eyes and
plant both hands on the rim of the sink. She'd seen this in
others and couldn't understand how they didn't know. Or
how they tried to pretend it wasn't so. Yet here she was,
doing the very same thing…and had been for a while.

Goodness, she was a hypocrite, just as Scooter had
claimed. The very thing she'd told her sisters to face,
she'd been denying.

Lifting her lids and once again staring at her reflection, she proclaimed aloud, "You're right. You, Josie Nightingale, are in love with Scooter Wilson." Then, just in case she still didn't believe herself, she repeated, "You're in love with Scooter. And have been for some time."

Nothing changed in her reflection, but something inside of her shifted. Yes, she was in love with him. Probably had been since his father had died and he'd quit school to take care of his family. She'd missed him immensely those first few weeks.

Her mind, which didn't need an image in a mirror to question things, pondered something else. What was she going to do about it? Tell him? Not tell him? Definitely not tell him. There wasn't anything she could do about it, and there was no need for him to know. Ever. Once Norma Rose returned from her honeymoon and took over at the resort again, she'd head to Duluth as planned.

Standing there, reflecting on many things and thinking about the future, Josie came to another conclusion. Scooter was the reason she joined the Ladies Aid Society. When she'd learned of Maize's absence that day, she'd offered to help. She'd wanted to help. Scooter had already had too many burdens.

A heavy sigh built deep in her chest, burning so intensely she had to let it out. Scooter had had a lot of burdens back then—he still did—and now she'd added several more to his shoulders.

"Josie?" Heavy rapping sounded on the door. "Josie, I know you're in there."

The sound of Gloria's voice increased the burning sensation in Josie's chest. Scooter was the reason she'd joined the crusade, but why had she continued? Freedom? That was a sham. Being under Gloria's thumb was far worse than being under her father's.

The lightbulb above the sink flickered. Maybe because of the pounding on the door, or perhaps because the light was signaling she knew that answer, too.

Giving her reflection one last solid stare, Josie nodded. She had experienced freedom—just in a difference sense. The society had given her an excuse, a reason for not caring about fashion or makeup or clothes or glossy magazines, which had transformed into a cause. Seeing all those girls who had nothing, and were doing what they could to survive, made her understand how lucky she and her sisters were.

Josie pulled the door open just as Gloria's rapping started up again.

"Where have you been?" the other woman asked. "Duluth? I told you not to go today."

Feeling more herself and more confident than she had felt in some time—since her arrest actually—Josie stepped into the hallway. "I know what you told me."

"And you know the rules," Gloria said, finger wagging. "They are to be followed at all times."

Scooter had already passed out all the rules she could handle today. "Or what?" Josie asked. "You'll tell my father?" Years of pent-up frustration rose inside her. It had to be released. There was no other option. "You'll tell him I've been driving up to Duluth every Tuesday? You'll tell him about the cases of condoms in my closet? You'll tell him you wanted us to drive up there during Twyla's wedding? You'll tell him all of that?" The words were rolling inside her, tumbling out of her mouth, and there were more to come. "Go ahead and tell him. Because I'm ready to do it myself."

"Josie," Gloria spat in her listen-to-me-or-else tone. "Hush up. You want this entire place to hear you?"

"I don't care who hears me," she answered. "You do."

"Don't threaten me, young lady."

"Why not?" Josie asked. "You've been threatening me for three years."

"I have not." Gloria's wrinkled neck was beetroot-red and her nostrils were flaring. "I've been the one covering for you."

"Covering for me? You were the one making me go." She hated arguing. That part of her would never change. "I'm sorry, Gloria, I—"

"As you should be," the other woman snapped. "I've never been so rudely spoken to in my life."

"I'm not sorry about that," Josie said, her anger renewing itself. "I'm sorry your husband slept with his patients. I'm sorry he became infected and ultimately died. I'm sorry you were hurt by it all, but none of that had anything to do with me. Not then, and not now." Shaking her head, she pointed out a fact they both needed to realize. "None of this is about either of us anymore."

Gloria's eyes turned beady and cold. "It's that Wilson boy, isn't it? He's gotten to you. I told Shirley to put a stop to him."

The fire returned to Josie's belly. None of this was Scooter's problem, either, or at least it wouldn't have been if he hadn't poked his nose in. "Put a stop to him? No one can stop Scooter when he puts his mind to something."

"Men," Gloria grumbled. "They're all alike."

"Are they?" Josie challenged. "What about my father? Where would you be if he hadn't given you a place to live when your house burned down?"

"I work for your father," Gloria retorted harshly.

"You write out prescriptions for people to obtain alcohol." The utter shock on Gloria's face made Josie flinch. The other woman was an excellent physician. People searched out her care for miles around. "I didn't mean to sound so cruel," she whispered. "I'm just so frustrated. What you've done, what we've done, has helped. Condoms are more widely used and protecting both women and men, but it's not enough. Our weekly visits haven't been enough for some time now." The danger she'd put herself and Scooter in today made her stomach gurgle. "There has to be another way, Gloria. Maybe it's time we tell Father. Maybe he could help us save those girls and—"

"No," Gloria said. "We can't."

Although she hated to admit it, Josie said, "We're in over our heads. I almost got caught today."

Gloria's curse could have rattled the windows. "That's exactly what I was afraid of. Where? What happened?"

"At the docks." Afraid to reveal too much, Josie said, "I got away and no one followed me." She also buried the guilt swarming inside her. Whether she'd promised Scooter or not, she couldn't sit around waiting for his phone call. There wasn't time for that. "We have to get those girls out of there, and stop Francine from kidnapping more. My father—"

"Your father's a bootlegger," Gloria said. "The men backing Francine are mobsters. Ones who make Galen Reynolds look like an angel. Why do you think I've worked so hard to make sure no one connected what we did at the docks to this place? Francine's men will target anyone involved."

Josie shivered. "What are we going to do?"

"Not panic," Gloria said. "And not tell your father. But

we are going to have to act fast. That fireball the other night says the connection has been made. The only reason for you not to be followed today was the fact they already know where you live."

Fear once again welled inside Josie. The resort was well guarded, but Scooter's station wasn't.

The door at the end of the hall opened and Norma Rose strolled in. "There you are. We're going to be late. Will you be joining us, Gloria?"

"No, thank you," Gloria answered. "I told your father I'd see to the guests here."

Lost, Josie glanced between the other two women. "Late for what?"

"We're going to Twyla's for dinner tonight," Norma Rose said. "Ty and Father are waiting downstairs."

"Go on," Gloria said, giving Josie a little shove as she lowered her voice and whispered, "We'll talk first thing in the morning. I'll have come up with a plan by then."

Norma Rose had stopped several feet away and was now frowning. "Are you all right, Josie?"

"I'm fine," Josie lied. Searching for an excuse, she added, "I'm just surprised. I thought Father and Ty moved Twyla's furniture to town today."

"They did," Norma Rose said. "It took several trips with Ty's truck and she wants to feed them dinner as a thank-you."

Gloria gave Josie another little push. "You two best get going. Don't want to keep the men waiting."

In a matter of minutes, Josie found herself in the backseat of her sister's Cadillac. Norma Rose sat beside her while Ty drove and their father rode in the front passenger seat.

"That's good," she responded to Norma Rose's glow-ing report of how well Maize had handled things as Ty drove out of the parking lot.

Norma Rose frowned. "Are you sure you're feeling all right?"

"I just have a headache," Josie answered. She did. A pounding one.

"I can see why," her father said.

Her insides hiccupped.

Chuckling, he added, "Spending all day with a dozen old biddies would give anyone a headache."

She nodded while discreetly exhaling a breath of relief.

"Where was your meeting today?" he asked.

"Anita Weatherby's," she answered by default. It was her regular explanation. "I must have gotten too much sun. I weeded her rose beds after the luncheon." Actually, that was probably why she had a headache. She hadn't eaten all day.

"Did you ask Gloria to give you something?" her father asked, concerned.

"Yes," she answered. Another lie, but Norma Rose had been frowning ever since finding her and Gloria in the hallway. "It's already easing up."

Father reached over the seat to pat her knee. "Driving Dave's car could have brought on a headache. It's a rough-riding thing."

Josie throat locked tight.

"Dave said yours wouldn't start so you took his to your society meeting. He had to call Scooter to get yours running."

That explained how Scooter knew she'd gone.

"I've called Big Al. He promised to have several for you to look at by the end of the week."

Telling fibs in order to cover up her activities had

never been easy, and she hadn't liked it, but the sincerity on her father's face filled her with such guilt her hands trembled. She couldn't continue this. Just couldn't. "Daddy—"

"No arguing, now, Josie-girl," he said, twisting back to look out of the windshield. "I know you don't care about such things, but I do. I can't have you driving around in a car that's not dependable. Any number of things could happen. Besides, those old ladies you're friends with depend on you to haul them around." Turning toward Ty, he continued, "Speaking of cars, Ty, isn't it about time you got rid of that old Model T? That thing about rattled the teeth right out of my head today."

Norma Rose was still frowning and Josie pretended to be interested in the discussion taking place between Ty and her father. There was a deep layer of trust between the two men. It was clear by the way they were so relaxed and comfortable talking with one another, even when arguing about Henry Ford's thoughts on producing only black automobiles. Father trusted Norma Rose, too—that was evident by the way he always drew her into the conversation. Josie's empty stomach revolted, sending bile up her throat.

Once he learned about all she'd done, her father would never trust her again. Not the same way he trusted Norma Rose. Not like he'd trusted her at one time, too.

She turned her gaze to the window, and her heart skipped a beat as Scooter's station came into view. Dread filled her, caused by the danger she knew he was in because of her. Nothing looked unusual. The Closed sign hung on the door, but he was always closed by this time of the evening. He was probably at his mother's house eating supper. It was a mile up the road that curved behind his gas station.

Another jolt of fear made her tremble. Scooter, his mother, Maize and little Jonas were all in danger because of her. Josie glanced around the car, taking in the other passengers. Everyone was in danger because of her, and by morning it might be too late. No matter what Gloria or Scooter had said, there wasn't time to wait. Something had to be done now.

Chapter Fourteen

Anticipating a call, Scooter was halfway down the stairs before the phone jangled a second time. He'd left a message for Ty to call him as soon as possible. It was his only hope of making sure Josie didn't leave the resort. Increasing his speed, he grabbed the earpiece just as the third ring started. "Scooter here."

"Eric? Eric Wilson, is that you?"

Hope floundered when he didn't recognize the voice. "Yes, it's Eric. Who's this?"

"It's Clyde Odell. The cops just raided Francine Wilks's warehouse. They took the girls and Francine and her men downtown, but, Eric, there are some things I think you need to see before the cops clean out the joint. How fast can you be here?"

"I can be there in a couple of hours," Scooter answered.

"Meet me in the US Steel parking lot," Clyde said, and then the line went dead.

Scooter's blood turned icy. Clyde wouldn't have called unless it was serious. It had to be about Josie. Francine must have had something on Josie.

Taking the stairs two at a time, Scooter raced upstairs

to grab his coat, hat with earflaps and goggles. It would be well past midnight before he arrived in Duluth and even in the summer months riding the motorbike at night was chilly. In the winter months he drove his delivery truck, but it was as slow as driving through molasses.

In mere minutes, he was on the road, heading north. There was next to no traffic and he expected there wouldn't be all the way at this time of the evening. That wasn't a good thing. The desolate road would give him plenty of time to think.

Josie was his main topic of thought, which wasn't unusual. Not lately anyway. She'd occupied a good portion of his thoughts, both when he was awake and sleeping, for days on end. Actually, she'd lived in his mind for years. There was this whole little corner there that had been reserved just for her.

He would have to do something about that.

Kissing her had made her presence in his mind bigger. If only she wasn't so unique. So one-of-a-kind. Josie stood out from her sisters like a peach in a barrel of apples. Or a Buick in a line of Model Ts. Quality. That was what Josie was. With fine lines, and smooth and precise curves, she had showroom shine like no other. Josie was no assembly-line car. She was built solid, inside and out. He probably couldn't count the number of eyes she'd caught or the heads she'd turned. She probably couldn't, either, but only because she never would have noticed.

Josie didn't want to catch anyone's attention. Didn't need to. Her mind was on other things. Things she believed in. He couldn't fault her on that. Her heart was in the right place. Her head usually was, too. This whole saving-the-world thing had just gotten bigger than she could handle.

He understood that trying to get a grip on something so big, so large, could easily take over a person's life. If they let it. A person had to take life one step at a time. Things didn't seem so big then, so consuming. Pretty soon, almost before they realized it, a milestone could be reached. Then another one. And another one.

Maybe if he had explained all that to Josie, she'd understand it more. He didn't want to stop her from doing the things that mattered to her. She just needed to be safe while doing them.

Then again, maybe if he wasn't so stupidly stubborn, she would have accepted his help. After all, no one wants to eat when someone is shoving food into their mouth.

That was just him. He saw a problem and wanted to fix it. If a car was misfiring he wanted to know why, and he wanted to know how to make it run smoothly again. He'd stayed up many a night tinkering on engines until they were running perfectly. People, though, weren't like cars.

He wasn't like Josie, either. He didn't want to save the world. He just wanted to save her. But she'd never asked him to, and wasn't impressed by his actions. She'd pointed out the problem he was trying to fix wasn't hers. It was his.

Riding down the highway, which was growing darker by the minute, with nothing to draw his attention away from all that was going on inside him, admitting she was right was easy. It was his problem. The moment Ty Bradshaw had pulled into the gas station with Norma Rose sitting next to him, Scooter's heart had started backfiring. Up until then he hadn't worried much about all the men who visited the resort. Roger hadn't let any of them near his daughters. Ty's arrival had changed that and now Josie was the only Nightingale girl not claimed.

Why did he have to love her? Of all the women in the world, why her? It was a problem he couldn't solve, and it was driving him crazy.

With so many questions rambling around in his head, he arrived in Duluth before he knew it. The streets were quiet, but the dock area was humming. Clyde was right where he'd said he'd be. Scooter cut the engine and removed his hat and goggles.

"We'll take my car," Clyde said. "Francine's place is several blocks from here. No sense walking when we can drive."

Scooter climbed in the Buick, and within minutes they arrived at their destination. The warehouse was old, and the first thing that assaulted Scooter's senses was the smell. He coughed and spat.

"I know," Clyde said. "The rooms those girls were in were despicable. Some of them were little more than babies, and not one of them had any clothes." After cursing, he said, "They'll be returned to their families as soon as possible." The man gestured toward a long hallway. "It gets better up here, just hold your breath."

Scooter was already holding his breath. The smell of urine was stronger than in Dac's dairy barn on a rainy day. His nose and eyes were burning. "What is it you want me to see?"

"You'll see," Clyde said. "I'll verify the information if you need me to."

A shiver rippled Scooter's spine. What on earth would he need verified? And with whom? The police? He hadn't done anything illegal. Ever. Other than speeding, namely on his motorcycle after whisking Josie away from the docks, the closest he came to breaking a law was fueling up tanks and revamping bootlegger's cars. There were no laws against either of those things. He'd purposefully kept his nose clean. He'd encountered enough problems in his life and had never warmed to the idea of some foolish mistake taking away all he'd worked for. The temptation had been there a time or two, especially when he saw the kind of cash Dac collected from running shine. Stuffing old Humphrey had cost Dac plenty of jack and though Scooter would have done it for free, Dac had paid him well to mount the bull in the back of his truck. Dac had called it an investment. Scooter had called it foolish.

Who was the fool now?

Clyde pushed open a door. Scooter paused on the threshold, taken aback by the luxury. Thick carpet covered the floor, silk curtains framed the windows, oil paintings hung on the walls and the room was full of fancy white-and-gold furniture. The place put him in mind of Nightingale's Resort, apart from the police officer sitting behind the desk. His blue uniform and shiny brass buttons were as out of place as Scooter always felt amid the glitz and glamour of Nightingale's.

"Eric, this is Chief Reinhold, Duluth's finest," Clyde said. "Chief, this is Eric Wilson."

"I recognize him from the photos," the chief said, rising to his feet. "It's nice to meet you, Mr. Wilson. Thank you for coming."

Not sure why the man would be thanking him, Scooter asked, "What photos?"

The man pointed to a scattering of newspaper articles and photographs laid out on the desk. One finger narrowed in on a specific picture.

Scooter picked it up. "This is from the Fourth of July," he said. "People were snapping pictures left and right. Babe Ruth was there." The photo had been taken when

Roger had introduced his family to the crowd. A hard ball formed in his stomach. He was standing next to Josie in the picture. Someone had drawn a circle around her face.

"So was Francine Wilks," Clyde said. "Have a seat, Eric. The chief will explain."

Picking up a newspaper clipping, the officer handed it across the desk as Scooter sat in one of the available chairs, Clyde in the other. The chief sat down, too.

"That is Ray Bodine," Chef Reinhold said, indicating a man's picture in the clipping. "A mobster from New York. Bodine's gang and the one Francine is connected to have been at war for years."

"It started over neighborhoods," Clyde added, "and has continued on to bigger things. Operations they've created across the nation."

The chief nodded. "It seems Francine followed Bodine from New York to Detroit, then Milwaukee, Chicago, St. Paul. The difference was she set up prostitution rings while Bodine was focused on bootlegging whiskey from Canada."

Scooter's guts turned sour. Not showing any reaction, he said, "Says here Bodine was arrested."

"Yep, recently, in Wisconsin," the chief said. "By an undercover agent the feds keep well hidden. Even Prohibition agents don't know the man. What we do know is Bodine was after the Minnesota Thirteen trade. The finest bootlegged whiskey in the world."

The chief's gaze, slowly moving from Clyde to him, had the air on Scooter's arms rising even before the man said, "And everyone in this room knows where that comes from."

Scooter once again refused to let any reaction show. If they thought they could weasel information out of him about Roger Nightingale, they were shopping in the wrong place. Both men were looking at him carefully, cautiously. Lifting his chin, he shook his head, "Sorry, but that's got nothing to do with me. And it's going to stay that way."

"Oh, yes, it does," the chief said. "More so than you realize." Lifting a sheet of paper off the desk, he held it out for Scooter to take. "One of Francine's main men wasn't captured tonight. We think we know where he went."

Chapter Fifteen

Josie's head was pounding and she truly couldn't take much more. Time was being wasted. They'd already eaten supper and had spent far too long bowling—something Twyla insisted everyone had to do.

"It's almost midnight," she muttered, when her sister insisted everyone had to go upstairs to see her and Forrest's apartment.

"Do you still have a headache?" her father asked, placing an arm around her shoulders.

"Yes," Josie answered. If she hadn't had one before, she did now. Francine Wilks and her men knew where both she and Scooter lived. She had to get back to the resort and talk to Gloria. There was no reason the society couldn't drive up to Duluth and rescue those girls just like they had with Maize. It had worked then and would work now. She'd mulled over it all evening. They could use Colene's big car, no one would recognize it. The only problem was she still didn't know exactly which warehouse to target, but with several of them looking, they should be able to find it. Ultimately, they had to put a stop to all this before someone was hurt.

"Why didn't you say something?" Twyla asked. "I have headache powder. I'll get you some."

"No," Josie said. "It's not that bad." Headache powder not only soured her stomach, it put her to sleep. That she didn't need. Pulling up a smile, she added, "Lead the way."

Twyla led them toward the front door of the Plantation. The building was huge and the front boasted white pillars that stretched three stories high. Once a nightclub catering to gangsters from all over, the place now hosted a bowling alley that was quickly becoming more and more popular.

Once on the second floor, Twyla graciously threw open a door. "We put most of my things across the hall." Smiling, Twyla glanced up at Forrest, who stood by her side. "Until I have time to rearrange things."

Josie followed the others, including Forrest's mother, into a clean but rather small apartment filled with furniture that had seen better days. Josie made note of that fact only because of all the girls, personal possessions—and the quality of them—meant the most to Twyla. But her mind was mostly focused on getting back to the resort. Maybe she could borrow Twyla's car. That way she could stop at Scooter's place, just to make sure he and his family were safe.

"This is the living room," Twyla said, "as you can tell. Over here is the kitchen and…"

Josie's gaze had gone to the far wall, where two windows overlooked the back of the building. A painting hung between the windows, and she moved closer as if interested in it. She wasn't, she wanted to see if Twyla's car was parked out the back or not.

"I'm so glad Twyla found that picture in the basement," Karen Reynolds said, stepping up beside her. "It was one of my father's favorites."

Josie shifted her gaze from the parking lot, where the moonlight revealed Twyla's car was parked, to the painting depicting an Indian brave, knife drawn as he rescued a maiden from a huge white bear. "Kis-se-me-pa and Ka-go-ka," she said offhandedly.

"You know the story?" Karen asked.

Anyone who had grown up in the area or lived here for any length of time eventually heard the legend of how White Bear Lake had got its name. Mark Twain had even referred to it in one of his many books. "There are several legends with different endings," Josie said. The brave killed the bear. The bear killed the brave. The bear killed both the brave and the maiden. All three died— the bear, the brave and the maiden. No matter which ending, the legend of the great white bear had given the lake its name.

"They were from different tribes," Twyla said, having joined them near the window. "He was a Chippewa brave. She was the daughter of a Sioux chief, and they were in love." Twyla sighed heavily. "Her father was about to attack the Chippewa and she went to warn him. His brave act of saving her from the bear proved his love and they lived happily ever after."

"Where'd you hear that version?" Josie asked. Her sister's tale was an idealistic mixture of all three popular tales.

"That is the correct version. The most romantic," Twyla said, moving forward to straighten the picture. "I don't know why it doesn't want to hang straight. It's always tilting to one side, as if that side is heavier than the other."

"Maybe the wire on the back needs to be tightened," Josie offered, uninterested, while attempting to come up with a logical excuse to borrow her sister's car.

"I never thought of that," Twyla said, lifting the picture off the wall.

"I didn't mean right now," Josie said.

As Twyla spun the picture around for Josie to examine the back, the cardboard backing became separated from the frame. Acting quickly, Josie grabbed the bottom before it fell all of the way out.

"Here," Forrest said to Twyla. "I'll take it."

As he lifted the picture, Josie tried sliding the cardboard back into place. "It's stuck."

"Set it on the table," Karen said, "before the glass falls out."

Josie held the bottom until Forrest lowered it onto the table in front of the couch. Then she stepped back to give him room to work. Leave it to Twyla to make the story of killing a bear romantic.

Scooter had rescued Josie several times lately, but it hadn't been a romantic gesture, and he hadn't done it because he was in love with her. He'd done it because he had a family to feed. A family he loved so much he'd left school and all his friends behind in order to make enough money to keep everyone fed and clothed. He'd hate her forever if something happened to any one of them. She wouldn't blame him, considering it all would be her fault.

"Something's under the cardboard," Forrest said.

Josie considered pointing out that it would be the picture, but didn't. Her mind was focused on too many other things. Including how she could get Twyla's keys.

"Forrest! That's it!"

Karen's shout had everyone looking at her, including Forrest, who'd just pulled the backing all the way out of the frame.

Snatching up an envelope that had been exposed, Karen opened the flap and started crying. "It's them, Forrest. It's them."

Confused, Josie glanced around.

Everyone looked baffled. Twyla asked, "What are they?"

With hands shaking, Karen pulled out several pictures. "These," she said, sifting through the pictures.

"Who are they of?" Twyla asked.

Karen glanced up at Forrest before she handed him one of the pictures.

He took it and examined it thoroughly before he showed it to Twyla. "Pictures of my real father."

Josie took another step backward, near to where Norma Rose stood. Twyla had told all the girls that Galen Reynolds wasn't Forrest's real father a while ago. That his mother had been pregnant when she'd returned to Minnesota from New York. Norma Rose's shrug said she didn't know any more than that.

"Oh, Forrest," Twyla said, wrapping an arm around his back and lying her head against his shoulder. "You look just like him. Except his hair is darker and you're more handsome."

Josie wanted to groan. Once again she felt an inkling of jealousy toward the love her sisters had found.

"What's his name?" Twyla asked Karen.

"I don't know," Karen said sadly.

Josie wouldn't have had to pass out condoms to prostitutes to know how sex worked, and she couldn't fathom how a woman could not know a man's name after they had completed that act. Those thoughts also brought her mind right back to Scooter. An immense sense of dread was filling her stomach. Francine's men could be at his station this very minute. She tried to quell her growing fears by telling herself Scooter was well aware of that. He'd said as much on Sunday when he'd told her to not leave the resort, and again today.

"We never told each other our real names," Karen said. "It was a game to us. We were young and…" She sighed longingly. "So young and so in love."

Once again Josie felt like an outsider, a bystander, but this time she didn't mind. While the rest of her family was engrossed in the tale of Forrest's long lost father, perhaps she could sneak away. She wouldn't get far without car keys, though.

Everyone had gathered closer around the table, and Josie took a step backward. She didn't have keys, but there was a phone in Forrest's office downstairs. She could call Gloria, or even Scooter.

Norma Rose then let out a little gasp. "I've seen this man." Spinning around, she held the picture up. "You have, too, Josie."

Josie glanced at the picture. Her throat locked up in time to cover her wheezing.

"When? Where?"

Anyone in the room could have asked that question. Josie didn't care who had spoken, but she wanted to know when Norma Rose had seen the man in the picture. It was of a younger version, but the picture held a striking resemblance to the man from US Steel who'd delivered Dave's Chevy.

"Years ago," Norma Rose said. "Right after Mother passed away. He stopped at the house asking for her."

"He did?"

The question came from several people.

"You remember, don't you, Josie? You and I were the only two home," Norma Rose said. "I'm sure it's him. He was very sincere and sad when I told him she'd died."

Karen was crying again. "I used your mother's name to write to him. With Rose's permission. I knew Galen would intercept any mail I received. All I knew for sure was that he worked for a carriage company, so I wrote to every one of them in New York. I gave a description of him, and asked that if he knew a girl from the school I had attended to please contact Rose Nightingale in White Bear Lake, Minnesota." Wiping at the tears rolling down her cheeks, Karen looked up at Forrest. "And he did."

Josie took several steps back. She didn't remember the man from years ago like Norma Rose, but the burning sensation in her stomach made her certain this was the man from US Steel she'd met today.

"We'll start searching for him," her father said. "Put my men on it right away."

"Where?" Karen asked. "Where would we start?"

"The pictures, Mother," Forrest said. "You thought they'd give you clues as to where to look."

"Yes, yes," she said excitedly. "I'm just so happy that my head is not working."

"Ty, come and take a look at these," her father said.

Josie's head was spinning faster than the conversation surrounding her. She stepped farther back. Her internal struggle was tearing her apart. This man could very well tell her father all about the way he'd helped her and Scooter escape today, but this was also her chance to make sure Scooter was safe, which was far more important. "Call Scooter," she said.

The room went silent as all eyes settled on her.

"He can tell you where that man is."

Chapter Sixteen

Scooter had never imagined his motorcycle could go so fast. His cheeks were on fire from the wind whipping at his skin, and Nightingale's Resort had never looked so good. He was happy, too, to see lights on. It had to be close to three o'clock in the morning.

Of course there were lights on. He'd called before leaving Duluth. Roger hadn't been home, but Bronco had been. Scooter had told him enough that Bronco promised to send men over to his mother's house and to scour the resort's grounds.

Scooter cut the bike's engine at the same time he pulled it up onto its stand. Bounding off, he ran to the front doors while checking to assure the folded sheet of paper was still in his coat pocket.

The stack of papers Chief Reinhold had given him had been ransom notes. For Josie. As far as he, Clyde and the chief could figure out, Francine had learned who Josie was the day she got arrested for speeding and had been planning her kidnapping ever since. The fireball and the incident in the boathouse had most likely been attempts to get her alone.

It appeared Francine had been following the gangster Ray Bodine and his activities closely. With his arrest, she'd decided she wanted a piece of the bootlegging conglomerate Roger oversaw. The woman had penned several ransom notes. Some asked for money—large amounts of money—while others asked for shares of Roger's business. One demanded the entire operation.

Each one had stated stipulations and rather graphic details of what would happen if her instructions weren't followed.

The door swung open before he reached it. Recognizing Ty, Scooter asked, "Where's Josie?"

"In her bed, safe and sound."

Relief washed over him, yet he asked, "You sure?"

"I'm sure," Ty said. "Roger's in his office, waiting for you."

Scooter crossed the threshold. Josie was going to hate him forever, but she'd be alive. Maybe someday she'd come to understand he'd done this for her own good. Forcing her to trust him, to let him help, hadn't worked out, so he wasn't counting on that anymore.

Josie was so different from the other women he knew. When his father died, his mother and sister had immediately relied on him to make it all better. To take care of them. Josie wasn't like that. She never would be. Unfortunately, that was just one of the many things he loved about her.

The door to Roger's office was open. Scooter didn't pull it shut, knowing Ty was right on his heels.

Roger stood and planted both hands on his desk. "What the hell is going on? And why do I have the feeling I should have known about it long before now?"

"Because you should have," Scooter said. "You're going to want to sit down for this."

Roger slapped his desk. "Start talking, boy. I get home tonight and Bronco tells me you called and said someone's after Josie. Who and why?"

"Did you tell her that?" Scooter asked.

"Not a chance. I sent her up to bed."

"And you checked?" Scooter asked, "Made sure she's there?"

"Of course I checked."

Scooter let out a sigh of relief, and then dug in his pocket. "This is just one, and because there were a dozen others, I was allowed to take it."

"What is it?" Roger asked, reaching across the desk.

Scooter had envisioned starting this conversation at several points in the long stream of events, and finally settled on beginning with the highlights. "It's a ransom note," he said, giving it to Roger. "Francine Wilks wrote it. Mind you, she's in the Duluth jail right now, but she penned several versions of that note, all similar. All asking for money in exchange for Josie."

"Josie?" Roger paled and lowered himself onto his chair, reading the note. When he looked up he asked, "This woman's in jail right now?"

"Yes," Scooter said. "She'd discovered Josie was your daughter when she was pulled over for speeding in Duluth. Francine Wilks is from—"

"I know who she is and where she's from," Roger said. "Ty's told me everything he's discovered, but said you'd tell me more."

"She's in jail. However, she was here for the Fourth of July party and took pictures of your family," Scooter said. "And yesterday, she tried to kidnap Josie."

"To hell you say," Roger bellowed. "Josie was at her Ladies Aid meeting all day yesterday. Ask Gloria."

Scooter wasn't here to hash all that out. There were more important matters to address. "J. P. Morgan, the owner of US Steel, wasn't impressed with the number of deckhands he was losing in Duluth and sent Clyde Odell to see what was happening. I met Clyde yesterday in Duluth. He'd discovered Francine's prostitutes would entice the deckhands to their rooms and then fill them full of hooch. Some they dumped into Lake Superior were too drunk to wake up before they drowned. Clyde told the Duluth chief of police that J. P. Morgan wanted that to stop, and Francine's place was raided."

"Just like that?" Roger asked, skeptical.

"Money talks," Scooter said. "You know that."

"Who's this Odell fellow and why haven't I ever heard of him?" Roger asked.

"Because he just moved here last week," Scooter said. "But you'll meet him. Turns out he's Forrest's real father."

Roger grabbed something off his desk. "He's the man in this picture?"

Scooter took the photo and examined it. "Yes, he's older now, but that's him." Later he would ask how Roger obtained that picture, but right now, there were other things Roger needed to know. "Clyde called and asked me to drive up to Duluth tonight because they'd found these ransom notes. The chief believes he has enough other evidence against Francine, but is holding the notes just in case."

"In case of what?" Roger asked.

"In case she's told her family in New York her plan." The matter couldn't be more serious to Scooter, and he let his gaze display that to Roger. "They could already be on their way here."

Ty stood. "I'll go and make some calls."

"No," Roger said. "You're retired. This is something that's best handled on the inside. I've been securing my interests for a long time, and have provisions in place for a takeover."

The hair on Scooter's arms stood on end as he glanced from one man to the other. The tension was heavy with what Ty and Roger weren't saying. Scooter had a distinct sense of being trapped in the middle. Not just between Ty and Roger, but in a much deeper sense, too. He was about to find himself more imbedded in Roger Nightingale's business than Dac and his stuffed bull.

Then again, he already was in deep. He'd been trapped for some time now. In Josie's trap.

If he'd seen Ginger in the back of Brock's truck while throwing the tarp over it, he'd have marched her straight in to her father. When he saw Twyla heading to town in Dave's Chevy, he'd instantly called Forrest. Because he wouldn't want to see any of the girls in danger, but he hadn't proclaimed himself as their guardian. Not like the way he had Josie. He hadn't gone to her father because he'd been worried about his own hide. Sure, one word from Roger could destroy all he'd built, but he'd been there before and could start over. Hard work never scared him. He hadn't said anything, because he was protecting her. Josie being hurt scared him stupid, because he loved her more than anything else on this earth.

An eerie feeling gnawed at him once more, so he asked, "You're sure Josie's in her bed?"

"Yes," Roger said. "I'm sure."

She was going to hate him more than she already did,

but so be it. He wasn't a quitter and wasn't about to start being one now. Her life meant far more than his heart.

Scooter placed both hands on Roger's desk. "There are two more things you need to know. One of Francine's men is still on the lam, and Josie hasn't been going to society meetings every Tuesday."

Josie had never imagined she'd find herself trapped up a tree, but here she was, high up and hidden among the long and tangling veins of the weeping willow tree next to Gloria's cabin and she couldn't figure out a thing to do about it. She was too far away from the resort to scream for help; no one would hear her, other than the man she'd climbed the tree to get away from. He was as well hidden as she was; the only difference was he didn't know she could see him.

She'd panicked when she'd seen the stranger and had shot up the tree. This time she should have listened when she'd been told to stay put. She might have done so if she'd been told why.

Back at Twyla's apartment, her father had gone downstairs to call Scooter about Forrest's real father, and when he'd come back upstairs, he'd ushered Ty into the hallway. Shortly afterward they were all rushed home, where Bronco met them.

The tension in the air had been so heavy her heart had dropped clear to her heels. The fact Norma Rose had accompanied her upstairs and gone to bed in her own room rather than going for a walk with Ty had told her something was happening. Something bad.

When her father had checked on her three times within a short time period, she'd feared that something involved Scooter. Unable to withstand that thought, she'd plumped her bed with pillows to look as if she was still sleeping and had crept down the back stairway, all the way to the basement.

Built to look like little more than a storage space for all the things the resort needed, the underground portion of the building had more hidden rooms than a fly had eyes. The Minnesota 13 her father distributed from producer to seller was delivered to the barn in crates and barrels earmarked as furniture or building supplies. A portion of it was transported via a tunnel and stored in the basement, to be served to customers upstairs. The majority, however, was repackaged in the back rooms and then sent down another tunnel that led to the one cabin that was never rented out. It appeared to be like all the others, just farther away and hidden by the woods surrounding it. Bronco lived there and guarded the trapdoor under the back steps like a soldier. That tunnel was the one Twyla had used when she'd snuck out to meet her friend Mitsy.

There was another tunnel that very few people knew about. It was the one Josie and Gloria had used on the Fourth of July to reach The Willow cabin without being seen. That was the tunnel she'd used tonight.

She'd quickly found the false wall that gave way to the door, and had hurried down the long earth corridor. The tunnel ended with a ladder that led to the inside of the outhouse behind Gloria's cabin. The tiny hut was concealed by the cascading limbs of the willow tree, and also had a large Do Not Use sign affixed to the door, which appeared to be locked tight with a huge padlock.

She'd just exited the outhouse and had been about to cross the yard to Gloria's cabin when she saw the man sneaking around the other side. He wasn't one of her father's men, she was certain of that, so she'd scrambled to the base of the tree and quickly climbed up, staying close to the trunk so the leaves wouldn't rustle.

To her utter dismay, he'd shot under the tree, too, where he now sat on the ground, Tommy gun in hand.

Critters could be heard scampering in the woods and an owl hooted every now and again, but the man didn't so much as twitch. Therefore, neither did she. She didn't move a muscle, other than her heart, which she thought could burst from fear with the way it continued to pound. The familiar sound she'd heard a short time ago had increased her fears. Hearing Scooter arrive on his motorcycle had brought tears to her eyes. She was glad to know he was okay, but more afraid than ever that he'd once again come to her rescue. The ability he had to do that was uncanny, but this time it was sure to get him killed.

This was definitely one of her more stupid plans, but in her bedroom, full of worry about Scooter, going to Gloria had been the only thing she could think of doing. Now all she could hope for was sunrise, which would be in a couple of hours.

When the thud of running feet sounded, she knew her luck had run out, and the sound of Scooter's voice shouting her name confirmed her worst fears had come to light.

Josie opened her mouth to shout his name, to warn him to stay back, but the man beneath her beat her to it.

"Scooter, is that you?" the man asked, stepping out from under the dangling willow branches.

"Yes, it's me, Owen," Scooter shouted in return. "Put that gun down."

Owen? Owen Lester? She'd been sitting in the tree above Dac's little brother? What was he doing here? She could no longer see him, but recognized his voice.

"Sorry," Owen said.

"Have you seen Josie?"

"Nope, I've been here, guarding this cabin just like Bronco said," Owen told him. "Dac wasn't home so Bronco hired me as an extra gun."

A thud and clatter sounded. Josie couldn't see, but it sounded as if someone had just kicked in Gloria's door.

"Where's Josie?"

That was Scooter shouting again.

"I don't know," Gloria said. "What's happened?"

"If you're hiding her, so help me, woman!"

Josie's stomach fell. That was her father's voice.

"I'm not, Roger, I swear," Gloria said. "I haven't seen her since she left for Twyla's with the rest of you."

"She's not hiding me," Josie shouted, trying to push out of the branches of the tree she'd planted herself into. The tree seemed to have swelled up around her and wouldn't release its hold.

"What on earth are you doing up there?"

Of course Scooter would find her. Even in the dark, she could tell it was him standing at the tree's base, look-ing up.

"How did you get up there?" he asked.

"Well, I certainly didn't fly," she answered, still try-ing to move. Her bottom was wedged solidly on three sides.

"Climb down," he said.

"I'm trying."

"You all right, Josie-girl?"

She closed her eyes against the frustration welling in-side her. "Yes, Daddy."

"I'll get her," Scooter said.

"Bring her to my office when you're done," her father said. "Right now Gloria and I are going to have a conversation."

Josie squirmed harder, determined to get free before Scooter reached her. He was scaling the tree faster than she had managed, and she'd been quick.

The crack of the branch beneath her was completely unexpected. The sense of falling had her screeching and grabbing for something solid, which turned out to be Scooter's shoulders as one of his arms caught her around the waist.

"I've got you," he said.

With her mind and body completely enthralled with him, Josie wasn't aware of much until her feet touched solid ground. Even then it was a moment before she realized they were out of the tree and Scooter was kissing her. It was so pleasurable, so fascinating, that it was close to consuming every part of her. Not wanting to, but knowing she had to, she twisted out of his arms. The need still pulsing on her lips had her pressing a hand against them. Her heart was pounding, too, and air didn't want to stay in her lungs. Feeling suffocated, she parted the willow branches and stepped out into the moonlight.

"You aren't even dressed," Scooter pointed out.

She had forgotten that. In her hurry to leave her room, she'd only taken the time to throw a housecoat over her short nightdress. "I have extra clothes at Gloria's," she explained. "I figured I would change there."

"Before you went where?" he asked.

Not about to admit she'd been set on going to look for him, she said, "Someone still has to rescue those girls."

"No, they don't."

"Yes, they do. Of all people you should realize how much danger they are in."

"Were in," he said. "The police raided Francine's warehouse tonight. The girls will all be returned to their families as soon as possible."

"How do you know that?"

"Because I was there earlier," he said. "Clyde, the man from US Steel that delivered Dave's car to us, called me and asked me to drive up."

"Why?"

Scooter took a hold of her elbow. "Come on, you need to go back to the resort."

Wrenching her arm away, Josie held her ground. "No, I don't. I don't *need* to go anywhere, what I need are answers. Why did he ask you to go to Duluth?"

"It doesn't matter why he called me," Scooter said, grabbing her arm again. "All that matters is that those girls are safe." He pulled her forward, forcing her to walk. "And you will be, too, once you get inside the resort."

"What?"

His growl said he didn't want to have to say more, yet he said, "One of Francine's men is still on the lam. He could be anywhere."

That explained why Bronco had hired extra men tonight. Another realization hit as Scooter pulled her past Gloria's cabin. "You told him. You told my father everything, didn't you?"

Scooter figured he'd lost several years off his life tonight. Roger had assured him Josie was in her room, but his gut had kept telling him she wasn't. With the other man's permission, he'd gone to her room, just to check. Finding her bed empty except for a line of pillows had stopped his heart. When it had kicked in again, so had his feet. The only place he could think to look had been Gloria's cabin.

Drawing a deep breath, he slid his hand down Josie's arm to hold her hand as they walked.

Before finding her bed empty, he'd told Roger everything. About Josie's activities in Duluth. About Gloria and the other ladies in the society, including his mother. About Dave's car and how he'd gone to Duluth to find her.

Then he'd asked one thing of Roger.

Permission to marry Josie.

Roger had said that was up to her.

Scooter stopped and turned to face her. "Yes, I told him everything," he said. "Your father knows all about your Duluth runs and why you did it."

She frowned. "Why I did it?"

"Yes, why." He reached up to cup her cheek with his other hand. "The young girls have been rescued, Josie, and Francine is in jail. Once her last gunman is captured, it will all be over. You'll never have to worry about any of it again. Not even Gloria. Your father is talking to her right now."

She lifted her chin while looking at him deeply, thoughtfully. "And he said you are to deliver me to him when you're done." Her brows knitted together as she asked, "Done with what?"

He may never before have experienced the bout of nervousness that raced across him at that moment. He knew there might be a better time, but he was too impatient to wait. "Asking you to marry me."

She took a step backward. Except it was more of a stumble, and he dropped the hand from her cheek to catch her shoulder so she wouldn't fall.

"Marry you?"

The astonishment in her voice wasn't exactly what he'd hoped for. Still, he nodded.

"Oh, that's ducky, Scooter," she said. "Just ducky."

Annoyed at her insolence, he dropped his hands to his sides. "What kind of answer is that?"

"A no," she snapped. "I won't marry you. Not now, not ever." She shoved at his shoulders with both hands. "Have fun telling my father that." Spinning around she started marching toward the resort.

"Josie—"

"You don't know why I did anything. Neither does my father." She spun around to face him. "Just stay away from me, Scooter. Just stay away from me." Turning toward the resort again, this time she ran.

He took a step to follow, but stopped. It wouldn't do any good. Not to him or her.

Chapter Seventeen

For someone who'd claimed sulking never did anyone any good, Josie now acknowledged that was yet one more thing she'd been wrong about. She'd made a list. Might as well add sulking to it. While sulking, one could come up with a hundred and one reasons why they were right and the rest of the world was wrong. People also tended to ignore sulkers, and that was not a bad thing.

Everyone thought she was sulking because of the extra cleaning chores her father had given her, along with forbidding her from attending society meetings for the next two weeks. That was her punishment for her Duluth runs. Everyone knew about them, right down to Moe, who looked upon her sadly and shook his head.

In truth, Josie had expected more penalties for being a part of Gloria's cause, and accepted everything with her head held high. Even while her father had her closet cleaned out.

She felt no regret or shame for what she'd done. If not for her trips to Duluth, those girls would still be locked in that warehouse. True, she owed their rescue to Scooter and Forrest's real father, Clyde, but it wouldn't have happened if not for her.

It had been two days since she'd seen him, since he'd asked her to marry him, but the pain inside her was still as raw and real as that night. Yet she continued to tell herself she'd given him the right answer. He'd never understand why she'd done it all. Why it was something she had to continue to do.

She may have considered not answering the knock that sounded on her bedroom door, but her father didn't leave that as an option. "Josie," he said, pushing the door open, "we need to talk."

Turning, she dropped her feet to the floor but didn't rise off the cushioned window seat. "About what?"

He walked in, closing the door behind him. "I just got a call. Francine Wilks's last man was just arrested in Duluth."

"That's good," she said.

"Yes, it is." He sat down on her bed. "It also means you can leave the resort if you wish."

Lifting her chin, she said, "I thought I couldn't attend meetings for two weeks."

"You can't attend society meetings for two weeks, but you can go and visit people if you want to."

She turned to glance out of the window. "Who would I visit?"

"Your sister, for one," he said. "I'm sure there are others."

"None that I can think of," she muttered.

"Gloria would like you to look at some property in town. She's thinking of opening a dispensary there."

"I don't know anything about being a doctor," Josie said.

"But you know plenty about pouting." His black-and-burgundy suit stood out boldly against her white bed-spread.

"I'm not pouting," she said. "I'm simply accepting my punishment."

"Rubbish." He shook his head. "I may not be very good when it comes to broken hearts, but I know a lie when I hear one."

Blinking at the sting in her eyes, she asked, "Who has a broken heart?"

"You."

She wanted to shake her head, but her neck had seized up.

"I was as surprised as Scooter when you said you wouldn't marry him," her father said. "I don't understand why you refused."

"Norma Rose will be leaving soon, and—"

"Don't give me that excuse. Norma Rose hired Maize, and that is working out very well from my understanding. I'll be here, so will Gloria."

Josie was too full of hurt to take much more. "Are you saying you don't need me?"

"No, I'll always need you, just as I'll always need your sisters, but I'll never stand in your way, just as I didn't stand in their way when it came to marrying the men they love."

Tears clouded her vision. "It doesn't matter if I love Scooter or not, I can't marry him."

"Care to tell me why?"

All the reasons she'd come up with in the past two days shot forward in her mind. "Because he lied to me—he told you everything when he promised he wouldn't. Because he thinks it's all over now, that I'll never have to go to Duluth again." Fury was building inside her and she leaped to her feet. "It's not over. Francine may be gone, but there are other girls there who still need help. Other girls who don't want to be there, but don't have a choice."

Reaching out, her father took her hand and pulled her over to sit on the bed beside him. "And that's what you want to do, help those girls?"

"Yes," she said. "I want to buy a house, a safe house, where the girls could live while they find other work."

"Then do it."

"I'm going to," she said, "as soon as Norma Rose gets back from her honeymoon."

"There's no reason to wait until then," he said. "You have plenty of money in the bank—I should know, I put it there." Grinning, he continued, "Use some to buy a house and hire someone to run it."

"You wouldn't mind?"

"Of course I wouldn't mind," he said. "I'll give you regular donations to keep it going. I have a few friends that will, too."

"You will?"

"I've known for a long time that running this resort isn't for you. You have to go with what's in your heart, Josie. If you really want something bad enough, you'll find a way to make it happen, no matter what." Lifting her chin, he added, "But that doesn't mean you have to give up on other things."

"There are no other things."

He stared at her long and hard, before letting go of her chin. "If you say so." After kissing her forehead he stood up. "I'm going to Twyla's for dinner. You're welcome to join me."

"No, thank you," she said. "I have some planning to do."

Nodding, he walked away, but stopped after pulling open the door. "I'd have helped you and Gloria with those girls if you'd have asked."

"You would have?"

"Yes." He took a step but then stopped again. "We never know what someone will say until we ask them."

A shiver rippled up her spine.

"I have one more question, and then I'll leave."

She nodded.

"Does Scooter know you want to keep helping those girls?" When she didn't reply, he said, "Perhaps you should tell him."

She opened her mouth, but closed it when her father started talking again.

"I've already told him how indebted I am to him. If not for him, I may have lost you. He saved a lot of lives. I'd think you'd want to thank him for that."

As the door clicked shut, Josie rubbed the base of her neck, where deep inside her throat burned. Pushing off the bed, she walked to the door, but then turned and walked to the window, where she spun around again. Feeling caged, she left the room and took the back staircase down to the kitchen. The resort wasn't busy, but there were a few guests and the waiting staff was busy carrying out platters and plates to them. Bypassing the activity, she ducked into the storeroom and then out of the back door.

The same door she and Gloria had used on the Fourth of July, leaving Scooter standing there alone, promising to wait for her. Tears once again formed in her eyes, and this time, she let them fall.

She crossed the lawn to the road that led past Uncle

Dave's cabin, noting that his Chevy was gone. The very car Scooter had found a way to get back home so she wasn't caught. Following the bootlegger's road, she walked past the boathouse they'd been locked in together. The tears were still falling, but they weren't painful now. Before she realized it, the Bald Eagle depot appeared. She walked around the building and then along the tracks. Town was four miles ahead. She had no desire to go that far, but couldn't seem to stop walking. It was as if her feet had a mind of their own, knew where they were going.

When she finally stopped, her heart was beating fast. Not because of the exercise, but because of her location. She stepped over the iron rails and into the row of trees that separated the train tracks from the highway. Scooter's station sat on the other side of the road.

The ditch was steep. One misstep could easily twist an ankle. A grin stopped as it was being formed. Scooter wouldn't come to her rescue. Not this time.

Choosing her steps carefully, she made her way down the ditch and up the other side. The gas station was built close to the road on the other side, and she could clearly see the Closed sign hanging on the door. It was late, already past closing time.

A clap of thunder had her glancing skyward. How had she not noticed those dark clouds? Storm clouds. Having been at his station many times, she knew the back door was rarely locked.

She ran across the road and made it inside Scooter's station before the rain hit.

Rain was the last thing he needed. No, Scooter thought as he wiped the water off his face with one hand, the bolts of lightning striking the ground all around his bike were the last thing he needed.

The storm rolled in fast. There hadn't been a drop of rain when he'd left the Plantation. He could have stayed. He'd been invited to the evening meal, but Clyde had told him all he needed to know. Francine Wilks's last man had been found hiding under one of the piers. Josie was safe. Spending the evening with her family was something he didn't need right now.

He'd known she'd be mad at him for telling her father the truth. His timing could have been better, when it came to asking her to marry him. Then again, it had been a pipe dream anyway. In the midst of all the craziness, he'd lost sight of his station in life. He'd come a long way since his father's death and would continue to work hard until his dying day. He had a lot more than many others, a home with food on the table and heat when needed, reliable transportation and enough money that he didn't worry when falling asleep every night. All that was enough for some. Enough for him in many ways. Just not for Josie.

His common sense had gotten away from him, that was what had happened when he'd asked her to marry him. Of course she'd said no. No woman would want to live in a dingy room above a gas station. And even if the three bedrooms at his mother's house hadn't already been taken, Josie was used to living in much finer conditions than he could offer.

A dip in the road, full of water from the rain cascading down, caught him off guard, and he wrenched on the handlebars, struggling to keep the bike upright. After a couple of moments when the back tire fishtailed, the cycle straightened out and he pulled the bill of his hat down a bit farther, wishing he had his goggles. At least he was almost home.

Less than half a mile later, he pulled into his gas station. While rounding the building to park the bike under the lean-to built for that purpose, the side door caught his eye. It wasn't shut. The latch didn't always catch, but he'd purposefully checked that it had closed before he'd left.

He parked the bike in its normal spot. The rain was so loud he doubted whoever was inside could hear him approaching. It could just be a traveler who'd taken refuge from the rain, but then there would have been a vehicle parked nearby.

Scooter entered via the open door and crossed through the mechanic's bay—where the main light switches were located near the door that led into the other room of the station.

He pulled his hat off and dropped it on the workbench that lined the wall as he strolled forward. Once at the door, he threw it open and pulled on the long cord for the lights at the same time.

Overhead, the bulbs flickered as the light grew stronger and right before him, standing next to the desk he used to write up orders and pay bills, Josie slapped her hands over her mouth, muffling a squeal as she stumbled backward.

Expecting anyone but her, Scooter stopped dead in his tracks. It wasn't until a smile—one that made his heart flip—overcame her startled expression that his mind clicked into gear. "What are you doing here?"

Her coy little shrug and the way she tugged at the hem of her white blouse didn't help the way his body was reacting to seeing her. The britches hugging her hips teased him, too. They always had. The fact she never dressed like her sisters may have been part of the reason he'd forgotten the big differences between the two of them. Dressed as she was, he could almost believe Josie wouldn't mind living above his station—at least until he could build her a proper house, which he would do. Or would have done if she'd have said yes to his proposal.

Fighting the urge to step forward, he growled, "A man can only take so much, Josie. Don't push me too far."

"Push you too far?" she asked. "I haven't pushed you. You were the one pushing, the one telling me what to do—"

"Because you were too foolish to see it for yourself," he interrupted. "You were too busy worrying about saving the world to realize how much danger you were in."

"I know," she said quietly. "You were my saving grace, always there to rescue me."

Her confession broke things loose inside him. As did the way she approached him, slowly and purposefully.

"You're my hero, Scooter," she said. "My hero."

He had no response to that. She was here. Standing right before him. The instant that all hit home, he caught her shoulders, pulled her forward and planted his lips against hers with all the intensity of the storm crackling and booming outside.

Scooter didn't stop with one kiss. Nor with several. He kissed her over and over again. Especially when her lips softened and parted for their tongues to meet in a way so primitive he could almost imagine what Eve's first kiss must have done to Adam. It was pure sweetness, heavenly and uniquely forbidden all at the same time.

It wasn't until he realized the desire filling him was

a new danger to her now that Scooter ended the kiss. He couldn't, however, convince his arms to let her loose.

"What are you doing here?" he asked.

Her arms were around his neck, her fingers playing with the ends of his hair. "You're wet," she said.

The blush on her cheeks told him she hadn't been sure what to say, had just let something roll off her tongue. The desire to let his tongue play with hers again had him biting the inside of his cheek and he was having a hard time controlling all the other desires springing forth.

Tugging her hands away by grasping her elbows, he dropped her arms to her sides and spun around. Shrugging out of his wet coat, he marched forward before he changed his mind.

When he picked up the telephone earpiece, she asked, "What are you doing?"

"I'm calling your father."

"He's not home," she said.

"I know," Scooter said, "I saw him at the Plantation before I left." He gave the crank a whirl to connect to the operator.

A boom rattled the window. "Hang that up," she insisted. "You could get struck by lightning. Everyone knows that."

That did happen often enough, yet he turned to face her. "I'll take my chances."

"Ducky," she said smartly, "water's a conductor of electricity. Lightning is electricity and attracted to the high poles. You're dripping on the floor with the phone in your hand."

Scooter spun to talk into the mouthpiece, waiting for the operator. "Come on," he muttered.

"The operator's not going to answer," Josie said. "They have an iota of common sense."

A snap and crackle in the phone line sent a shiver through his body. Scooter slapped the receiver into its holder and unbuttoned his shirt, ripping off the wet material covering his tingling skin. He dropped the shirt to the floor as he backed away from the phone.

Footsteps made him whirl around. "Where are you going?"

"Home," Josie said.

"Home?"

"Yes, home." She lifted her chin. "I thought maybe we could talk, but I see the only person you ever want to talk to is my father."

He caught her arm before she opened the door to the mechanic's bay. "How'd you get here?"

Nose forward, not glancing his way, she said, "I walked."

He twisted her around to face him. "Why?"

"Because I felt like going for a walk," she snapped.

Hope was once again blooming inside him. "To here, so we could talk?"

"Yes, but I've changed my mind."

Her tone was sharp, but tears glistened in her eyes. Regardless of all that had happened, or perhaps because of it, his heart was spilling out all the love he'd worked so hard to keep concealed. His fingers slipped down her arm and then folded around her hand. Pulling her closer, he wrapped his other arm around her. "Come here," he whispered.

As the warmth of her cheek came to rest on his bare chest, she sniffled softly.

The tingle beneath his skin had nothing to do with the phone or the lightning. Ignoring it, he gently rubbed her back. "I'm glad you're here. I've wanted to talk to you, too. I need to apologize."

She sighed heavily. "For telling my father everything?"

"No." Resting his chin on the top of her head, he added, "I had to do that, Josie, and I'm not sorry." Increasing the intensity of his hold, he added, "Francine's last henchman was arrested this morning. They found him under a pier near her warehouse."

"I'd heard that," she answered.

The storm outside was increasing its wrath. Wind and rain had the windows rattling and the lights overhead flickering. Scooter tried to concentrate on that—what was happening outside of the room, not what was happening inside him—but the feel of Josie snuggled against his bare skin was impossible to ignore, and impossible not to react to.

He kissed the top of her head, hoping the action would help satisfy a part of the desire rippling through his veins.

She leaned back slightly. A tiny frown made her brows knit together. "What did you want to apologize for, then?"

His throat locked tight. He wasn't sorry he'd asked her to marry him, was just full of remorse it couldn't happen. At least right now. If he worked hard, doubled his income, he'd be able to build a house and then he could ask her again. The possibility of that had him lowering his mouth to hers again. This time he didn't release her lips for a very long time. Not until his lungs were burning. Even while drawing in air, he didn't lessen the hold he had on her hips, how he kept them pressed against his. A gentle rhythm had overtaken them both. A dance given birth by the music of their bodies, drawing them together with teasing and lusty promises. More over-powered than he'd been by anything, ever, Scooter slid his hands around to her backside and pressed her more firmly against him as they kissed again.

Chapter Eighteen

The intense burning and throbbing coming from her very core was as exciting as it was foreign. Once before, the night of the fireworks, while dreaming about Scooter, Josie had experienced this unfamiliar need. She'd awoken that night, withering beneath the sheets and squeezing her thighs together. There'd been a great craving inside her, a need that had burned like no other.

It was there now, too.

Kissing Scooter, twirling her tongue with his, made that need spike, as did his hands, the way they squeezed her behind and pressed her more firmly against him. She could feel him, and thinking of that, realizing what she felt, made her heart quicken and her breath catch. Her breasts felt heavy, too, and her nipples stung in a rather spectacular way. The pressure of them against Scooter's bare chest was encouraging all of the wonderful chaos inside her to grow.

As if he knew what she was thinking, his hands roamed up her side and his thumbs rubbed the sides of her breasts before working in between their bodies to caress the very tips of her nipples. She could very well have been the one dripping wet and talking on the telephone. The jolt of pleasure that shot through her was as bold and hot as lightning.

Scooter's lips moved off her mouth, over her chin and down her neck, leaving a tingling trail of kiss that made her giggle.

"We need to stop, sweetheart," he whispered, while still kissing her neck. Up one side and down the other.

Being called such an endearment by him filled her with sunshine and optimism. "No, we don't," she insisted. "I like kissing you."

"And I like kissing you."

His whole hands, not just his thumbs, were working their magic on her breasts now, and the pleasure made her groan. She had to press her hips harder into his. The longing in her center was growing more needy. Scooter caught her backside again with both hands, holding her tight against him.

Breathing beyond the sensations filling her was practically impossible, yet she asked, "What did you want to apologize for, Scooter?" She had to know before she could go any further.

His lips were working their way back up to hers. "For making you so mad," he said between kisses. "Someday I hope you'll realize your safety will always come first and foremost to me."

She caught his lips with hers, kissing him even while smiling. His answer had certainly made her happy, and gave her hope. Lots of it. She was even able to understand that telling her father had been just one more way he'd rescued her.

The smell of him, made more powerful by the rain that still dampened his skin beneath her fingers, excited her. Closing her eyes she breathed in deeply, luxuriating in ways she'd never fathomed.

Scooter's lips left hers. When they didn't return, she opened her eyes. His lids were closed, but when he opened them and looked at her intently, he shook his head.

"What?" she asked, not giving in to a little quiver prickling up her arms.

"We have to stop."

Although she knew what he meant, she asked, "Stop what?"

"You know what." He took a step back and drew his hands away. Grasping her arms, he lifted them off his neck. He kissed each of the backs of her hands, before lowering them to her sides.

A loud crack of thunder made her flinch.

He squeezed her hands. "It's quite a storm out there," he said. "A real downpour."

Her insides screamed with a longing more commanding than she'd ever encountered. Scooter's breathing said the feeling was just as strong for him. That made her smile. He was right, though—with all this kissing, she was getting ahead of herself.

"A real downpour," she repeated. "Your britches are wet. They got my clothes wet."

He let go of her hands. "Sorry. I'll run upstairs and get you a towel."

As he started up the steps, she asked, "A towel? You have a bathroom up there?"

"A bathroom, kitchen and bedroom," he answered. "All I need."

She nodded, even though he was already halfway up the steps. For some reason, she'd assumed there was just a tiny room up there. A place for him to sleep in between filling up bootleggers' vehicles that ran shine for her father. Not an apartment.

Excitement zipped up her spine, and Josie raced up the steps.

The low ceiling was lit with two bulbs hanging on wires. One was in the kitchen area, complete with cookstove, cupboards, a small refrigerator and table and chairs. The other light hung over the bed, where Scooter was. He had his head upside down and was rubbing his hair with a towel. The muscles on his arms bulged beneath his skin.

"I was going to bring the towel down to you."

"I…uh…" Spotting the bathroom over his shoulder, she asked, "Could I use the bathroom?" A moment to put everything together was exactly what she needed.

He stepped aside and waved an arm. "Of course."

Walking past him sent a tantalizing shiver through her center. Her toes curled in her shoes. She might not be experienced, but she was knowledgeable. Very well informed when it came to certain things.

Josie closed the door behind her. Her eyes locked on her image in the mirror. The challenge was there, in her reflection. *Now what?*

She saw her grin form in the mirror. "Watch and see," she whispered, unfastening her britches while kicking off her shoes.

Stepping out of her pants, Josie draped them over the edge of the bathtub and then shrugged out of her blouse. She started to remove her camisole top, but stopped, recalling how often she'd seen the girls on the third floor wear little more than camisoles while opening their doors.

The set of underclothes she had on was white, not

nearly as eye-catching as the red or black ones the other girls had worn, but they were made of silk and trimmed with a delicate lace.

She straightened the straps over her shoulders and then stepped closer to the mirror and pinched her cheeks. Licking her lips to make them shine, she bit down on the bottom one.

Her image had a glow she'd never seen before, and her heart thudded madly. She jolted slightly when thunder made the building rumble. Then again, it could have been the excitement inside her. Josie turned around and grabbed the doorknob.

"Did you find…" Scooter's voice faded as his gaze went from her head to her toes and up again.

"A towel?" she asked, leaning one hand against the door frame. "My clothes are wet. They need to dry." Running a hand across the damp silk of her top, she said, "Even my underclothes are wet."

"Josie." He shook his head and drew a breath while taking a step backward.

Her breasts, as small as they were, felt teased in a unique way by his eyes and the soft fabric flowing loosely over them. Looking him up and down appraisingly, she said, "Your pants are wet. You should take them off."

"This isn't funny, Josie," he said. "Go get dressed."

"No."

"Yes."

"Why?"

"Because…" Scooter ran a hand through his hair. "Because I say so."

Stepping forward, she kept her eyes locked on his. "Telling me what to do didn't work before, Scooter, and it won't now."

Holding up both hands, as if that could stop her, he said, "You don't know what you're doing, Josie."

"Yes, I do," she said. "But I also have a confession to make."

He swallowed visibly. "A confession?"

She nodded. "I wasn't mad at you for telling my father everything. I'd have told him myself, if not for Gloria. I knew we were in over our heads, but the way you kept coming to my rescue made me believe we could find a way to save those girls without my father's help." To make sure she held his attention, she reached up and pushed one of the thin straps of the cami top off her shoulder. "You saved them and I need to thank you for that."

Scooter's gaze danced between her face and shoulder. "No, you don't," he said. "Clyde saved those girls, I didn't."

"But you found Clyde," she said, pointing out the truth. "Found a way for it all to happen." Taking a single step forward, she whispered, "I'm counting on you to help me with other things, too, Scooter."

He was shaking his head and had retreated all the way across the room. Grasping the table behind him with both hands, he said, "So you were mad at me for asking you to marry me."

She bit her lip to disguise the smile that fought to gain control of her lips. "Not hardly," she said. "I was mad because you said it was all over. It's not. I want to keep helping girls on the docks. Even though Francine's been arrested, there are still girls working there who don't know they have another choice. I know passing out condoms isn't enough. I want to buy a house in Duluth, where those girls can live while looking for other work, or going to school, or whatever they need."

"You do?"

Taking another step, she nodded. "Yes, I do, but that doesn't mean I can't have something else that I want."

"Which is?"

Stepping up, right in front of him, she rested both hands on his bare chest. "You."

"Me?"

She nodded. "There may be times we both come to regret it, considering we're both too stubborn to readily admit what's good for us, but...what do you say we get married?"

He caught her beneath the chin. "What?"

"You heard me," she said. "But don't say yes if you expect me to stop making trips to Duluth. I love you, Scooter, but helping those girls is something I have to do. Just like Norma Rose has to be in charge, and Twyla has to wear the latest fashion, and Ginger has to have cherry-flavored lipstick. It's who I am." He was frowning, deeply, as if he didn't understand what she was saying. "I could have stopped making those trips at any time. One word to my father and it all would have ended, but I didn't want it to end. I'd found something I was good at."

"You're good at a lot of things, Josie."

The undercurrent of his tone told her what he was thinking of. She grinned, but asked, "Will you help me, Scooter? Help me help other girls?"

"I'd help you build a bridge to the moon if that's what you want, Josie Nightingale."

"You would?"

"Yes." A smile curled up the corners of his mouth. "I love you, Josie," he said. "More than I love motorcycles and monkey wrenches."

She giggled. "That much?"

He grasped her waist and pulled her close. "Yes, that much. I bailed you out of the hoosegow, didn't I?"

"Yes, you did," she agreed.

"I have a confession to make, too," he whispered, barely kissing the tip of her nose.

"You do?"

He nodded, "Your call from Duluth was exactly what I'd needed. All of you Nightingale girls were off-limits. Completely. Everyone knew that. But then, Norma Rose started dating Ty, and next thing I knew, Twyla and Forrest were off flying together. When I heard about Ginger and Brock, I knew I had to do something before someone else snatched you up."

Elated, she wiggled a bit closer to him. The sigh that escaped moments before their lips met was the most wonderful exhale. The kiss that followed was pretty spectacular, too. Downright amazing. It may have stopped raining for a time, while they'd been talking and kissing, she couldn't say for sure, but the crack of thunder and the flash of lightning that brightened the room beyond the lightbulbs said the heavens were opening up again.

The tension he'd emitted earlier, when she'd first stepped out of the bathroom, was completely gone. It had been replaced with a heady, sensual feeling that filled the air between them. It tickled her, inside and out, and made her remember why she was standing before him in nothing but her underclothes. After licking her lips, she asked, "So, should we get married or not?"

He chuckled and kissed her briefly. "Why not? I sure don't want anyone else marrying you."

That sounded exactly like the teasing Scooter she'd known years ago, back in school, when they'd both been free of the burdens placed on them after the deaths of her mother and his father. Embracing the playfulness, feeling rather carefree herself, she said, "Well, I don't want anyone else marrying you, either. Especially none of the women who stop by here regularly."

"What women?"

"The ones who don't need gas or air in their tires, the one who just want to watch you wash their windows."

"No one—"

"Oh, yes they do," she insisted. "I've heard them whispering about it."

"Well, I don't want you marrying any of the men who fill the resort continuously," he said. "I've heard them whispering about you."

She grinned and ran her hands down the front of his chest. "I don't know about any men other than you." Trailing one finger along the waistband of his pants, she added, "Because you are the one I want to marry."

His hands framed her face and he gently tilted her head back. "I want to marry you, too." Having lined up their lips, he leaned closer and kissed her deeply.

When they parted for air, Josie was gasping. The love, the need inside her, was powerful and relentless. She slipped her fingers inside the waistband of his pants. "Your britches are still wet. We should hang them to dry beside mine."

Scooter grasped her waist and picked her up. With barely a step, he spun around and set her on the table. "You don't let up once you've set your mind to something, do you?"

Shaking her head, she admitted, "No, and my mind has been set on one thing since I left the resort." Tugging him forward, she hooked her legs around his. "I love you, Scooter, and I want you. All of you. Now and forever."

Using one finger, he drew a line from the tip of her chin downward, between her breasts, which made her nipples tighten. His finger kept going, down to her stomach, and then back up, where it circled each breast, one at a time.

"I feel the exact same way."

She leaned back slightly, giving him more space to continue teasing her. It was most enjoyable. "I always knew we thought a lot alike."

He kissed her chin. "We do. My mind's been set on one thing, too. For weeks. Months. Years." His lips followed the trail his finger had forged. The heat of his mouth created utter turmoil inside her. Breathtaking and incredible madness spread through her so fast, she didn't question a single impulse that sparked inside her.

His mouth had found one nipple, tasting it right through the silk. The pleasure was so great that she quivered. Unable to stand much more, she grasped his head, making him stop. Leaning back, she then grabbed the hem of her top.

Scooter groaned and pressed a hand to his heart, as if he couldn't wait to see what she was about to uncover. She laughed and so did he.

Slowly, hoping it was as tantalizing for him as it was for her, she lifted her top, almost uncovering her breasts, but then tugged it down again.

"Oh, you are a tease," he said huskily.

She laughed and ripped the top over her head. Flinging it at him, she laughed again when it fluttered to the floor.

Scooter grasped her arms and lifted them over her head. Gathering both of her wrists together with one hand, he used the other to play with her already taught nipples. "Let's try this instead." Leaning down, he kissed her breasts until she was so full of delicious and rather wicked sensations she had to lock her heels against the backs of his legs to keep from slipping off the table.

He let go of her hands, and she grasped his shoulders as he lifted her, pressing her against him. "I love you, Josie," he whispered, "So very much."

"I know," she whispered, barely able to breathe. "I. Love. You. Too."

He laughed when she finally got the whole sentence out. He was masterful. So skillful in the ways he touched her, kissed her, teased her, that she'd grown boneless. Every part of her was throbbing, begging for his attention.

Scooter lifted her completely off the table and kissed her thoroughly while he carried her to the bed, where he laid her down. The separation from him, even though she knew it would be brief, left her feeling lonely and more than a little desperate.

"Hurry, Scooter."

"I am," he answered, unfastening his britches.

Every ounce of her being was on fire, anticipating what was to come. What they were about to do. As that thought hit home, Josie shot upright. "Do you have a rubber?"

The expression on Scooter's face, and the way he froze, hands on his waistband, had Josie letting out an expletive she'd never imagined using. "I've passed condoms out by the dozens and now when I need one they're miles away," she groaned, throwing herself backward, her head bouncing against the pillow on his bed.

Scooter held up a hand. "I'll be right back."

The thud of his footsteps running down the stairs had her shooting upright again. "Scooter, wait!" she shouted. A door slammed below. Sighing and looking heavenward, she moaned and flopped back onto the bed. The drug-store was closed at this time of the evening. Her stomach fluttered at the thought of Scooter buying condoms. Mr. Kemper wasn't known for his ability to keep secrets. Everyone would soon know if Scooter bought some. Josie rolled to the edge of the bed, frustrated. Although she would gladly bear any number of Scooter's children, she would prefer they got married before one was conceived.

The door downstairs slammed again. She was still sitting on the edge of the bed when Scooter reentered the room, water running down his chest, arms and back.

"It's still raining," she said. The idea of being stranded inside with him and not doing what they'd been about to do was overly depressing.

"Yes, it is," he answered, smiling.

Her gaze shifted to what he held up. "My bag!"

"I found it at Francine's warehouse," he said, dropping it on the bed. "The chief let me keep it." After kissing her forehead, he added, "It was still in the saddlebag on my motorcycle."

"We never know when luck is on our side, do we?" she asked, pulling a box out of the bag. She also said a tiny prayer for the several other boxes still in the bag.

Scooter pulled off his boots and then stepped out of his pants, kicking them aside as he climbed onto the bed. He immediately went to work again, kissing and teasing her until her body was once again begging for more, for all of his glorious attention.

He gave it, all of it, even long after he'd eased her camiknickers over her hips and down her legs.

Excitement had her breathing unevenly and her heart throbbing when he left her long enough to open the box. She watched intently as he opened the package. Intrigued, she couldn't pull her eyes away as he shed his underwear and rolled the condom on.

"I've dreamed of this," she admitted. "Of me and you."

"So have I," he said, climbing over the top of her.

Smiling, she reached up and held his face between her hands. It was then a hint of uncertainty plagued her. "I'm not sure what to do."

"I am," he whispered.

"Good," she answered. "Where do we start?"

"Where do you want to start?"

She shrugged. "Kiss me?"

"Forever," he whispered, leaning down to take her lips.

Without further ado, he masterfully orchestrated their coupling. Josie had seen beautiful things in her life, lived with them daily, but she'd never experienced beauty. Not like this. Scooter's masterful entrance was a completion she'd never have understood without experiencing it. His love was evident in each caress of his hands, each kiss of his lips, and his extreme devotion was made apparent by the way he whispered words of love as their bodies fell into a rhythmic dance fueled by their shared dedication to one another.

Josie welcomed all the yearning, all the amazing cravings and delightful ache of hunger that grew inside her. Their bodies merged, became one, like they had when they rode his bike together, leaning and swaying in perfect harmony.

A divine desire spread through her entire body, becoming so great, so demanding, she tossed her head from side to side and bit down on her bottom lip. Pleasure-filled groans were rolling in her throat, escaping now and again, along with gasps when she couldn't fully catch her breath.

Scooter's arms were strong, his shoulders broad, his entire body much more powerful and larger than hers, yet he was infinitely gentle while commanding her body through one amazing phase and into another. He took her to places that couldn't be of this earth and kept her there, holding on to nothing but him. Thinking of nothing but him.

The phenomenal tension he created inside her was reaching a peak, she was sure of that, but had no idea what to do next.

"Breathe, Josie," he said. "Just breathe."

She hadn't known she was holding her breath, and as she let it out, a great release happened. It was a feeling of freedom so great and powerful it consumed her wholly and left her euphoric.

A wealth of pure bliss fanned through her, filling her with such harmony she sank deeply into the mattress below her. Scooter was sinking, too, his glorious weight resting upon her lightly.

He kissed her, softly, sweetly, and then slowly rolled onto his side, pulling her close. Beyond the pounding of her heart echoing steadily in her ears, the music of the rain still falling upon the roof above made her smile. She'd always liked the sound of rain, and would even more from now on.

"We'll live here, won't we?" she asked. "After we're married?" A tinge of heat filled her cheeks. The idea of his mother or sister, or little Jonas, hearing the commotion they'd just created could prove to be rather embarrassing.

Scooter's eyelids jerked open as if all of his cylinders had misfired. He stared at the ceiling for a moment, wondering if the roof had sprung a leak. Something had shocked him back into reality as fast as cold water thrown on his face.

"Yes," he said, trying to sound normal. Although he was about the furthest he'd ever been from that particular state. He and Josie would be married, as soon as possible, which could very well be the longest few months of his life.

Chapter Nineteen

It was very late by the time the rain ended. Scooter didn't bother checking the clock. No matter what the dial said, he was taking Josie home. He'd made mistakes in his life, but that didn't mean he had to keep making them. Having her snuggled up to his back, with her arms wrapped tightly around his waist as he dodged puddles on the road, didn't help his resolve.

He'd seen the taillights ahead of them, and wasn't surprised when he saw Roger walking across the parking lot. Or Gloria. They'd arrived at the Plantation shortly before he'd left. Before it had started to rain. Before he'd found Josie at his station. Before—

"It looks like you two made up," Roger said.

Scooter had pulled up next to the main doors of the resort and cut the engine.

Josie giggled next to his ear as she climbed off the motorcycle.

Scooter set the stand beneath the motorcycle and climbed off. "Josie was at my station when I got there," he said, nervously trying to explain what he was doing bringing her home so late. "I had to wait for the rain to end before bringing her home."

"We waited, too," Roger said. "That was a real cloud buster. You have any hail at your place?"

Scooter had no idea if it had hailed or not. "Won't know if there was any damage until daylight," he said, trying to answer indirectly.

"It was the size of grapes in town," Roger said as he moved forward and wrapped his arms around his daughter. "How you doing, Josie-girl?"

Smiling, she nodded. "Good. Wonderful, actually."

Stepping back, Roger gestured toward the door. "You two come into my office," he said. "So we can talk."

"I'll say my good-nights here," Gloria said, leading the way through the double doors. "It's been a long day."

There was no tension in the air, or underlying message in Gloria's tone, which had Scooter hoping she and Roger had settled things between them. The man had not been impressed that Gloria had involved Josie in her scheme. Scooter experienced a slight punch to his gut as he wondered what Roger would think of Josie's desire to buy a house in Duluth. He'd help her with that, just as he'd said, whether her father approved or not.

A tiny smile appeared on her lips and her eyes softened much like they had earlier, back in his bed, as she looped her arm through his while saying good-night to Gloria.

Side by side, he and Josie entered Roger's office.

Taking off the coat he'd insisted she borrow, Josie draped it over the back of a chair before she sat. "You were wrong, Daddy."

Scooter glanced between her and her father as he took a seat in the other chair.

Roger had already sat down. Elbows on his desk, he tapped the tips of his fingers together. "About what?"

"Not being very good with broken hearts."

The gaze she sent his way had heat rising to Scooter's neck.

Turning back to her father, she said, "You knew exactly what you were doing."

Roger laughed. "I was young and in love once, too, you know."

Scooter wasn't sure what the two of them were talking about, but had an inkling it involved him.

Leaning back in his chair, Roger then asked him, "Did she tell you about the house in Duluth she wants to buy?"

"Yes," he answered.

"What do you think about that?"

Scooter reached over and squeezed Josie's hand. "That if anyone can make a difference for those girls, it'll be Josie."

Roger nodded, but then lifted a brow. "There will be no shenanigans this time. No pulling the wool over anyone's eyes."

Scooter looked her way, bracing himself for her reaction. "I won't have to, Daddy," she told her father while looking at him. "Scooter will know all about it from the very beginning."

"That's how it should be," Roger said. "Gloria's interested in helping you. So is Karen Reynolds. She's moving to Duluth on Monday, when Clyde goes back up there."

"She is?" Josie asked. "Isn't she still married to Galen?"

Roger shrugged. "Where there's a will, there's a way, Josie-girl. Nothing is going to stop Karen this time, and I say good for her. Good for them. Karen wants to talk with you before she leaves. She said she'll look at some property there and Clyde says he'll have two large donation checks for you when the time comes. One from US Steel and one from J. P. Morgan."

"Really?" Josie asked. "That's awfully nice of them."

"If not for you and Scooter, he'd have had a harder time convincing the police to raid Francine's warehouse." Roger turned to him then. "Speaking of US Steel, they own a lot of trucks, use a lot of fuel. Clyde thinks you should consider opening a station or two in Duluth. I'm interested in financing them if you do."

"You are?" Scooter asked, the ability to build Josie a proper house instantly foremost in his mind.

"Sure am," Roger said. Leaning forward he waved a hand. "Bootlegging has been good to me, but it'll come to an end. I'm aware of that. But steel, automobiles, gasoline—those are all here to stay."

"I'm interested, all right," Scooter said.

"Good," Roger said. "We'll set aside some time to talk more about it next week. Get things going." He glanced between the two of them. "A man fighting to give his wife the life she deserves is a man to reckon with. I've been there." His expression grew solemn as he glanced around the room. "And would give everything I own to be there again. Rose, your mother," he said specifically to Josie, "died before I had any of this. Our life together was that of scrimping and scraping. We never lived alone. Moved in with my parents on our wedding night, and they all three died within days of each other, in that very house."

Scooter tightened his hold on Josie's hand again, and offered a consoling smile when she squeezed his in return.

"I'm assuming you two will be announcing a wedding date soon," Roger said.

"Yes, sir," Scooter answered.

"We'll wait until Norma Rose returns from her honeymoon," Josie said. "I'll be here to help you with the resort while she's gone."

"We've already talked about that," Roger said.

"I know what you said, Daddy, but—"

"But you don't think I can do it without you?" He chuckled then. "I know this place is Norma Rose's baby, and I'm glad of that. Just like I'm happy you are branching out to follow your dreams." Puffing up his chest, he continued, "But let me assure you, I can run this place if need be. And let me assure you, there was never any threat of the Eastman gang taking it all away from us."

Scooter flinched slightly. Retaliation for Francine's arrest was still a real threat.

"Your secrets made me realize it's time for me to come out in the open a bit, too," Roger said. "To my family. I've told Forrest and Twyla, and will tell Ginger and Brock everything when they come home for Norma Rose's wedding."

"Tell us what?" Josie asked.

"That I'm not a gangster," Roger said. "But I do business with a few of them. They like the product that I provide them, and we all make a lot of money from it. The men I deal with aren't about to let a band of underground thugs step in, and never will. The only thing that could have taken me down was the government, and that didn't happen because the federal agent that could have done it was after a mobster named Ray Bodine, not me."

"The undercover agent the feds keep well hidden," Scooter replied.

"Yes, the one who turned in his badge to marry my oldest daughter."

"Who? What? Ty?" Josie asked all in one breath.

"Yes, Ty," Roger said, then laughed. "And you thought you had consequences falling in love with Josie, Scooter."

"They seem pretty minimal now," Scooter said.

"They always were minimal," Roger said. "It's just that when some things consume our minds, they grow much larger than they really are." He stretched his arms out to his sides and let out an exaggerated yawn. "Well, I think I'll call it a night." Standing, he held out a hand. "Welcome to the family, son."

Scooter stood and shook Roger's hand. "Thank you, sir."

Stepping around his desk, Roger kissed Josie's cheek when she stood. "Catch the lights after Scooter leaves, will you?"

"Yes, Daddy," she said. "Good night."

Roger pulled open the door before he turned around. "You know there's an old saying that women marry men who remind them of their fathers. Handsome. Intelligent. Suave."

The grin on Roger's face caused Scooter to chuckle. "Can't say I've heard that one before."

"Me, neither," Josie said.

"You haven't?" Roger shrugged. "Maybe I just made it up."

"Maybe you did," Scooter replied.

His gaze was on Josie then. "He has one up on me, Josie-girl. I never had to bail your momma out of the hoosegow."

Josie's blush was so endearing, Scooter wrapped both arms around her waist and tugged her into a solid hug. "I'd do it again," he told Roger, and her. "I just hope I won't have to."

"You two are incorrigible," Josie said, although she was laughing along with the two of them.

Roger stepped out of the room, but before he completely closed the door, he said, "Let me know if you want me to tell Norma Rose you'll be getting married before her."

The door closed before either of them could respond.

Josie's mind was twirling so fast she could very easily be going batty. There was so much to think about, to process. Thank goodness Scooter's arms were around her, keeping her grounded.

"He was joking."

Taking a step back, mainly so she could think, Josie asked, "What? Joking about what?"

"About telling Norma Rose you were getting married before her," Scooter said.

Josie purposefully held his gaze. The spark in his eyes was mesmerizing, and promising, which had her insides dancing the Charleston, but there was also a hint of something else. Distress maybe.

He took hold of her hands. "We can wait as long as you want."

"As long as I want?"

"Yes."

His kiss was glorious and she didn't want it to end, but she sensed he was kissing her in order not to have to talk. Pulling her head back, she asked, "How long do you want to wait?"

His silence made her stomach bubble.

"I love you, Josie," he said seriously. "I sincerely do, and what I have to say isn't easy. I want us to be married as soon as possible."

"But…" she said, her nerves kicking in. After all they'd been through, all they'd talked about, she couldn't comprehend where this conversation might lead.

"But I believe the earliest it can happen is this winter. Hopefully."

"This winter?" she repeated. "Hopefully?"

"Yes."

Josie willed herself to remain calm. A difficult thing. "Why?"

"I'm hoping by then to have a house built."

"You have a house," she said.

"No, I don't." He let go of her hands and brushed the hair back from his forehead. "That's my mother's house. I don't want us to live with her. It would be too crowded."

"I asked if we'd live at your station," she pointed out, "and you said yes."

"I know, but after thinking about it, that's no place for you to live."

Josie stepped back. She thought Scooter had understood her. Completely. "After thinking about it or after bringing me home?"

"I don't want to wait, either, Josie, but—"

"But," she interrupted. "You said I say that all the time. I don't. You do. But this. But that."

His smile could have meant to be consoling. There was just no soothing her. There was no changing her mind, either. "Scooter Wilson," she began, wagging a finger before his face, "let me tell you a few things about myself, things you'd best remember. I don't care about a lot of things. I don't give a wit about fashion or makeup or flashy parties with fireworks. I don't care about fancy houses or food I can't pronounce. None of those things have ever made me happy. And that's what I do care about. I want to be happy. I am happy when I'm with you. Therefore, I am not about to wait until next winter, until you build a new house. *But*—" she emphasized the word on purpose "—if a new house means that much to you, I'll help you build one. I'll pound nails and sew curtains and fill it with all sorts of useless furniture because I love you. That is what I do care about. You. Loving you. I care about becoming your wife. And that I want to do now, not months from now."

He took a hold of her hands again. "You may say all that, Josie, but when it comes to living above a gas station, you'll think differently."

"No, I won't. I know myself, Scooter, and you know me, too."

"Yes, I do," he said. "I know you're used to the finer things in life."

"Used to and wanting them are two different things." She shook her head. "Don't do this to yourself, Scooter. For once in your life, put what you want first." The conversation with her father came to mind. "Do you know why Clyde and Karen were separated all those years ago? It was because her father refused to allow her to marry a poor man. When he discovered Karen was pregnant with Clyde, he forced her to marry Galen Reynolds. Something he soon regretted."

"How do you know that?" he asked.

"Twyla told me all about it yesterday." Josie leaned forward and pressed her lips to his briefly. "I love you, Scooter."

"I love you, too, Josie, and I want what's best for you."

Pulling her hands out of his grasp, she ran her fingers up his arms and onto his shoulders, while stepping close enough that she could feel the heat of his body. "You are what's best for me," she insisted. "Living in your apartment will be best, too. Given there's so much we have to do." When he frowned, she said, "You told me you'd help me buy a house in Duluth for those girls."

He nodded.

"That will take time," she said. "We'll have to find someone to manage it, maybe Karen Reynolds could help since she'll be living up there anyway. We'll also have to figure out where you want to build more gas stations. After we do all that, then we can decide where we want to build a house. Here by our families, or up in Duluth." She shrugged, not really concerned over that at all. "Or wherever."

"Josie—"

"A house is the least of my worries, Scooter. Marrying you is what I want. Please, don't make us wait for that," she whispered, touching his chin with the end of her nose. "Please. My plan will work. Trust me, like I trust you."

"I do trust you," he said huskily. "And I know what you're doing."

She glanced up and grinned at the shine in his eyes.

"Teasing the hell out of me," he said, grasping her hips. His kiss demanded a response, and she gave it freely. The greedy need she had for him was hotter and more fiery than the huge mortars he'd lit on the Fourth of July. It was impossible to contain, too. She imagined it would be this way for years to come, and was ready to start enjoying their love every day.

If he needed proof of that, she'd gladly give it. Parting her lips, she swept her tongue inside his mouth. As brilliant as any fireworks, the passion they'd shared just a few hours ago reignited between them. Just as bold, just as hot. Just as consuming.

Scooter's kisses, his hands roaming her back, his hips pressing into hers, said it devoured him as much as it did her. With a low growl, he pulled away from the kiss and took a step back, as if the distance would help him.

She took a step back, too, hoping the distance would make him see the light.

The smile that appeared on his face came slowly at first, but grew as he shook his head. "Fine."

"Fine?"

He nodded. "We'll go and get a marriage license tomorrow."

"I knew you'd see things my way," she said, moving back into his arms.

"You make it impossible not to," Scooter said, his lips already pressed against hers. When they both needed air, he added, "Besides, the apartment is small enough that I'll be able to keep one eye on you at all times."

Josie laughed. "Just one?"

The members of the Bald Eagle Ladies Aid Society outdid themselves decorating the resort balcony, where Josie and Scooter were married just two days later. Oh, and there were fireworks that night. At least there were for Josie.

* * * * *

REQUEST YOUR FREE BOOKS!

◆ HARLEQUIN®

ℍ ISTORICAL

Where love is timeless

2 FREE NOVELS PLUS 2 **FREE GIFTS!**

YES! Please send me 2 FREE Harlequin® Historical novels and my 2 FREE gifts (gifts are worth about $10). After receiving them, if I don't wish to receive any more books, I can return the shipping statement marked "cancel." If I don't cancel, I will receive 6 brand-new novels every month and be billed just $5.69 per book in the U.S. or $5.99 per book in Canada. That's a savings of at least 12% off the cover price! It's quite a bargain! Shipping and handling is just 50¢ per book in the U.S. and 75¢ per book in Canada.* I understand that accepting the 2 free books and gifts places me under no obligation to buy anything. I can always return a shipment and cancel at any time. Even if I never buy another book, the two free books and gifts are mine to keep forever.

246/349 HDN GH2Z

Name   (PLEASE PRINT)

Address   Apt. #

City   State/Prov.   Zip/Postal Code

Signature (if under 18, a parent or guardian must sign)

Mail to the **Reader Service**:
IN U.S.A.: P.O. Box 1867, Buffalo, NY 14240-1867
IN CANADA: P.O. Box 609, Fort Erie, Ontario L2A 5X3

Want to try two free books from another line?
Call 1-800-873-8635 or visit www.ReaderService.com.

* Terms and prices subject to change without notice. Prices do not include applicable taxes. Sales tax applicable in N.Y. Canadian residents will be charged applicable taxes. Offer not valid in Quebec. This offer is limited to one order per household. Not valid for current subscribers to Harlequin Historical books. All orders subject to credit approval. Credit or debit balances in a customer's account(s) may be offset by any other outstanding balance owed by or to the customer. Please allow 4 to 6 weeks for delivery. Offer available while quantities last.

Your Privacy—The Reader Service is committed to protecting your privacy. Our Privacy Policy is available online at www.ReaderService.com or upon request from the Reader Service.

We make a portion of our mailing list available to reputable third parties that offer products we believe may interest you. If you prefer that we not exchange your name with third parties, or if you wish to clarify or modify your communication preferences, please visit us at www.ReaderService.com/consumerschoice or write to us at Reader Service Preference Service, P.O. Box 9062, Buffalo, NY 14240-9062. Include your complete name and address.

HH15

A fresh pot of coffee, hot toast and the last pot of what
Phipps assured her was Mrs. Semple's best strawberry
conserve would surely soothe a troubled male breast at
breakfast time, Tess thought. Halfway up the back stairs
she remembered her apron and went down again to take
it off and straighten her cap, which showed a tendency to
slide on her tightly coiled hair.

"You look the part, Miss…er…Mrs. Ellery," MacDonald
said with an encouraging smile that only confirmed that
what she *looked* was in need of encouragement.

At Alex's door she knocked. *I must stop calling him
that, even in my head.*

"Come." It was hardly welcoming. Perhaps the jam had
been a mistake, too obvious a peace offering.

Tess walked in, wishing this was rather less like being
summoned to Mother Superior's study and that she could
manage a confident smile. But that still made her cheek
ache. "My lord." She bobbed a curtsy, folded her hands
and waited.

"For goodness' sake, Tess, sit down and stop play-
acting." He was using the point of a paper knife to flip over
a pile of gilt-edged cards on his desk.

"I am not. I am endeavouring to behave like a proper housekeeper in front of your staff and any visitors."

"You cannot be my housekeeper. You cannot stay here." Alex jammed the paper knife into a jar of pens. "You are most certainly not going to come into contact with any visitors."

"I am perfectly competent and they taught us housekeeping and plain cookery at the convent. This is a small house—I can manage very well."

"That is not what I mean." His gaze, those hazel eyes shadowed, was on her mouth. His own lips were set in a hard line.

They had felt firm, yet soft on hers. Strong, yet questioning. They had asked questions she... Tess closed her eyes and Alex made a sound, a sudden sharp inhalation of breath. She blinked and he was still staring at her.

"It's about that kiss, isn't it? You think I was throwing myself at you." The words were out before she could censor them. She had been so certain he knew it had been a mistake, so certain that he had disregarded it with an ease she could only dream of managing herself.

"No. Yes. Partly." Alex had his elbows on the arms of his chair. Now he clasped his hands together as though in prayer and rested his mouth against his knuckles, apparently finding something interesting on the surface of the desk. When he dropped his hands and looked up she could see neither amusement nor desire in his expression. "You should not be in a bachelor household, it is as simple as that. I am not in the habit of pouncing on my female staff and, although I can find explanations for what happened the other night, they are not excuses, not acceptable ones."

Don't miss
HIS HOUSEKEEPER'S CHRISTMAS WISH
by Louise Allen, available November 2015 wherever
Harlequin® Historical books and ebooks are sold.

www.Harlequin.com

THE WORLD IS BETTER WITH

Romance

Harlequin has everything from contemporary, passionate and heartwarming to suspenseful and inspirational stories.

Whatever your mood, we have a romance just for you!

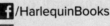